PELICAN BAY

JESSE GILES CHRISTIANSEN

PELICAN BAY

Copyright © 2013 by Jesse Giles Christiansen. All Rights Reserved.

No part of this publication may be reproduced, stored in a retrieval system, or transmitted, in any form or by any means, electronic, mechanical, photocopying, recording, or otherwise, without prior written permission from the authors.

This is a work of fiction. Names, characters, places and incidents either are the product of the author's imagination or are used fictitiously. And any resemblance to actual persons, living, dead (or in any other form), business establishments, events, or locales is entirely coincidental.

www.jessegileschristiansen.com

FIRST EDITION TRADE PAPERBACK

Imajin Books - http://www.imajinbooks.com

July 20, 2013

ISBN: 978-1-927792-12-4

Cover designed by Ryan Doan - www.ryandoan.com

Praise for Pelican Bay

"Christiansen offers a tale sure to entrance readers—a story of love and wisdom and the mystery of a forgotten graveyard under the waters of PELICAN BAY." —Man Martin, author of *Paradise Dogs*

"A riveting read sure to please mystery lovers. Christiansen pulls readers into the world of PELICAN BAY with vibrant characters, evocative imagery, and a tantalizingly mysterious sea captain. A seafaring mystery tinged with Southern Gothic appeal, PELICAN BAY offers a fast-paced story, hooking readers with a mysterious captain, a forgotten graveyard, a series of accidental deaths, and a coastal community with constant storms on the horizon. Dark clouds loom on the horizon in PELICAN BAY —and mystery lovers will enjoy the resulting storm." —Elizabeth Craig, author of *Death at a Drop-In*

"With beautiful prose and a fresh voice, Jesse Giles Christiansen's PELICAN BAY, is a wonderfully written sea-side page turner. Take heed, Christiansen has got serious writing chops." —Jeff Bennington, bestselling author of *The Secret Tree*

"PELICAN BAY is a story full of suspense and intrigue that will stay with you long after you've finished reading the last word. While the dialogue is distinct, it is the prose that is volatile and sublime in equal measure." —Jacinta Rao, Howtotellagreatstory.com

"An old undersea cemetery, a secret love, mystery and intrigue await you in PELICAN BAY. Jesse Giles Christiansen has written a well-crafted story of suspense that will keep you turning pages!" —*The Dark Phantom Review*

This novel is dedicated to my late uncle, Thomas Joseph Burke, who was a dear father, loving husband, heartfelt poet, and stalwart man of the sea.

Acknowledgements

I would like to thank my friends and family for their untiring encouragement.

Thanks to Annie Proulx for writing *The Shipping News*, a book whose reverberating sounds of the sea and Newfoundland and unabashed, beautiful prose helped inspire this book.

Many thanks to my editor, Todd Barselow, for his unswerving truthfulness.

And finally, to the wonderful author and publisher, Cheryl Kaye Tardif at Imajin Books, for believing in my novel and constantly challenging me to be not only a better writer, but a better career author.

PROLOGUE

Aspen Langsley fell prey to a dare, for he was small and awkward for his age and always eager to be anything but that way.

The year was 1931, and the gaunt arms of the Great Depression reached even the forgottenness of Pelican Bay, South Carolina. Were it not for the fish that still happily fed near their shores, or the big bags of flour that stout elders had put away for meager times such as those, they might have emaciated themselves right into the great sea.

Aspen awoke from a terrible nightmare that he had had ever since he was four years old. The haunting dreams started after picnicking with his parents on Pelican Bay Beach where he first saw the old fisherman standing, like a petrified pirate, atop a nearby dune. And when he had them, they were always about the old man. That growling, chuckling barnacle—the crusty ambassador of Pelican Bay. His nightmare always had the same awesome echo of slimy figures swathed in the clothes of Vikings, their winged head gear the iron ghosts of prehistoric gulls, and their rotting, creased faces like pages of little oval history books written in indecipherable font. And always in front, leading them more by his oceanic presence than by anything else—without exception—the old man.

They were coming to punish the townspeople for thinking too much about things that were better left alone.

Aspen did not understand how he could succumb to such a dare, how he had to confront his worst nightmare like a tiny son of Superman facing a truckload of kryptonite. But his father, a great fisherman in his own right, Captain John Langsley Sr., always told him that wars were mainly fought by very young men who were hungry for honor. And facing the scary old fisherman in his dreams always felt like a dark war, the battlegrounds the ornery sea and the misty mire of his psyche.

They started stripping Aspen of his honor early on, right from the first grade.

Though Aspen was undersized from the beginning—for a while the Langsleys feared they might have birthed a little person—he was too many inches behind his peers. He also held too much weight for his age. By seven years old, he had boy breasts and was ridiculed for it as relentlessly as the beach was by the vicious Pelican Bay tides. His mom would try to make up for it when she often said, "Don't worry Aspen. Your body's going to catch up one day and that fat will turn into big muscles. You'll see."

But Aspen would never see—never see beyond the sleepy blackness of that dare on an unexpectedly chilly June night.

Freckly Chucky Olinsworth was the worst by far. "You have bigger breasts than my sister," he would say. But who was Chucky to say anything? Unlike Aspen, he was the same size as the other kids, but was covered in noisy red freckles from head to toe. He looked like a walking Alabama night sky seen through a red-lensed telescope, and besides, he spoke with the voice of a mosquito giving its existential view through a megaphone.

Then there was Bert—short for Berton—Hodges. He was tall for his age, but ridiculously gangly and so pale that in the summer, when Pelican Bay's skies were not usually bruised, you could see blue veins swimming underneath his skin like a school of baby bluefish. Bert's hair was as black as a starless night or Pelican Bay's absence on any map—so black against his sickly skin as to make him look like a male Goth. "Can I have a feel?" he would always say. Then he would cop one immediately in spite of Aspen's answer. Chucky would join in until Aspen lay on the ground squirming and screaming under the twirling sting of descending twin-titty-twisters.

The dare was born of ghost stories on an early summer eve, a windy dusk blanketing the dunes in view of the old fisherman's just-lit lantern, flickering like a lost soul. His boat was moored to the slippery docks in the near distance, creaking like it always did—a wooden brontosaurus with arthritis.

"You know who's a ghost for real?" Bert said, his dark hair a dune-tip shadow waving in the breeze, a dancing black flame, his eyes darting off to the captain's bobbing boat.

"Shut up," Chucky said.

"I want to know," Aspen said.

"Of course you do, dip shit," Chucky rifled, the stiffening wind now carrying his voice away.

"Have you ever seen him up close?" Bert went on.

"You're an idiot," Chucky said.

"I saw him once," Aspen said, "when I was four. His face is the oldest face I've ever seen."

Chucky laughed. A bullish laugh. Aspen felt a punch coming. Crossed his arms. Cowered for it but it did not come.

"A few years ago I was fishing with my dad and saw him bathing in the ocean near the shore by the old docks. His face looked to be in its twenties," Bert said.

"This is complete bullshit," Chucky said.

"Well, maybe so. You can sit here jerking off and telling stupid stories all night. But if you want to see a real ghost," Bert concluded, "then you need to go out and talk to that old man."

"Ha, ha. What a bunch of morons," Chucky said.

"I believe it. He gives me the willies," Aspen said in a loud whisper. His gentle blue eyes, now almost lost to the engulfing blackness of Pelican Bay, looked near raving.

And the punch finally came.

It seemed to Aspen that they always came without warning. They were like the ominous Atlantic storms that seemed to enjoy bullying Pelican Bay. A jinxed boy, a jinxed town. But Aspen preferred a bad storm over the punches or the insults. He preferred the honor of dying in a storm.

"I've got better things to do," Chucky said, starting up.

"Yeah? Better than watching Aspen go out there and say hi to the old man?"

Chucky sat back down again on the cheek of the dune, his eyes flaring, an evil smile burgeoning.

"You can forget it," Aspen said, rising, his voice trembling a little, betraying the fear underneath its counterfeit bravado.

Another punch. This time from Bert.

"Chicken. Bock, bock, bock," Chucky said, marching around the dune, flapping his arms in grotesque mockery.

The old man's lantern suddenly went out for a moment and goosebumps ripped at the boys' flesh.

Suddenly the lantern was lit again. They all looked at each other, wide-eyed.

"You want to be a real man?" Bert asked. "You want to be treated like one of us?"

"Yeah. You want to stop being a pussy your whole life?" Chucky added, laughing obnoxiously.

Now Aspen looked at them, then out toward the docks, then back at each of them. "I don't have to prove anything."

Chucky grabbed him and he struggled. Bert came up in front of him and said, "We haven't twisted those titties in a while."

"Don't! I don't have titties!"

"Prove it," Bert said.

"Yeah, show us you're not a girl with titties."

Bert reached for Aspen's nipples while Chucky held him.

"Okay! Stop! I'll do it."

"You will?" Bert said.

"He's lying," Chucky said.

"Give me that lantern," Aspen said. "I'll go out there and say hi to that old ghost—and you'll see that I'm not a pussy—that I'm just as tough as you guys."

"Yeah right. You're full of shit," Chucky said.

"No. I think I believe the chicken shit. Give him the lantern," Bert said.

The onyx cloak of a Pelican Bay night was almost upon them. Aspen looked back toward the dunes and his friends had been swallowed by the dark. As he took his first step onto the docks, he looked ahead at the old man's boat, a buoying shadow of archaic oak, a symphony of moaning ropes and petulant planks, a sputtering lantern, which was perhaps a disembodied pirate debating between this world and the next.

He stopped just near the boat, struggling to maintain his footing on the slimy dock boards.

"Hello. My name's Aspen. I've come to talk to you."

Nothing.

"I mean you no harm." Aspen's voice was soft and gentle, even when blasted and pitched. He was to be a little orphan Oliver replaying his debut dramatic role for all eternity.

Still nothing.

And then suddenly the darkness grunted. So near him. So near. And there was a sea stench that the young boy could have never known existed until that night. His every youthful sense was insulted, his every thought was of dark, oaky places, his every feeling that of waking in an ancient tomb under the sea.

As his virginal feet began to turn they slipped into the air and the back of his head hit the dock. The next thing that he knew he was immersed in a drastic, salty wetness and sucked under the docks by a wicked current. He was dizzy in the cool, black sea. His head hurt immensely.

Suddenly an arm reached down into the water and groped around. It was as thick as a fallen oak log, the arm of a sea god, but as hairy as a fishing grizzly.

Aspen clung to the dock beam under the water, eyes open, a child apparition under the sea, his hands shredded by the toothed barnacles that munched upon his fleshy palms, his lungs already aching, his darkening mind wanting to surrender, his frail body, always too small, always too weak, wanting to quit.

Many seconds passed. Seconds of absolute fear.

Aspen finally found in himself the courage for one reach. But when he stretched for the great arm, it suddenly abandoned its search.

Sleep now.

No more insults.

No more fretful, desperate young life.

Just peaceful sleep. Dreaming with the sea, of the honor of all those who have warred with it and lost.

But better than no honor at all.

CHAPTER ONE

I must have been dreaming, or at least it felt that way, when I first saw the peculiar rocks darkly festooning the ocean floor just beyond the shoreline. They started to appear after the recent storms that had rocked Pelican Bay, South Carolina, black freckles left by Mother Nature to remind Morgan Olinsworth and me, Ethan Hodges, of how small we were in the grand scheme of things.

"Look, off to the right, you can see them under the water. They're so strange. Why are they suddenly showing up? Have you tried to dive down and see them?"

"No," Morgan said, "but if you look a little farther out, they're in front of you, too."

I looked carefully in front of me and I could see bulky shadows lurking below the surf, their stony heads protruding from the ocean floor.

It was becoming dark now, nearly too dark to see. Morgan's pale face was almost an early moon—one of those early moons that seems too close to believe. I wanted to kiss her. I had this feeling all the time, but we had been just friends for as long as I could remember.

No one was too friendly in Pelican Bay, and there were so few of us to go around. Morgan headed up the tiny library. She tended to it so carefully, the way that I wish she would me, but she was painfully shy and never really took to people that much. She was the silently proclaimed mayor of our town. Pelican Bay was anything but amiable—and it had no mayor or elected officials—not even a sheriff.

Pelican Bay was beautiful to look at, though, especially on early mornings. When you thought that all hope was lost, the sun would poke its head right out of the sea, glowing just over the horizon, a giant, orange-haired mermaid waking to face the day.

"Let's get our masks and snorkels and dive off the shore tomorrow morning. I really want to see what's down there."

"I don't know," Morgan said.

"Ah, come on—it'll be Sunday. The library will be closed, anyway."

"Maybe. We'll see."

Now it was almost fully dark, and Morgan's face was getting lost—that same moon becoming conscious of itself, experiencing painful shyness and retreating far, far away. Sadness caressed my heart like a rogue winter breeze, and I could hear its breath, hazy strands of pink at the edge of the sea.

"We should head back," I said.

"Good idea."

We said nothing on the way back to town on the foot-worn path through the wild grass and sporadic beach roses, now just dull shapes in the night. I imagined that we were now under the sea visiting those same strange stones. There was a symphony underwriting our silence, and I always felt that we communicated better when nothing was said. But then we would have these conversations that dove deeper than the deepest part of the Atlantic Ocean—deeper than the Puerto Rico Trench.

The little lights from the windows of Pelican Bay's cottages reminded me of ghostly lanterns of old frigates languishing upon a black sea. In that moment, I felt so thankful for those little windows. We gazed at the few stars, now materializing magically above, jealous stars, like those little windows in Van Gogh's famous painting.

"Will you at least think about tomorrow? I'm really curious, aren't you?"

"Let me see how my dad's doing, okay?" Morgan said, her voice the night whispering to me. "He's been a little down lately."

"Why don't you bring him along? The ocean might do him some real good."

"We'll see."

That was the best that you could ever get out of Morgan. In fact, if she ever made any abrupt decisions, there are none of them etched upon my memory. To be with Morgan, you had to be in the moment. She was a spirit that never accepted that she had to live in the real world—always fighting earthly existence, fearing that having to make decisions might somehow surrender the possibility of heaven.

"Good night, Morgan."

"Good night."

I glanced off to my left and I could see a few lights from boats lingering in their usual places in the little harbor hosted by Pelican Bay.

There was an old man, Captain Shelby, who lived on his boat year round, even in the coldest winters when the waves, so cold that it seemed that they might be frozen were it not for their ceaseless motion, would beat against his floating house, knocking to be let in to dream ancient dreams with him.

Captain Shelby was like the pelicans of Pelican Bay—he had been there as long as anything else that our town could remember. And when you peered into his face, if you had such nerve, there was a steadiness indescribable, as if the calm of the sea held its story there, whispering its words through eyes a shade of blue just lighter than the ocean about him. His wrinkles seemed set eons ago, pages written in the history before history. They called him Captain Shelby because he had commanded a fleet of commercial fishing boats in his heyday.

I looked to him for answers about Pelican Bay. I had a lot of questions now, questions that had gone unanswered for too long, questions that could no longer be submerged.

Captain Shelby knew a lot, sometimes everything, it seemed. He helped me back when I had questions about my mother and father, why they had gone missing from Pelican Bay, declared lost at sea, leaving me with my paternal grandmother, Sidney Hodges, to raise me. He said that the great sea would swell up and claim a lot of people. And sometimes the sea would just become vengeful on its own and take people, even when there was no special storm battering our shores and petite bay. As the old man used to say, "It's the still and silent sea that drowns a man."

In Pelican Bay, the sea was the Hand of God.

Seeing that one of the wavering, almost floating boat lights was Captain Shelby's, I headed his way. I had to pass near the docks to get to my grandmother's cottage, anyway. I had another question for the old man—one that even he might not be able to answer this time.

He met me on the dock, as if he already knew that I was coming.

"A bit dark to be out, isn't it, me Son?"

"Yeah—it just got dark so fast today. Is winter coming already?"

"Maybe she's been called early by the sea," he said in his gravelly voice. "So what's on yer mind, me Son? Better tell me quick, or it'll be too late to go to town and I'll have to stow ye out on the deck with some of me old blankets. You'll have to sleep with the pelicans tonight."

I barely stifled a chuckle. His eyes widened and seemed to pick up flecks of unseen light still hanging on from somewhere.

"Morgan and I were out walking on the beach and we saw those old stones. They're so creepy."

"What are ye at now? Better stay clear of them stones. They're dangerous. That's all there's to it. You'll break a leg or bust yer head and the sea'll claim ye."

"Yeah, but—"

"Some things are better left alone. I'll put to the sword those that disagree. I don't know how those dark bjargs got there. They don't seem to go there. Maybe the Great Hurricane brought 'em in—from God knows where, and only God Himself should ask why. Maybe the last few storms finally exposed 'em. Like me said, some things are better left alone."

"But they're just so—weird."

"What ye should be worryin' about is why that pretty librarian won't marry ye. The summer moments always pass quickly."

Silence followed, perhaps summoned by my discomfort over his statement. Captain Shelby knew it and, when he lit his pipe, he smoked our salty silence in it.

"I don't think she loves me."

"Well, ye sure spend enough time together. There's mingling in friendship when a young man can share his whole mind with another. Might as well be married, I say."

"We're just friends."

The old fisherman let himself chuckle out loud. It could have been the sound of approaching thunder.

"I did ask her to dive down and check out the stones with me tomorrow morning. She said she might."

"Bad enough ye can't leave them bjargs alone. No place for such a dainty lady, I say." Captain Shelby was looking across the sea. He had an obvious annoyed expression, his eyes focusing on something far off now. "Ye shouldn't be askin' fer trouble. Lost yer parents to the sea, isn't that enough? Anyway, ye best be gettin' on home now. 'Tis dark as molasses out here. Take this flashlight. Ye can bring it back to me tomorrow."

"Okay."

I took the flashlight and turned back toward town. I had not gone but ten paces when he spoke again.

"You'll stay away from them stones, if ye know what's best!"

CHAPTER TWO

It is amazing how different Pelican Bay can appear early in the day. It is as though you have traveled at night in your dreams along the coastal highway, waking up in another town and calling it Pelican Bay out of sheer habit. It was probably on account of the brightness of the mornings, when there was no storm. Pelican Bay could be as bright in the morning as it was dark at night—the place where the sun kept her bed.

Everything was so much clearer, and I felt the same thing that I always felt on those crisp Pelican Bay mornings.

I knew that I loved Morgan.

I wished that the sea could claim my love for Morgan, the same way that it had claimed my parents years ago. Nothing good ever came of it. Loving someone that does not love you in return is as pestilent as a seagull incessantly chasing and then running away again from the sea. Besides, my grandmother always told me that it is not good for a man to spend so much time with a woman who does not love him back.

"Honestly, I don't know why the two of you spend so much time together," she would say.

"We're friends. She's my best friend. It's really no big deal."

"I really worry about you, Ethan. Your best friends are a woman who spends all day with you but won't marry you, and a crazy old man who talks to the pelicans."

"Captain Shelby's not crazy."

"Not crazy, dear? Then why does he talk to the pelicans?"

"You talk to Sam all the time and you're not crazy."

Sam was our white Siamese cat.

"That's different."

I was heading to Morgan's cottage now. We called all the houses in Pelican Bay cottages. They were your typical beach houses but so weathered from the ocean, and so small, that one day we just sort of took to calling them cottages and it stuck. We did not have enough of a town to gather the audacity to refer to things as large as houses.

I rarely called Morgan on the phone, mainly because she was no good over the phone, but also because she rose earlier than the sun and was always busy doing something, fiddling here and there, in the kitchen, or in her beach rose garden. If not, her long, handsome nose was buried in a book. Whatever occupied her fancy, she became oblivious to everything else. In fact, she was apt to forget people even when they were standing right in front of her.

Morgan was a short, trim young woman with shiny but almost coarse, ash-blonde hair, pale skin all over, and eyes an almost transparent pale blue. But what I loved most about her was her face. It was the most unassuming and plain face that I had ever seen on any woman—and this made her unfathomably beautiful to me.

"I honestly don't get what you see in that girl," my grandmother would say. "She's the homeliest thing I've ever seen. You could do so much better, Ethan—honestly. What's wrong with Elizabeth in Gull Bay? She's just as smart and she's classically beautiful. She's single, you know."

I knocked on the door several times but there was no answer. Morgan rarely answered the door right away, and sometimes she did not answer at all. She lived with her dad, but he was partially deaf and always took out his hearing aids when he slept. But even when he could hear perfectly fine, he also rarely answered the door, especially if it was me. Her mom had passed just a few years ago, but the sea did not claim her, like many of the others. Cancer did. Everyone thought it sad but expected how the Olinsworths went from answering the door to not answering the door.

I walked around to the side of their cottage and found Morgan working in her garden. It was late summer and her beach roses, proud Rugosa Reds, were in full bloom, their orange-red hips dancing to the music of the Atlantic breeze. She had started her beach rose garden after her mom had died. I thought about how much Morgan was like her beach roses. Beautiful, but grown outside the city, amid sandy wild grass, haunting the dunes. They had to be sought out.

"Hi Ethan."

"Good morning, Morgan. Are you coming with me?" She was not looking at me, staring instead at the mask and snorkel in my hand, and then out to sea, her pale face betraying the morning sunlight vaguely like a dying star a million light-years away.

"I don't know. My dad's not awake yet. He was pretty depressed last night. You know, this coming Tuesday's the day that my mother died." She could not look at me. She was looking at her beach roses now.

"They're beautiful, just like you."

"Please don't say things like that, Ethan."

"Sorry," I said, looking down and away. "Well, I'm going to head down to the beach. It's such a clear day again, and we haven't had a storm in over a week. I bet I'll be able to see those strange stones even better today."

Morgan looked out to sea again, wistfully this time, then made direct eye contact with me for almost three seconds, which jolted me a bit. Direct eye contact with Morgan was as rare as two weeks without storms in Pelican Bay. I felt that she wanted to say something substantive but was too self-restrained. I melted.

"Look, why don't you see if your dad would like to come down with you—it would sure do him a lot of good."

"Okay—I'll see. That does make sense."

Morgan turned abruptly, went inside, and closed the door.

It was pretty clear and there was hardly a surf. You could see the gloomy stones along the ocean floor, just beyond our bay's shelf, down deep. They resembled the shadows of countless hoodlums, huddling, preparing to swarm Pelican Bay for its few priceless heirlooms.

What are those things? They're just too orderly looking to be random stones.

The lack of an answer prompted me to begin removing my shirt and shorts.

The ocean was cool, as cool as the pale blue sky above the horizon, as cool as Morgan's eyes when she took to staring right through you. As the ocean climbed my body like wet, ubiquitous vine, I put on my mask and snorkel and submerged my head, now breathing through my snorkel. My feet could still touch the bottom.

The stones were much farther out than I had thought, a good thirty feet, at least, from the shore. They became smaller, the closer that I came to them, perhaps engaging in some defensive shrinking mechanism, undiscovered sponges of the deep restricting out of bashfulness. They made me feel self-conscious too, embarrassed to be attempting to pillage the sea of her secrets.

Soon I was right over them, and I emptied and filled my lungs for my first dive.

It was a long way to the bottom, and I could feel the pressure of the water increase, my ears popping. Pelican Bay could have been an extension of the sky and, the same way that our town was lost to the dark, a local diver lost his sense of up and down to the sea. I might as well have been launching my body into outer space. My lungs were tiring already, and my lust for life made me want to return to the surface. But another part of me felt as though it could stay under water all morning.

The stone closest to me finally came within arm's reach. It was not some random rock washed in by the Great Hurricane, as Captain Shelby had thought, or some prehistoric ocean boulder peppering Pelican Bay. Though crudely shaped and roughly etched, it was a gravestone.

I rushed for the surface, my arms and legs flippers of primal fear flailing against the weight of the sea. My head popped up out of the water and I blew the salty contents of my snorkel out behind me, a baby whale having stayed under too long.

I did not look back until I reached the beach.

CHAPTER THREE

I sat on the beach trying to gather my wits, staring out at the waves as they rushed in. Fond childhood memories piggy backed on their frothy shoulders—memories of surfing on Pelican Bay Beach as a boy.

After my parents had died, I practically lived on the beach. The beach was where I had lost and found myself once again. I loved to just sit there building great sand walls against the indefatigable surf. I felt that there was no sense building a castle, if I could not protect the imaginary people inside from being decimated by the sea. Maybe some part of me believed that, if I could build a wall of sand strong enough, I could somehow save my parents, too, and all the other Pelican Bay victims of the incessant storms that ink-blotted the pages of our town history.

I failed miserably time and again.

But that did not keep me from trying.

I would show up with a fresh spirit all those summer mornings when the rusty school bell remained graciously still and Sidney would pack my favorite peanut butter and jelly sandwiches and her delicate cream cheese and cucumber sandwiches with the crusts removed, which always made me laugh. She would put them all in a picnic basket with a jug of fresh tea and plastic cups and off we would go, leaving little and big footprints through the wild grass-moled dunes.

Sidney would sit with her fine, pale shoulders and big, funny white lace hats and read hefty novels like *Pride and Prejudice*, *Jane Eyre* and *Wuthering Heights*, filling me with infinite gratitude for the long summer days that allowed me to stare at the sea and stubbornly build sea wall after sea wall, all destined to flood, crumble, and collapse—as I guess we all are.

And as I look back on those days, I often think that I built in myself a certain tenacity to think the unthinkable, to comprehend the incomprehensible, and to love the unlovable.

I eventually turned my focus to the waves, to the cause of the inevitable destruction of my sea-walls. I would stare at the waves for hours, sometimes understanding their hungry loneliness for the inhospitable shore. I loved their sound. I loved their beautiful uniqueness. I loved how they looked so ineluctable up close, but yet appeared like heaped failures to erase the land from the distance.

I soon turned my focus to riding the waves, rather than trying to stop them. Now this is a good philosophy of life, I imagine. We cannot stop the waves of misfortune, but we can learn to ride them so that misfortune somehow feels like fortune.

I started riding them with just my body. Sidney would sit there half-reading *Pride and Prejudice*, half-watching me, worry like the white sunscreen on her fragile-skinned, English nose. "Oh Ethan, dear, those waves are too big right now—you could be injured. Oh, dear, dear. What if the undertow grabs you? I don't like it at all! Oh, my, my." I do not know if Sidney worried more about Jane Bennet or me.

Before long I switched to a body board, which allowed me to get on top of the waves for the first time. Sidney was much happier with this mode of personal sea transportation. "Oh dear. Hang on Ethan! Well, at least it's harder to bruise or crack your ribs this way. Oh, dear, dear. Ethan, you come in now, the surf's getting much too high!"

I'll never forget my first real body board ride. It must have lasted for at least five seconds. Wow. For the very first time, I felt that perhaps I was moving somewhere in life. Maybe I could climb a wave and ride to Europe—anywhere other than Pelican Bay. But then I knew that I would quickly realize that I was leaving Morgan, and pine to return.

How many long, wonderful days I spent that summer mastering the body board, becoming a bronze-skinned son of Apollo. I would sneak out when the surf began to rise quickly, prelude to another abusive Pelican Bay storm, my friend Pete often persuaded to join me. Those were thrilling days, bruised-sky mornings and black, gusty afternoons when the 7-foot waves we rode made us feel that we might just skip the shore and ride into the vast mainland. I often fancied myself showing up at a Carolina farmer's doorstep and regaling him with my surfing story. Sometimes Pete and I would catch each other's glances atop the waves and cheer to one another. Oh, the days!

When I was ready to graduate to a surf board, Sidney would hear nothing of it. She absolutely, explicitly, forbade it. I can hardly blame her, although Sidney always worried way too much over me. This was where Captain Shelby first became an active part of my life.

Little did I know that he used to watch me surf on many occasions, through his old piratical telescope, to and from his almost daily fishing trips out to sea or to his Secret Spot. When I was about twelve years old, sitting on Pelican Bay beach at dusk, frowning at an unusually calm sea, my weathered body board tossed aside and half-buried in the sand, he approached me.

"Me can't decide which is flatter, yer face or them waves out there."

The gravelly voice jarred me slightly, but I knew immediately who it belonged to.

"Hi, Captain Shelby. I'm not supposed to be out here alone."

The old man chuckled. "Sidney has ferbid it, eh?"

"I'm also not supposed to talk to you."

The old fisherman laughed. "Are ye scared of me?"

"No. I guess not. Not at all."

"I would never harm ye, Son. Never." Some silence as the old man sat down next to me and we looked out to sea together. It was a peaceful moment, and I realize now that I have never felt more serene than in those quiet moments in the presence of that great man. "I've seen ye surfin' many a time."

"Yeah?"

"I surfed with me body when I was a young strappin' scopie."

"Really?"

"Eh. There be nothin' like the throat of the sea—her throbbin' rush. But when the sea stretches her arms, ye need a big board to ride her true, I say."

"I know. But I'll never get a surfboard—not with Sidney around," I said, putting my head between my knees.

"That be right true, but we scopies all be pirates below deck, Son, and sometimes what them duckies don't know won't be after hurtin' 'em."

My heart suddenly felt lighter. "What do you mean?"

"We could build us a right genuine surfer board. Thee and I, together."

"Really?"

"Out of beach pine so she be light but strong."

"Yes!"

"And with a coatin' so she be right smooth and a rudder and special curves so she glides like a fancy schooner over the sea."

"That would be great, Captain! When can we start?"

The old fisherman regarded me with big, childish eyes, the awesome wrinkles around them seeming to suddenly disappear. In that moment, I learned for the first time that our souls never age—they are the rooms of our identities, which are themselves eternal. And the windows of our houses, our eyes, displaying our dearest memories, stay open and unaltered even though our walls may crack and eventually crumble. It was also then that I first noticed how dark the old man's eyes could become at night—the shimmering ultramarine blue of many leagues below the sea.

"Come by me skip on the morrow just before dark."
"Okay Captain. Thanks!"
"Go on boy."

The next day when I came by the old docks that seemed to magically hold themselves together by the spirit of the sea, or the will of the old fisherman, or both, Captain Shelby was eagerly waiting for me with the smile of a child early for show and tell. He had already inspected and stowed away his fishing nets and was walking slowly around a piece of beach pine wood about seven feet long atop a section of old canvas on his main deck. He was whistling a wistful, beautiful melody that would lullaby my soul for many, many years—as I would learn that it was a ditty about a lost love. The sky was bright for incipient dusk, and I fancied that the old man was bosom buddies with Pelican Bay's Spanish orange sun, asking her to stay awhile, if he whistled a soothing tune for her. And she did stay forever it seemed.

"Hi Captain! Is that piece of wood for the surfboard?"
"Eh, Son. 'Tis a fine hunk a skógr, I say. She be right properly aged fer what we be after."
"That's great! Where did you get it?"
"From Fisherman's Island, near me Secret Spot."
"Fisherman's Island?"
"I'll show ye where it be one day when ye be older. 'Tis a raw island—full of snares for a little greenhorn like thee."

I hopped aboard the old man's boat. He had already carved away most of the bark and asked me to hold the large piece of wood in place as he sawed away top layers.

"How did you get to be so strong, Captain? I couldn't even move that saw."
"Ha! Yer arms be young and untested by the sea, Son. I've tugged many a squirmin' net of fiskr from the deep and rowed many a weighty skip in me day. I've also heaved many men from the crooked sea."
"Wow."

The old man cackled and it sounded like strange echoes of the saw, as if his marrow and the tree's marrow were connected in some way.

"I never even knew pines grew that big around here."
"Everything be large on Fisherman's Island. Why, I've seen flyin' bugs the size of yer hand."

My face wrinkled into a baby version of the old man's. He noticed and laughed again, seeming to guffaw craggily with the motion of his sawing.

"What color are ye after yer surfer board bein'?"

"I didn't think about that."

"All me has is black and white paint. Bad colors fer yer board, I say. Brighter colors be better so ye don't lose yer board and it be easier to spot thee in a crooked surf."

"That makes sense. How about light green?"

"Go on boy! May be a hard color to find in Pelican Bay." The old man stopped sawing and sniggered. "Seems to me the land folk are always after havin' fancy colors, when the colors of the sea and the trees be right handsome enough, I say. This pine wood be a pretty yellowish color and she'll take the stain right well."

"I never thought of it that way. Okay, Captain. I trust you. Besides, the wood is pretty."

The old man beamed and his eyes smoldered against the setting sun, looking tannish-brown in that moment, almost chameleons to the raw color of the wood that he went back to sawing again.

When I came back the following dusk, I could not believe my eyes. The captain was not about his deck as usual, and, when I climbed aboard to knock on his main cabin door, I saw it. I froze. What a work of genuine, beautiful craftsmanship. What wisdom and patience and love and inconceivable skill must have gone into it.

How did he finish it so soon? His boat was not at the docks all day? It's truly a miracle.

My first real tears of joy in my whole life found my eyes. I'll never forget that moment as long as I live. The surfboard was a deeply pleasing blend of natural tan with a light yellowish hue, its fresh stain glimmering in the sun, and I realized that the color was the same color as the old man's eyes the evening before when they seemed to intertwine with the setting Pelican Bay sun. The surfboard curved down on its sides and front and curled up slightly in the back. The rudder looked as though the fin of a shark had been confiscated, petrified, colored, and affixed somehow.

As I walked up close, I saw the beautiful graphic that Captain Shelby had carved into the top of the surfboard at its center. The carving was incredibly detailed, perhaps burned into it with the aid of the sun. It was a young boy with windblown hair sitting on the beach before approaching waves, staring out to sea.

It was me.

Tears of joy were streaming down my face now. I could not seem to stop them.

"Did me not render it to yer likin', Son?"

"It's amazing. I can't believe it."

"She be me first surfer board. Ye gettin' on okay?"

"Yes Captain. I just can't believe that you made this for me. It's the best surfboard in the whole world."

"Well, she be yers now to skim the vagrs—uh—*waves*—as yer heart sees fit. Only ye may be after keepin' her here on me boat to mind the nerves of yer grandmudder."

"Yes," I said, wiping away my tears. "Captain, I don't know how I'll ever be able to thank you for this. No one's ever done anything like this for me before."

"Ha! That's me scopie—so articulate and such. Ye got a good heart, and a callin' to the sea. 'Tis if ye be me own son."

Now my mind turned to trying out the surfboard. It was all that I could think about. Nothing else day and night. I wanted to bring the surfboard home with me and sleep with it in my bed, give the most beautiful heirloom of my childhood its own pillow and blanket, hug it through the night as I dreamed of surfing on it, riding tall waves by the windows of my friends' cottages, waving to them as I passed.

Every remaining day that summer, even into early fall, I tried to find a way to get out to Pelican Bay Beach without Sidney knowing.

What a challenge.

How many excuses can an intelligent young boy invent? The answer may be infinite, but the quantity achieved always significantly depends on the desire to excuse oneself. Thinking back now, learning to surf on the marvelous surfboard that the old fisherman had made for me lists as one of the top desires of my life, right next to wanting Morgan to love me back, to becoming a published writer, and perhaps my deepest desire of all—for the old man to find peace and happiness.

Every dawn and dusk, unless a storm surge gave the building of the sea too many floors to climb, or the ocean became too chilly in which to rumba, one could find Ethan Hodges surfing Pelican Bay Beach, more often than not far down the coast from our town, as far away as my impatience could bear.

I would pick up my surfboard from Captain Shelby every day before the jaundiced fingers of dawn scratched the horizon. He never seemed to sleep very long—at least not in my memory—and when I approached the docks, the old fisherman was always mending his nets or tending to his tackle, ready to pierce the flickering black sea of early morn to plunder her squirming bounty. He would hand me my surfboard and chuckle like a thousand coffee pots, the eyes of an old pirate tugged from the deep. "Mind yerself, Boy," the old man would growl. "The sea be a fickle wench who may love ye in the morn and curse ye in the eve." "Yes Captain!" I would yell back, grabbing my surfboard and mindfully yet quickly negotiating the wretched docks back to the dunes.

In the fleeting bastions of twilight, before blackness kidnapped Pelican Bay with its dreamless wit, I would creep up the docks and hand my surfboard reluctantly back to the old man. He would say with enthusiasm, "Have ye stood up yet, me Boy?" to which I would say, "Not yet, but so close!" and then I would ask, "Catch any fish today?" to which he would reply, "Eh boy, them fiskr be under me eternal spell."

It was not Captain Shelby who helped me to finally stand up on my surfboard, but Pete. He had his own surfboard, the same length as mine, a light blue color, a birthday present from his uncle who earned handsomely captaining a fishing boat out of Lighthouse Point. I watched Pete from shore, the way he would paddle frantically, as if a shark were chasing him, the way he would get on the shoulders of the wave, sea rushing behind him, and then swoop his legs and plant his feet all in one magical motion similar to gathering one's feet from the ground in a martial arts fight. Amazing. He taught me the move on the beach a few times, but Pete was not a natural-born teacher. Not at all. His eagerness to paddle out to sea, especially on strong swell days, always toppled his precarious patience. He would begin to talk quickly, looking longingly out to sea, his bronzed face drooping, his eyes melting, and I would finally lie. "I got it, Pete. Thanks. Go on out." "Great! Thanks!" he would yell back.

The day that I did stand up for my first ride was one of the most exciting days of my childhood, a day that I have remembered when facing the often daunting challenges of life. We all seek to understand and assuage our fears, but one cannot overcome a fear until he believes that he can. I learned that mastering fear is a matter of faith, not understanding.

I kept thinking about something that the old man would always say at every sunset that I returned my surfboard to him. "The sea be in all our veins, Son. Be one with yerself and she'll let ye ride her any way ye be after."

That morning I picked up my surfboard from the old fisherman and he did not say anything, but there was a prescient glimmer in his eye.

The sun had risen but the sky kept no visible record of it. The sea swelled quickly and dark clouds littered the sky. October was close, making her ghostly presence known to all those upon the sea, from Charleston on up to Massachusetts. I had no business out there. Captain Shelby must have known this, for I felt his presence as I paddled out beyond the insidious surf that morning, more than perhaps I ever had up until that moment. "The sea be in all our veins." I felt that he was watching me from somewhere, that he and the horizon were by hook or by crook one entity. "Be one with yerself."

I sat on the most beautiful surfboard in the world, sat on the etched mirror of myself, just beyond the break, watching the murky waves rise higher and higher. I waited too long. Light rain stung my torso and face. Some towering waves had already come. Come and gone.

What am I waiting for?

Finally, the right wave came. I do not know how I knew that it was the right wave. Some things you just know, and to doubt that sort of transcendental knowledge would be to forget one's self. So I turned and paddled with all my life. I rose like a human tempest and was rushed forward by the prehistoric thrust of the sea. In one seamless motion I was on my feet, unsteady at first, then firmly planted and immediately wondering why I had been so fearful till then, and a second later, why anything else in the whole world mattered at all.

The ride to Pelican Bay Beach seemed to last forever. I felt like I was on top of the world, skipping on a ski atop a great live globe. In the distance I saw a small group of people on the shore, one of them pointing at me, another waving his arms similar to attempting to signal an aircraft. One of the people appeared to be yelling something through cupped hands.

My wave dropped suddenly while I was still a good twenty feet or more from the shore. My heart fluttered as my surfboard was ripped back with such ominous force as to send me hurling forward into madly hurrying and swirling sea. I heard a distant scream as I fell, as if the cry of a gull being tugged by a chasing storm. I wanted to be a gull, to have the wings to fly up and land on my board again to finish my glorious ride.

But God did not make us with wings.

I was swallowed by the sea, jostled about by the mighty muscles in her esophagus, spiraling down into the blackness of her stomach. I have always wondered how the sea could have been so deep so near shore. Since that time I have developed an immense respect for the sea, much like a veteran lifeguard who has lost countless precious items to her. I understand now the sheer supremacy of the allied assault of a storm surge and high tide. I have lived with the sea, been held by her, felt the thrill of her love, the iciness of her retreat, and the gall of her temper.

There was no sense in trying to breathe. The sea filled my lungs instantly and after a twinge of the body, everything was rather peaceful. I was cradled by the arms of a charity-faced woman with sad dark eyes and long, flowing hair. I ate cream cheese and cucumber sandwiches with a white-nosed English woman. I helped an old man build the most beautiful surfboard in the universe and cried tears of joy.

And then there was a staircase that led down, down, down, and a serene light somewhere at the bottom. I was not afraid at all. I felt no anger toward Pelican Bay, just a forlorn longing for her grass-speckled, shimmering dunes.

I took the first few steps down the stairwell.

The next thing that I knew I was lying on my back on the main deck of the old man's fishing boat, experiencing the miserable suffering of having tried to drink the Atlantic and now coughing it up.

"That's it! Get on the go! Come back, me Boy! There ye be, me gutsy surfer boy!"

The old fisherman's legendary face came into focus. "What happened, I—"

"Get her out! That's me scopie! Ye can't breathe the sea!"

"Oh my God, I don't—"

"That's okay, Son. Take yer time. Take a rúm."

"How did you—?"

"I turned back early from me fishin' trip when the sky took crooked. I saw ye surfin' and a bad feelin' surged in me throat. 'Twas a wind of fortune fer thee I arrived in time."

"I was down so deep, I—"

"Save yer breath, Son. Eh, thee were deep in the belly of the sea's undertow."

"Where's my board?"

"Ha! Me knew it! This here scopie just outwitted death and he be worryin' after his surfer board! She be on her way to Charleston—likely already in Gull Bay by now." I felt a sadness wash over my body even worse than death. The old man noticed, his eyes shining with empathy. "I'll scout for her when this crooked weather be gone. If we can't find her, I'll make ye another one."

"You're the greatest man ever, Captain," I said, coughing again.

"Go on boy."

"I have to go. I'm late for school," I said, abruptly sitting up.

"Ha! That's me Boy! But ye better take a rúm fer a while, eh?"

"No. I really have to go. I don't want to get you in trouble for this. Sidney hates you."

The captain laughed—a laugh fringed with melancholy.

My problems had only just begun. It had been Pete and a few other kids standing on the beach watching me that squally morning. Pete had rushed to school and told one of our teachers what had happened.

The teacher called Sidney.

Before I could get past the dunes, both the Pelican Bay Volunteer Fire Department truck and the Pelican Bay Hospital ambulance had pulled up, sirens howling, as if every Atlantic gull had teamed up to tattle on me. Sidney came running up frantically with Pete's parents. She wore a yellow raincoat and I remember her blue eyes looking dreadfully dim under her hood, and her wrinkles seeming so numerous and entrenched.

"Ethan! Oh dear! Are you all right? Oh dear, dear! Come here!"

"I'm okay. I'm okay."

"I was worried sick, dear. Are you sure you're all right?" she asked, hugging me fiercely enough to almost press the lucky life out of me.

"Yes. I'm okay."

"The teacher said you were surfing. *Surfing*? With this storm surge?"

"Yes, I—"

"How many times have I told you not to surf alone? And you're too young for a board! We've discussed this a dozen times! Oh Lord help me!"

"Well, I—"

"I don't want to hear it! Where on earth did you get a *surfboard*?"

"Well—uh—you see, I—"

"Oh dear, dear! Well at least you're all right. I didn't have to lose another loved one to the sea. Thank God," Sidney cried, looking up at the scoffing sky. "Thank God!"

I was grounded for two months after that, and my surfing days were over for many years. I still love to surf, and I have had other rides since then—but none like that first ride, that blustery morning, the old man both giving me my life and saving it when I was in danger of losing it.

But the greatest thing that I remember from being twelve years old was not my first ride on a surfboard. The greatest thing that I remember was the surfboard and the man who handmade it—the second time the center picture etched with him sitting next to me on the beach, his face handsome, resembling mine, only older and wiser.

CHAPTER FOUR

Morgan came walking up the beach after a few minutes, waking me from my deep childhood memory. The sun caught her hair in such a way that it looked ablaze with golden fire, forming a luminescent halo around her head.

"You won't believe what I saw, Morgan!"

She fell suddenly to a lowered-brow expression, cynicism flashing in her eyes, her lips slightly twisted, the way she always looked when we talked about ghosts or UFOs.

"Let me guess, those are pieces of a marooned alien spacecraft down there, right?"

"Very funny. Try guessing again."

"Look, my dad's still pretty depressed. I'm not really in the mood for—"

"They're gravestones."

Morgan's face changed to blankness now. Her eyes became wide and her eyebrows high, as if somehow helping to search her mind for what to say. She looked quite innocent.

"That's impossible," she finally got out.

"Go see for yourself, if you don't believe me."

Morgan looked out at the gravestones, pudgy shadows absorbing the quickly approaching noon sun. Her expression of wide-eyed innocence remained, only now fear overcoming it like a sliding black curtain closing a child-acted stage drama.

"Ethan, this isn't funny, you know—and I'm not particularly in the mood for diving down to find some old barnacle-ridden stones, just so you can see me in my bathing suit."

"I wouldn't joke about something like this. You'll just have to take my word for it."

Morgan exhaled hard and quickly, shaking her head, bringing her gaze once more to the mysterious gravestones. She was curious, and there is no stopping a curious librarian.

She began to undress slowly and I looked away. Oh, I wanted to peek so badly. I loved Morgan's body. She was more slim than curvy, but this made her bosom, willfully shaped and hearty, more of a centerpiece. I finally sneaked a look and she caught me out of the corner of her eye, shaking her head again, but not too vigorously.

"Will you at least come with me and keep an eye out while I dive?" she asked.

"How can you think for a moment that I wouldn't?"

Morgan turned her head and looked into my eyes ever so briefly, offering a faint smile. The sun shone in her eyes and they looked as white as the spots on the dunes naked of wild grass behind her.

She followed me out toward the underwater cemetery. I had not seen her in a mask and snorkel since we were kids. She looked so funny, her pale features and ghostly eyes so unfit to my picture of a frogwoman. I laughed inside. As the sea eclipsed our bodies, I put my mask and snorkel on too, putting my face under the water, watching Morgan's skinny yet cute butt help her legs move her along.

A dark gravestone below loomed in front of her, and I was worried what her reaction might be. If I was frightened at first, she would be too. She had trouble watching scary movies, even as benign as *Poltergeist*.

Her librarian's curiosity proved too much, and she immediately dove down. There was a sudden rush of bubbles when she first arrived at the gravestone, a few jerks of her body, all its parts in a controlled chorus of panic. But she hovered about it for a good ten seconds or so. I started to become worried and began my way down, too. Before I could make it only a few feet, she had started back up again. She was swimming fast, and as she grew closer, a unique expression impregnated her eyes.

Our heads suddenly popped out of the ocean, as if buoys that were temporarily held down. We both removed our masks and snorkels immediately, kicking our legs to stay afloat, breathing vitally. Morgan stared right at me, her eyes the widest that I had ever seen them. Her plain face looked ageless buoying on the rippling ocean.

"Edmund J. Bigsley," Morgan said.

"What?" It was hard to get out more than a word or so at a time with our lungs still recovering.

"I saw a name."

"On the gravestone?"

"Yes. Ethan, I'm scared. I want to go back."

"Okay."

I followed her back to shore. I had never seen her swim so fast. Before long we were sitting on the beach. The surf began to grow, as if indignant for her dark secrets being breached. Morgan was trembling. I reached both of my hands out and began warming her shoulders with them.

"I'm fine. Really. You don't have to do that. It's just creepy out there. Macabre."

"I wish I had a dime."

Morgan laughed her little laugh—so quiet—almost a whisper: "Hee, hee."

When we were in high school, I was so impressed with her already immense vocabulary that I started giving her coins for certain words. In twelfth grade I once gave her a whole quarter for the word, *verisimilitude*. Morgan read more books than anyone. She imbibed them in days, magically retaining so many of them.

"So you saw a name on the gravestone?" I asked.

"Yes. Edmund J. Bigsley. I couldn't believe it at first. I still can't believe that there are gravestones down there. How could that be?" Morgan was more excited than I had seen her in a long time, and I felt more attracted to her in that moment than I ever had.

"Edmund J. Bigsley? Who the hell is Edmund J. Bigsley?"

"I don't know, but I'm going to find out."

"Let me guess, off to the library?"

For a split second vulnerability surfaced in Morgan's eyes, and I wished that I could take all those split seconds and build an unsinkable bridge between her and me.

"Hee, hee. But don't go thinking you have me figured out."

"You wouldn't catch me thinking that for a second. In the meantime, I'm going to go visit Captain Shelby and see what he knows."

"Good idea. Why don't you come by later and we'll compare notes?"

"Okay."

The sun was approaching high noon as Morgan dried off and began to dress. Clouds were gathering over the horizon, as if teaming up with the angry surf.

A storm was brewing. Pelican Bay was overdue for one.

It may be a while before we can see those gravestones again, I thought to myself.

I dried and dressed, too.

CHAPTER FIVE

It is more than a mere love of books that forges a librarian like Morgan. More than the surreal pounds of a hardback, the soft-callous feel of a cardstock page, as if a sail blowing a schooner of knowledge through her mind. More than the often dank and musky aroma of old shelves dwelling in her nostrils and more than those long words, like the black fingers of witches casting spells upon her psyche.

Much more. To be Morgan is to be born of plunging into the Land Between the Lines. To escape something.

And to love such a librarian requires a surrendering to her eccentricities, a bowing to her pathological quietness, an obeisance to a reticence that is utterly untreatable. If you cannot commit to this sort of dedication, then let her be. Let her wander in wonder among her books and live out her days in her own world without you.

I wish I had loved Morgan before she was a librarian. It would have been far easier. But it is too late now. There is no going back.

Her mother, a pale beach aristocrat, a sauntering, delicate, august wife of the town doctor, tried to kill Morgan three times.

Her name was Beatrice. Beatrice Olinsworth. She would have never tried to hurt her daughter. Of course not. But brain tumors have a way of changing your personality. More often than not.

Beatrice was a splendid mother, a splendid wife, a splendid everything, until her strange behaviors began. "It really is not her fault," Morgan's father, Charles, would say. "She is not well. Not herself at all."

Beatrice loved to take Morgan for long walks on Pelican Bay Beach looking for shells and other raw art materials. To this day, many of her beach wood sculptures adorn shelves and coffee tables inside the Olinsworth home. But Morgan destroyed all the necklaces that her mother ever made her after the third murder attempt—casting them all into the sea as though she were letting the shells loose again, like nursed-back-to-health wild creatures.

And she would have cast all the sculptures into the sea as well, had her father not caught her in the act. To this day, Morgan is not allowed near the odd sculptures. They are not very good. But Beatrice thought they were all masterpieces—thought she would sell them all for a million dollars in Gull Bay, maybe even in Charleston one day. But she did not have enough time left to do so. And Charles would never part with them. Morgan hated to look at them. She could not even give them a glance in passing for the longest time. Now they are but dusty antiques—strange organs of the sea that no doctor, other than Charles, could ever give names to.

The first murder attempt should not have been such a surprise.

Morgan was twelve years old then and hated books. I always laugh at this fact. She told me stories about how her mother, a philistine, forced books and bedtime stories on her, though with excellent intentions, to the point of a kind of terror. And after her mother died she began reading books at first as a vengeance, and then, like a time traveler whose time machine has been destroyed, became beautifully imprisoned in the Land Between the Lines.

The Land of the Lost.

Never to return again.

Morgan pitched a temper tantrum one night because she wanted to attend a school dance rather than finish *Pride and Prejudice*. Wow! What a mistake. Her mother had already become mercurial, crying during insipid TV commercials, going to bed insanely early or not at all, flying off into scary, obscure diatribes if the refrigerator door was left open by mistake. So it should not have been that much of a surprise when she tried to make her daughter swallow *Pride and Prejudice*.

But it still was.

Charles came in after too many seconds of it, hearing his daughter's muffled screams from the living room where he sat nodding off over a medical journal. He stood there before Morgan's bed, watching Morgan's eyes. Instinct just took over and he grabbed his wife and threw her to the ground.

Now Beatrice's eyes took on that same look.

Morgan already began to change after that first murder attempt. She talked less at school. The teacher had to call on her and make her answer questions, which had never happened before. She walked around Pelican Bay with her head down all the time. She always seemed to have a book open but never read a word.

And it was around this time that Morgan and I befriended each other. Or that I befriended her. Of course we had shared classes. In Pelican Bay, you shared every class with everyone. We had said hi to each other at town events, passing on Pelican Bay Street, and so forth. But it was around that time that we started hanging out together. Really hanging out.

I saw her sitting one afternoon in Bigsley Square, a frowning plot of neglected grass and unwieldy benches guarded by mammoth, ancient oaks, moss dripping from them, as if they had been mauled and would bleed gray-green forever.

I saw Morgan crying up a storm, teardrops so big, staining the pages in her history book in an attempt to alter history merely by smudging its lines. I came up and said, "Do you want to talk?" and she looked at me like I was crazy and said, "Go away."

As strange as it sounds, I really think that I fell in love with Morgan right there and then. There was just something about her face, though I should confess that I found it to be quite plain and ugly. Only there was something about the color of her eyes and the way those colossal tears welled up in them. When I looked into them it was like seeing a soft teal landscape through a foggy window, a sacred place that I wanted to escape into and never return from.

And I guess that I have always been living in Morgan's eyes. In that beautiful teal place.

I just kept asking her to talk and she finally told me what had happened, half-talking and half-crying. I cannot say that I understood all of it, other than her mother having just tried to kill her. But I have to hand it to myself. I listened carefully and did not judge her at all.

She finally asked me to sit next to her and she just let it all out. I fell deeply in love with her. I think that for her we had just become friends. It was so nice though. I do wish most of the time that I could go back to that first murder attempt, go back in time, and stop her mother before she tried it again. I think that it would have been much easier to love Morgan. But then another part of me thinks that it would not really be Morgan anymore.

The second murder attempt was much more serious though, I am afraid. I will never forget it because I was fishing with Captain Shelby when it happened.

That afternoon everything was impossibly bright, as if the sun were upset about something. As the captain's boat came into the bay, I saw the Pelican Bay Hospital ambulance's lights twirling like red licorice under the fuming sun. On the beach two paramedics were attending to a young girl whom I later learned was Morgan.

As the story goes, she and her mother were out on one of their shell hunts along the shore. I was always surprised that Morgan trusted her mother enough to walk alone with her again after the first murder attempt. But Charles had convinced Morgan that her mother was simply ill and would get better. And maybe this was so. Maybe a healthy Beatrice would have never tried to hurt anyone. Not even a fly.

They were walking, looking for shells, and suddenly Beatrice grabbed Morgan from behind, put a hand over her mouth and nose, and dragged her into the sea. Morgan was flailing and letting out a muffled, bubbling shriek, making those same eyes again. Eventually Beatrice gathered her wits and pulled her daughter to the shore. Her eyes showed the look of a hooked marlin. The only movement from Morgan was the sea leaking from the sides of her mouth, her long brazen hair like sunburned seaweed sprawled out on the sand.

Beatrice ran for home and told Charles, "Our daughter is drowning." Charles called Pelican Bay Hospital and then ran to the beach and performed CPR on Morgan, saving her life.

I did not see Morgan for weeks after this. She was kept out of school and her mother was sent away to a mental hospital, in Gull Bay, called Serene Halls. When I did see Morgan again, she would not look at me or talk to me at all, nor any of the other school kids. She was sent to the principal's office several times for not responding to the teacher.

I persisted and one day soon after, finding her walking among the dunes painted erratically with turning wild grass, she confessed all the details of her mother's second murder attempt. But this time she did not cry. Not a tear. Still, I felt even closer to Morgan. I loved her even more.

In a few months, Morgan had read more books than all the kids combined in Pelican Bay. No soul in our tiny town, or any town for that matter, would ever match such an astonishing feat of literary escapism.

While at Serene Halls, Beatrice, the once beach aristocrat, was diagnosed with a brain tumor.

Charles was livid and went to Gull Bay to argue with the psychiatrist that had sent his wife for advanced medical testing. "This diagnosis is not correct," he said. "What business do you have running these sorts of tests and worrying everyone to death? Who do you think you are? You're just a damned psychiatrist. For God's sake! Who the hell is in charge here?"

And then Charles went and argued with the Gull Bay Cancer Ward doctors. And his small town medical knowledge made him look small. And he finally gave into the diagnosis, coming back to his small town and feeling small and helpless and as angry as the Pelican Bay sun on that day that Morgan was almost drowned by his once royal-looking wife.

Charles brought Beatrice back with him, the latter having decided not to undergo radiation treatment. The tumor was well advanced and the prospects of success slim at best. Charles had found yet another thing to be angry about.

Those few days that Beatrice was lucid, those days that he canceled his patients and stayed home with his dying wife, prescient of a hermetic trend that would continue well after her death, such days he would try to convince Beatrice to go back to Gull Bay and undergo chemotherapy. Of course she refused, and he would become more furious and more raving.

Morgan would no longer be in the same room with her mother. She stayed more often than not at friends' houses and spent more and more time with me.

Of course I was very pleased with this.

There were days when Beatrice regained some energy, days when she looked almost normal, color returning to her face, a mermaid returning from a bath in the sea. On these days she would emphatically ask her daughter to go for a shell walk, or to read to her. Morgan always said no.

But on one fateful day, after her father had insisted that "she spend some time with her because there are only a few days left now and she'll never see her mother again," Morgan reluctantly gave in and went with her mother for a picnic on the beach. After all, her mother had not suffered any bizarre behaviors since Serene Halls, and she was on medication.

Morgan talks about this last day with her mother quite fondly, even though there was a third murder attempt. I think that we are all kickball captains when it comes to memory. We can choose who we want to play and who we want to sit it out. Thank God for this, for what happened to Morgan that last day makes me promise myself to never try and change her—ever.

It was a perfect Saturday. Not too hot—not too cold. It was one of those days when summer is saying goodbye and fall is whispering hello.

Hanging in the sky, a cloudless, brilliant sky, rare for Pelican Bay, that exuded the shades of blue of the eyes of both mother and daughter, were the merciless and greedy gulls. The two women had to throw their food behind a nearby dune in trade for peace and quiet.

Beatrice said very little, just oddly watched the gulls rip at the sandwiches and the apples. When the gulls had exhausted their luxurious scraps, Beatrice removed from the bottom of the picnic basket an over-sized box of assorted chocolates that Charles had given her when he came to Serene Halls the first time.

"Mother, what are you doing?"

"Nothing."

As she threw the chocolates at her daughter, the famished gulls multiplied exponentially. Their squawking became riotous.

Morgan began to scream, "Stop, Mother! Stop! Please!"

Finally, a few townspeople walking nearby came running over and shooed the hellish gulls away. But by then the chocolates were all gone, and Morgan's head and face were pecked to the point of what appeared to be mortal blood loss, her ash-blonde hair suddenly brunette. She could have been Tippi Hedren after her hundredth take in the filming of Hitchcock's, *The Birds*.

On her death bed, Beatrice confessed that she thought in that moment that her daughter was the angel of death.

CHAPTER SIX

Captain Shelby was taking a nap when I came across his boat around one o'clock in the afternoon. I could see his white canvas pants, the material like a weathered sail, rolled up atop sole-worn, brownish boat shoes. His torso, as if painted with a stained T-shirt, showed a happily protruding hairy belly, like fly-infested pork. A hopelessly faded captain's hat hid his crinkly face. He was on a self-fashioned hammock in front of his bridge. The rumblings of distant thunder could have been an amplification of his snoring.

"Better wake up, Captain. You're going to get wet."

He stirred.

"What? Well, me clothes could use the washin'," he growled. "Let me guess, been messin' around them stones again, eh?"

"How did you know?"

"It be all over yer face."

"You're not going to believe what we found!"

"Why don't ye take a breath and a rúm while yer at it."

"You'll never guess what's down there!"

"A man reaches an age where guessin's no longer fun or necessary."

"They're gravestones."

Were it not for the looming, unsettling thunder, there would have been perfect silence. Captain Shelby surveyed the sea, as if counting the seconds until rain. A deep worry, an old worry, fell upon his face, pushing out its old lines.

"Go on boy."

"That's how Morgan first reacted, but we dove and saw them for ourselves. In fact, Morgan saw a name on one."

The old man said nothing.

"Edmund J. Bigsley. Do you know the name?"

The old man looked out to sea again, squinting his eyes and shaking his head slowly. He was quiet. I looked out where he was looking and it appeared as though the ominous clouds were bringing the sky down into the ocean with them. Tiny drops of rain began to reach us.

"Can't be," he finally said, more as though talking to himself. "There be a Bigsley on a tombstone in town already—unless—"

"Unless what?"

"Listen, me Son, that cemetery down there may be very old—very old. And why she be washin' up now God only knows—God only knows."

Now it felt like the drops of rain were dressing me with a coat of fear.

"How old?"

"God only knows, I tell ye, me Son—God only knows."

And after saying this, the old man became so still, so pensive, staring out to sea once more. Goosebumps seemed to originate in my chest and spread through my entire body. I felt like I had jumped from the Titanic into the northern Atlantic.

"But I don't understand. I thought this town only had one cemetery."

"Eh boy—just one." Captain Shelby cleared his throat in a piratical way.

"But then how—"

"That there cemetery's very old. See, the name Bigsley, well, they're the forefathers of Pelican Bay. Built the town hall and that buildin' where yer girlfriend works."

"She's not my girlfriend."

"That there cemetery under the ocean could be part of this town. Pelican Bay goes back to the first English settlers that came after the fishin'."

"Really?"

"There been many a hurricane before the Great Hurricane. That means the shoreline ye see now around Pelican Bay ain't the true fit." Captain Shelby placed his hand on his chin, a worriedness resetting his face, and then scratched his head. "That means, me Son, that ye may have relatives out there under the sea—old relatives."

"Hmm. But why now? I mean, why is the cemetery washing up now?"

"Well, it's not really washin' up, to be correct, see? The shelf's worn a little thin. Must be all them recent easterly storms have exposed it— don't think it'll last for long, though. Look, she be an awesome westerly storm headin' our way." The old man pointed vaguely at the horizon.

"Could there be other things out there, too? I mean, you know—other buildings?"

"Eh boy! Big storms before the Great Hurricane took most of Pelican Bay with them one time or another—blew walls and doors and souls right out into the sea. There could be rubble down there—farther out—a town under a town."

I got goose bumps all over again.

"Have ye talked to yer grandmudder, Sidney?"

"No."

"Seems to me she may have dated a boy with the last name Bigsley—maybe—back in her school days."

The rain was really starting to come down now.

"Ye better get back and find some shelter, me Son. This storm be gettin' right crooked. Got me flashlight?"

"No. Sorry. I'll bring it tomorrow, okay?"

"Okay."

The dock was soaked with rain as I hurried back to town toward the library. I knew that Morgan would still be there. When she started researching, she could go on for hours.

Before I could make it to the shelter of the library's entranceway, the rain had become quite thick. I was utterly soaked with it. It was late afternoon and the sky was as dark as dusk, the air taking on a slight chill, as if from the old man's recent words.

I stood in the entranceway and rang the buzzer. It took a long time for Morgan to come to the door. I already had a mild case of the shivers.

"Wow—you're really soaked. Let me see if I have a towel somewhere. Just a second."

She came running back with a towel that looked almost as old as the library. But I was not in a situation where one might complain.

"Thanks."

The library was not well kept at all. Morgan could never boast of her organizational abilities. There were books strewn here and there, carts of them congesting old aisles. Piles of *New York Times* newspapers, tattooed with dates as old as my grandmother, sat on tables with little chairs pushed out, as if ghosts still thumbed through them. If Morgan had not been good about occasionally clearing the cobwebs, one might have quickly called it a ghost library. And the outside of the building was so worn that it might as well have been just another ghost building in another ghost town.

I took a seat, attempting to pat myself dry. Morgan looked at me. Her face was still possessed by such an eagerness, as if the storm had blown in a visiting historian with brand new facts about Pelican Bay. Facts that could change the course of our lives.

"I found out a lot, Ethan—I think—but it's mainly conjecture at this point. It could be that records have been destroyed or lost."

"That makes sense. Captain Shelby said something about hurricanes before the Great Hurricane."

"That could be. I'm sure that a lot of hurricanes have passed through Pelican Bay. Anyway, I couldn't find anything with the name Edmund Bigsley, but a James Bigsley, possibly a grandson or great grandson, built this library and other buildings. Ethan, do you realize how far back this dates Pelican Bay?"

And now my fading shivers were topped with new shivers.

"That's really something else," I said. "Captain Shelby kept saying that the cemetery out there under the sea has to be *really* old. Now this is all making sense!"

"Ethan, the building that we're standing in was built in the early 19th century."

"Wow. That means that the gravestones out there, from the town under our town, could be as much as—oh my God—wait—Jamestown was first settled in the very early 17th century, right?"

"The man knows his history. I'm impressed."

Morgan smiled at me.

And I liked it.

"That means that the underwater tombstones out there could be four centuries old."

"How fascinating!" Morgan chimed in like a loud church bell. She was looking right at me, huddling in, as if we were planning a town heist.

She let my lips touch hers for just a second, before pulling away. Her lips were always so soft, and on that late afternoon, our tiny town swaddled in vengeful rain, they tasted like a perfectly aged wine left by our forefathers, a crimson red adding an erotic second of color to a very black-and-white library. The tragic gravity between us always made me tremble at first.

"I asked you not to do that, Ethan. Why did you do that?" Morgan's face was tight and drawn.

"I'm sorry, it just happened," I said, frowning.

"I just don't think I feel that way about you."

"I know. It's just that, well—"

"Please don't say it! Please don't say it, Ethan!"

We were silent for the longest time, watching the carpet of rain outside, a fog if one looked carelessly. Pelts of rain making a thick, rhythmic knocking sound on the few windows in the library made me envision great ancestors carried in the rain drops, knocking to get in.

"Ethan," she said, rather softly and lowly, "I don't want to hurt you. Maybe we've been spending too much time together."

"Would you rather be with Henry?"

"That's not fair. Henry's been gone a long time, and I told you I don't love him."

"But he still writes you, doesn't he?"

"I don't want to talk about this anymore."

We fell silent again. The knocking rain carried the conversation on for us, the knocks eerie periods punctuating old sentences beating out the history of Pelican Bay.

"Ethan, there's something else that I found, or, I should say, couldn't find."

"What?"

"Well. I wanted to see if Captain Shelby's ancestors were among the forefathers who built our current Pelican Bay."

"And?"

"Ethan, I couldn't find the name Shelby anywhere—not anywhere at all."

"That's really strange."

My goose bumps were back again. The library seemed to darken further, somehow.

"Look, Morgan, there's probably some explanation, I mean—"

"Think about it, Ethan, what do you really know about him? You know, the townspeople all say that he's crazy."

"He's not crazy. Weird, maybe, but not crazy."

"Why does he live out there on that fishing boat all by himself? Why doesn't he have a cottage, like everyone else?"

"He doesn't like people that much, I guess."

"Why is he friends with you?"

"I don't know. Maybe I remind him of a son he lost."

"Where's Captain Shelby's wife?"

"He's never talked about any wife, but I imagine she could have died in one of the hurricanes."

"Ethan, we need to go to the cemetery."

I could not believe that she had said it. I stared at her with a lax face.

"But you hate cemeteries."

"Will you go with me tomorrow morning, in the light? Please?"

"Somebody must really have the 'research bug!' Okay, but this rain has to let up, and even if it does, we may have to wait a day or two. The cemetery's going to be pretty muddy."

"Thanks, Ethan."

She smiled again.

And I wanted to kiss her again.

"Do you still have that big umbrella here? Can I walk you home?"

CHAPTER SEVEN

The following evening I had my reoccurring dream about the first time that I met Captain Shelby. I was only nine years old.

I want to run away from Sidney, perhaps stirred by the cloudy sea that day. She sits erectly on an old blanket, a woman of crowning pale English beauty, adorned with a great white lacey hat that droops in the front and back as though she is living the perfect moment, erasing the tragic past and the craggy future of Pelican Bay with the hat's elegant bends.

I watch her all morning while building a great wall for a sand castle, a wall that is continuously swamped by the irascible sea. I want to escape that day, flee the black hole left by my parents and the smallness of my existence that live beneath the devilish smiles of crooked storms.

I watch and wait for my moment, which I think will never come. And it is more than the sea that stirs me—something a nine-year-old could never fathom.

I look at Sidney and she smiles back, her sky-blue eyes giddy oval gods. She looks up and down the beach, her long, pale, noble neck stretching like an East Yorkshire Kittiwake bird. I learned something noteworthy at that young age. The true grace of a woman's beauty awakens much later in her life. I also realized that Sidney was the most beautiful woman that I had ever seen.

Chance finally comes when a trickster wind swoops up out of nowhere and absconds with Sidney's scarf, a cloudy blue paisley thing of grace she seemed to always have with her. While she chases her scarf, I dash down the beach like a child sprouting his first run.

Sidney soon notices and shouts, "Ethan! Ethan! Where are you going?"

I do not answer. I am the tragic history of Pelican Bay given legs, avenging all pariah beach souls. Run, run, run. So fast. Yet I feel that I move only a few feet along the shore.

"Go on boy! What are ye at? The sea surge be in yer legs!"

The captain stands in front of me, palm held out, a yellowed map of all forgotten coastal towns. I stop and stare up, awed to the point of tears—a tiny soul wrecked by the great unknown. Yes. There he is. The greatest man I have ever seen or will ever know.

In a diminutive voice I try, "I—"

"Seems thee be lost, me Boy," he roars, an augmentation of the surf. I am breathing quite heavily. I stare into his eyes. It was the first time it ever occurred to me that, like the sound of the surf living eternally in a land-marooned conch shell, the ocean could live in one's eyes.

"I—"

"That be yer grandmudder yellin' for ye in the distance like a crooked gull, eh?"

"Yes." That is all I can get out.

"Ye must be Ethan then."

"Yes." I nod, a child helplessly agreeing with a Greek god. He is wearing a great coat that billows even though the wind that had brought me there has stopped altogether. "How did you know?"

"I knew yer parents."

"You did?"

"Yer mudder was a kind ducky. Her and yer old man was eatin' by the crooked sea on a skiff headin' back from Lighthouse Point." I never thought about the thunder having a human voice. Not until that day.

"I—I thought they died in a hurricane."

"Ethan!" Sidney yells again.

I look back at her. She seems so far away, her fine English voice swallowed by the surf, her billowy white cotton clothes converting her into a 17th century day-ghost.

"Ye knows yerself 'twas not a big contrary storm that took 'em."

"Yeah, but Sidney—"

"She be sparin' yer feelings, me Boy. 'Twas the hard luck of a crooked handleggr of the sea what took 'em."

"A crooked what?"

"Arm."

"You were there?"

"Eh boy."

"Did you try to save them?"

"Thee be a smart scopie!"

"Ethan, dear, wait for me! Don't talk to that man! I'm coming!"

"What happened, sir? Will you tell me?"

When the old man begins to tell the story, his face starts to look so young. This is what I remember most from all my dreams about him.

"There be things, me Son, that even a man of the sea can't be after controllin', see?"

I nod and he continues, but I can hear Sidney's feet in the sand approaching now.

"When the sea's after somethin', she'll devour it, and she was after yer parents that day—right contrary she was. Was on me way back from me Secret Spot and saw 'em just beyond the pass—saw the sea rise up like a rotten thumb. I rushed for 'em, but when I got there, 'twas just a capsized skip. I dove in. Was after findin' 'em, but they was gone like a couple a scared fiskr returnin' to the deep. 'Twas right sad. I be so sorry, me Son."

He must have seen how sad my little forlorn face was. There were big salty tears in the old man's eyes.

"Ethan!" Sidney yells one last time, catching up to me finally. She betakes Captain Shelby with great uncertainty, removing her hat, as if dubiously honoring a savage king. "I, uh—"

The old man laughs heartily, the sound of the sea coughing.

"I certainly don't mean to be rude," she says, "but—"

"Ha, ha. But what?"

"Ethan, it's time to go, honey. It's getting late and the sky is getting dark."

"Why so crooked, me Ducky?"

"Ethan, take my hand!"

My grandmother pulls me up into the dunes. I am crying along with the gulls that are pecking at a sun-baked crab. I look at the crab and suddenly want to be it. Dead. Devoid of memory.

As we climb a dune, I turn and look back at the old man and he waves at me. His face is old again and it seems so sad.

"Who is that man?"

"Captain Shelby. And you'll stay away from him, dear, if you know what's good for you."

CHAPTER EIGHT

The cemetery was still wet when Morgan and I visited it a few mornings later, and we had to wear galoshes. Morgan looked so demure in her galoshes. Her glasses just completed the look.
I, on the other hand, looked dreadful in galoshes.
Morgan laughed at me when I came to collect her. I laughed, too.
"How's your dad?" I asked.
"Well, tomorrow's the day, so what do you think?" Morgan looked at me straight-faced. "He hasn't left his room since last night. I think he's reading Edgar Allen Poe—not good."
"I'm sorry to hear that."
I really was, too, but her dad, Charles, never liked me very much. I tried to like him, and some days I really thought that I did. He was such an interesting man. He was well educated, caring, typically amiable, the town doctor, the only doctor, eternally in a white coat or a white shirt, always meticulously ironed, a fastidious man, balding but in a distinguished way, and almost always a gently smiling man.
But her dad wanted another man for Morgan. His name was Henry, a famous heart surgeon who now lived up in New York. He wanted his daughter to go with him to New York, but Morgan would not leave the library, would not leave her books. Sometimes I thought that nothing was more important to Morgan than her precious books. I loved books, too. But no one loved books as much as Morgan, for they were the keys to the kingdom of the Land Between the Lines.
If I love books and she loves books, why can't we both love each

other? I always thought to myself. But this was a bad argument, a bad argument indeed. Henry did not love books, and I *loved* that Henry did not love books. But Henry loved Morgan, and wrote her religiously, which made me want to hate religion, and Henry along with it. I always felt guilty for thinking that if I were a doctor, Charles might like me, too. However, I was the worst thing that I could have been. I was a writer.

"You look like a tall duck—a lanky groom for a pelican," Morgan said.

"Thanks a lot."

We both chuckled.

She locked their cottage door behind her and we sauntered down Pelican Bay Street, the town's main thoroughfare, where you could find the Pelican Bay Post Office, Pelican Bay Hotel, and of course, Pelican Bay Bank, which on account of Pelican Bay having a town population so small, might as well have been a giant piggy bank. We were headed toward Pelican Bay Church.

"I think I already know the answer, but why are we going to the cemetery exactly?"

"Somebody forgot to do his homework," Morgan said.

"You want to make sure your town records are accurate, right?"

"Bingo."

"But what's that going to prove, anyway? I mean, what if Captain Shelby came from another town—you know, moved here for the fishing?"

"But listen to your reasoning, Ethan. That would mean that he came to Pelican Bay *before* our oldest townspeople."

"Uh, yeah, I guess, if our town stories are true about him looking old to our oldest townspeople when they were young."

"But how could that be? Captain Shelby would have to be almost two hundred years old."

Morgan and I both stopped dead in our tracks and looked at each other, wide-eyed—wandering deer hearing a faraway car.

"Morgan, what if he's Pelican Bay's town vampire?"

"Stop it, Ethan. That's not funny."

We began walking again, but very slowly. A wind from the bay was beginning to whip up and made a whirling sound, almost as if walking along with us to eaves-drop.

"Or what if he's a ghost?"

I suddenly grabbed Morgan's shoulders from behind. She jumped slightly. I laughed out loud.

"Ethan, stop it right now. You're scaring me and it's not funny!"

"And you're the one who wants to go to the cemetery, my squeamish librarian!"

"I'm sure there's a perfectly logical explanation for all this. I just want to know what it is, that's all. Do you think I'd be going to the cemetery at night? And you're here to protect me, anyway."

I really liked the sound of that.

Really.

The Pelican Bay Church Cemetery epitomized the "old small town graveyard." There were still water pockets about the place from Sunday's hard rain, adding a marshy quality to it. Moss dangled from guarding cemetery oaks like dog-chewed old green winter coats. The headstones seemed to shiver in their places. Some of them were centuries old and quite faded, but modern compared to the tombstones under the sea. A few might have been special-ordered from England, perhaps by the well-to-do families of those times. Some were so covered with dirt and mud and grime as to make immediate reading of them difficult. All the gravestones were the color of coin-rubbed heavy lead pencil on dull-white construction paper. The small, white wooden church stood pleading, lonely, just beyond the graves.

"Why don't you start on the right, and I'll take the left," I offered cordially.

"No, Ethan, stay with me, please."

"Okay."

"We're looking for anything with the name Shelby on it—anything at all."

"I got it."

We had already scoured the bulk of the cemetery and the task was beginning to seem futile, when we finally came across a gravestone set a bit apart from the others, a gravestone pariah. Morgan stretched her beautiful, delicate hand out and stopped me.

"Look, Ethan, at that grave over there. The last name is partially covered, but it starts with 'S-H'. Quick, go inside the church and see if there's something you can borrow to clean off that stone."

"Okay, but it's kind of early still. I doubt that Minister Billingsley is there."

"Well, use your imagination, then. Look around the back of the church for something, anything. And don't be gone long. Promise?"

"Okay."

The church was locked, just as I had suspected, but I quickly came back with an old chimney brush that had been napping in the back near some cement steps.

"Quick, Ethan, clean it off!"

The tombstone read: Richard H. Sherman. We just stood and stared at each other.

"That's it, Morgan. We've checked them all."

"I just don't get it. How can this be? There has to be a plausible explanation. Even if generations of his have lived on fishing boats, which is unlikely, they would probably have gravestones."

"What if his relatives were all cremated and scattered on the sea?"

"It's certainly possible, but there would still be town records, and I have access to all of them."

"Eerie. Just plain eerie."

"You said it. Can we get out of here now? I'm really starting to get creeped out."

"Sure."

We began walking back down Pelican Bay Street toward the library. I let Morgan lead the way with her cute, shuffling steps.

"We need to talk to more townspeople. I'll see Minister Billingsley during lunch. Why don't you talk to your grandmother? She knows a lot about this town."

"Sounds good. What about Captain Shelby?"

"You better make sure you have all your ducks in a row before you confront that old man. How would you feel if someone accused you of being a ghost?"

"The whole thing's just downright creepy!"

"You can say that again."

"The whole thing's just downright creepy!"

"Hee, hee."

CHAPTER NINE

Sidney's hair was silvered by years of overwhelming concern for a parentless boy in a sea-battered town. She cared for me, as if I were the last beach rose in the last dune garden on earth. She was in her early seventies, of moderate height, a careworn, denuding smile, and a warmth and gentility all her own. She possessed the candor of a boat's bow, head to wind, but the touch of a ray of sunlight.

"Good morning, dear. Fresh toast and biscuits and homemade jam are on the table, and hot water for tea is on the stove."

"Thanks, Sidney."

"Where have you been off to this morning? Fate should have it with that librarian again."

"Yes."

"Dear Lord."

I looked at Sidney steadily.

"Okay, let's have it. What's on your mind this morning? It looks quite serious."

"Sidney?"

"Yes, dear," she said, spreading some boysenberry jam on a slice of white toast for me.

"Have you seen the gravestones yet?"

"No, but the whole town is talking about them. A lot of fuss over an old cemetery, if you ask me. You know our ancestors have had to rebuild over and over again. If it weren't for the spectacular fishing, I think settlers would have given up on Pelican Bay centuries ago. Nothing here but a disease of bad storms, one after the other."

"Sidney?"

"Well just speak your questions, dear! Why, you're getting me all spooked."

"Where did Captain Shelby come from? I mean, *really* come from?"

Sidney fell to silence, looking out the window. You could see the sea so clearly from our house, almost a bright blue today, as if blissful to be free of the recent storm. There was a two-foot surf, and you could even see a few rusty pelicans bathing just off shore.

She finished her cup of tea, a big sip, and then looked right through me.

"They used to tell stories about him when we were kids," she said, "but not too much anymore, maybe because our town population was cut in half during the Great Hurricane."

"I don't understand. What do you mean, *when you were kids*? You're over seventy."

"You heard me right, dear. In grade school everyone was afraid of that crazy old man. How he survived the Great Hurricane is anybody's guess. No one really knows how old he is. Have you ever asked him?"

"No. I don't know why. I guess it just never came up. I always thought he was very old. His face doesn't always show it, though."

"And what about me, dear? Do I look old to you?"

"No, Sidney, you're beautiful."

"You're just being sweet. But I love you for it, Ethan. I love you for it."

"So what did they used to say about him?"

"That he's an old ghost. A Viking."

Chills bathed me as seawater, like the old pelicans loitering off shore. My eyes widened, and I thought that they might tear up.

"A Viking?"

"Did you know the name Shelby is descended from the Vikings, from Old Norse, the language they used to speak?"

"No."

"We used to dare each other to go out to the docks late at night. They say a light is always burning out there on his old fishing boat. Legend has it a boy drowned on a dare. They say he went out there one night and saw old Captain Shelby coming toward him down the dock, grumbling something, only he was moving faster than any one could ever run. Well, the boy fell on the dock and hit his head. His body washed up a few days later."

"That's some story, Sidney."

"They say he pushed and then drowned the little boy."

"I don't believe it. I think he's a good man—highly eccentric, but good. I don't see what's wrong with him."

"Captain Shelby gives me the willies, plain and simple. There's something wrong with him. I think he's dangerous. Why is all this coming up now, anyway? What does he have to do with the undersea cemetery?"

"Morgan and I dove down and saw a name on one of the gravestones."

Sidney's stare intensified.

"Whose name?"

"Edmund J. Bigsley."

"*Bigsley*?" Sidney began scratching her head and a faraway look seized her again. "I know that name."

"Captain Shelby told me that you dated a boy named Bigsley?"

"He did? Well, Bigsley's a big name around here. They built most of this town."

"That's right. That's what Morgan said."

"I don't see the big deal. If the Bigsleys built this town, then their great ancestors' names are on those headstones under the sea."

"Here's the thing. There are no records of any last name Shelby at all."

The weight of the air in the kitchen seemed to change. Sidney just sat there quietly for a moment, her face inhabited, her eyes seaward again. The sky outside was darkening and a rogue breeze came through the window, leaving chilled bones in its wake.

"I don't understand, Ethan. That's impossible. His boat's been moored to that dock since I was a kid."

"Has he ever lived in town?"

"Not that I know of, dear."

"What about his wife and son?"

"Wife and son? That old man's been alone as long as this town's been a town. The poor fellow's just lonely, that's all. That's why he's always trying to talk to you and take you fishing with him."

"Think hard, Sidney. This is important. What did Captain Shelby look like when you were a kid? Can you remember?"

"Old. He's always looked old."

I rubbed my face with my hands.

"Ethan, don't go letting that vast imagination of yours run wild now. I'm sure there's a simple explanation."

"That's what Morgan keeps saying."

"Why don't you go ask him yourself? Just be careful, dear, okay? You know I don't like you around that old man. And don't go calling him a ghost. He's liable to fly at you, too, and send you below those docks with that poor little boy."

"That's really funny."

It began to thunder in the distance, as if the voice of the old man were acquiescing with Sidney.

"But it doesn't look like you're going to be walking out there this afternoon, or looking at those sunken gravestones anytime soon," Sidney said wistfully.

"Sidney, what if his name's down there?"

"God only made us to live so long, dear. Now drink your tea, and stay away from that kooky librarian."

"You know I can't do that, Sidney."

"And that's your greatest failing, dear. You fell in love with someone that you'll never be able to have and hold. She's too screwed up."

"That's not fair. What would your life be like if your own mother tried to kill you—not once, but three times?"

Sidney's eyes shut so slowly and then opened again. A whisper of sand leaving the scalps of the dunes might have relaxed the careworn wrinkles in her face. Her early spring eyes arrowed me and I melted.

"Ethan, dear, you confuse a writer's sympathy for love. That is your predicament."

Some moments of silence as the sky darkened further and began to growl again.

"Sidney."

"Yes, dear."

"Why do you hate Captain Shelby so much?"

"I don't hate him. He just makes me—uncomfortable. That's all."

"Why? Is it because he's so strange?"

"Partly." Sidney stood up and walked over to the window. The sky was as shadowy as twilight now and thunder called like a deep warning. "Another storm. What a shock."

I walked up behind Sidney and placed my hands on her shoulders. She trembled, heaved, and then reclined.

"Sidney, there's something you're not telling me."

"You're so smart, dear—just like your father."

"Is it about the kid that died in 1931?"

"No, dear."

"What then? Please tell me."

We stood at the window, watching the rain launch at us from the sea in enraged slants. It was as thick as a curtain of doom. Sidney closed the window and sat down again.

"Ethan, dear, there are many things, tragic things, that I was waiting until you were older to tell you. I've just kept putting them off. One of them was how your parents died."

"I still dream about that day Captain Shelby told me."

"I'm sure you do, dear. I was going to tell you. I'm still angry at that old pelican for telling a nine-year-old something like that."

"He didn't know any better."

"You're still so naïve, dear."

"Well, I'm old enough now, and I deserve to know." My face was quivering, tears rising just like on that day that I looked up into the old man's face for the first time.

Sidney's voice was trembling, and she spoke more softly than I could ever remember—a whisper, but so loud in my memory. "Captain Shelby killed your parents. Oh blessed Lord, please forgive me for this." Sidney was crying now, shaking.

"How do you know that?" I asked in the same defensive tone as the raindrops retreating from the rattling windows.

"I just know."

"That's not good enough! You need proof to make an accusation like that!"

Sidney stopped crying and looked at me with open eyes. "Your father was an excellent sailor. He could have handled even a tropical storm in nothing but a skiff. That old crazy coot had to have collided with them."

"But why? What reason would he have to do that? It just doesn't make any sense."

"They were too close to that creepy spot he goes to through that rocky channel, the place where, based on an old Pelican Bay wives tale, he goes to rejuvenate."

"*Rejuvenate*?"

"My mother told me a story when I was a very young woman—one of those strange stories that stays etched upon one's mind. Do you know what I mean, dear?"

"Yes."

"She was very chaste. If we said a cuss word or took the Lord's name in vain, even by accident, our mouths were washed out with soap and we had to say ten Hail Mary's. When she told this story I'm about to tell you, she would become so red in the face." Sidney chuckled. "It makes me laugh just picturing her telling it."

I smiled.

"My mother was an avid shell collector. Wait a moment, dear." Sidney got up and ran to her bedroom like a schoolgirl. I sat there waiting for her, sniggering to myself.

"Look at this."

"It's beautiful," I said.

"My mother made this necklace," Sidney said, beaming with pride and placing it around her neck.

"Wow. That's really nice."

"There are shells in that rocky channel, Ethan, shells that are far more beautiful, they say, than anywhere else in the world."

"I never knew that."

"Look at the colors of blue in this necklace. It has always been an old tale in Pelican Bay that the shells come from Captain Shelby's eyes. When they grow old, he throws them in the sea and the sea gives him new ones. They say the shells, just like his eyes, change colors all the time."

My eyes were colossal. I looked at the shells on the gorgeous necklace around Sidney's neck and said, "What a story."

"Yes, dear. Well, my mother had the fire of the Old Testament in her, my uncle always said. And when she was set on doing something, no woman, or man, for that matter, could stop her."

"Hmm—sounds like someone I know."

"That's funny, Ethan. Anyway, as you probably guessed, she was dead set on going into that dangerous channel to fetch some of those magic shells, even though my father had strictly forbidden it. But he was out on a fishing trip. Women always win one way or another, dear. Always remember that."

"I guess that's right," I said resignedly, looking down at my feet.

"You're so sweet, dear. Anyway, so there she was, in an old wooden skiff, paddling her way up the channel, as the story goes. She stopped several times to collect shells that she saw in the rock clearings, and by some miracle, the sea was very calm. You know, Ethan, the sea in that channel can rise in a heartbeat and feed you to the rocks. That's why I forbid you to ever go in there."

"I know."

"My mother spotted this shell that had washed up in the sand where the rocks broke near the end of the channel, right before the Secret Spot—a shell that glowed in the sun like a big rare blue diamond, she said. She rowed onto the sand there, and as she was collecting that special shell, she happened to look out just beyond the shore and that's when she saw it."

"Saw what?"

"A man was bathing in the sea, completely nude." Sidney began to blush—something I rarely saw. It was cute. "She said he was the most beautiful man she had ever seen. He was quite young and tanned and muscular and had long, shiny, curly black hair—as black as the deep center of the Secret Spot, a place believed to be a great trench. He spotted her and turned and his eyes were the same color as the shells, and they glowed."

Sidney stopped, her eyes extremely far away, her face enchanted and flushed.

"What happened?"

"She said that he began to walk toward her but she became very frightened and got back in the skiff and rowed away back down the channel."

"Did the young man follow?"

"She said she never looked back. She just kept rowing."

"Do you think the story's really true?"

"I don't know, dear. I'll certainly tell you this. That story became sort of an erotic folk tale quite popular among woman during those days, whispered whenever the men were not around or out of earshot."

"So you're saying that man was Captain Shelby?"

"Like I said, dear, an old wives' tale."

"Oh."

"What I do know is that old man guards that spot like a great secret—a secret perhaps he'd kill to protect."

CHAPTER TEN

I was not able to see Morgan again until the weekend. She had taken a few days off from the library to spend with her dad, who, according to the Pelican Bay Doctor's Building, was, "Out sick with a bad cold." I was dying to find out what Minister Billingsley had told her, especially to share the legend of Captain Shelby as it was told to me.

It was Thursday. The rain had stopped but the skies over Pelican Bay were still moody and the surf six feet high. There would be no diving for a few days. No solid answers.

There was only one place for me to go. And I had to. But some part of me was afraid.

But why should I be afraid? I've only felt good feelings around him, and I always enjoy talking to him so much. He's such a great man. He can't be a murderer. How ridiculous! Surely this is a misunderstanding—some detail we're all missing. We're going to laugh when it's all said and done.

I waited until the sun was almost setting to go and visit Captain Shelby, for he went out fishing almost every day. I wondered if it was true what Sidney said, that his fishing trips took him to a fountain of youth on some uncharted island.

He was mending a net when I approached, the silver lining of his old pipe catching the fading sun like a bait fish caught in his mouth.

"Hey Captain, how was the catch today?"

"Not much to speak of," he spit out coarsely, speaking from the free side of his mouth like a piratical ventriloquist. "I'm right crooked. The weather's got them fiskr hidin' from me—runnin' deep. But nothin' to brew me nerves over. I'll catch up. Always do. What are ye at today? Lookin' at yer face I see a book a questions, me Son, a book a questions. Best to search while the trail is new, eh?"

I jumped onto the old man's boat and walked over to him, watching him work on his net. I was staring at his face more than usual.

"Well spit it out, me Son, before the night swallows us again like a pelican a baitfish. I bet ye don't have me flashlight, do ye?"

"No. Sorry, Captain Shelby. I guess I've had a lot on my mind lately. I'll bring it tomorrow—promise."

The old man just kept mending his net, not seeming too concerned at all about the flashlight, more about finishing his mending before dark. Twilight was already upon us, but the sky was inextricably bright near the horizon.

"Well, uh, I was just curious about something, sir."

"Sir? Go on boy! This should be serious, I say."

"Well, I guess, sort of."

"Spit it out, me Boy. Spit it out!"

His swarthy snarl jarred me and my bones danced on their hinges. He was not looking at me at all, just barking at the sea, as if my voice were the verisimilitude of an unwanted fish scrounging his bait.

"May I ask how old you are?"

"Go on boy! Ha! Ye may, ye may! But all men have their secrets. Ye better beware. Brawl with a pig and ye take away his stink. Ha! How old do ye think I be?"

"I really don't know. It's so hard to tell. You look about seventy in the face, but, but—"

"But what?"

"There's no record of your family in town."

The night seemed to fall so quickly that I could barely see the old man's face now. He could have been any age at all—in the night. He stopped what he was doing and his eyes locked with mine. I thought that my bones might actually be humming.

"So, that's what ye been at, eh? Lookin' up me records?"

His eyebrows curled and a rage flashed across his face. I was patently frightened now.

"Uh, well, Morgan and I, see—"

"Look! Ye put them sunken bjargs and a librarian together and what ye got? Trouble, that's what! I told ye Boy, some things are better left alone!"

"I'm sorry. I didn't mean to—"

"That's right, nobody means nothin' at all. They're always after diggin' up all sorts a things. I suppose ye think I killed that little boy in thirty-one, eh?"

"No, I—"

"He slipped on the dock and hit his head. Before I could fish him out, the sea swept him away. Tried to look for him in the dark, but 'twas no use. Not me fault, I say! Not me fault!"

"I didn't mean to imply that—"

"Sidney been tellin' ye a mál bout me murderin' yer parents? She just be jealous cause yer mudder tried to help me once. God rest yer mudder's sweet soul."

"I didn't know my mother—"

"They won't be the last to toss their hopes and dreams to a crooked wave. I rushed for 'em. I can't save every creature enters the sea."

"I'm really sorry, sir, I—"

"Ye nosy kids can't let a poor old man be. The man that walks his own road, walks alone. Just cause a man keeps to himself and minds his own business, that means he be crazy, right? Crazy old Captain Shelby!"

"Look, sir, I'm really sorry. I was just curious, that's all. I mean, everyone says that you've always lived here, and—"

"Ye best be gettin' back, Boy, before ye slip in the dark and the sea claims thee, too."

I could barely see the dock to walk back. Halfway to land, I turned and I could not see Captain Shelby at all. I could not even see his old fishing boat. And for the first time that I could remember, there was no light lit at all. There was simply nothing—nothing but the dark.

CHAPTER ELEVEN

Early on Saturday morning I walked over to Morgan's cottage. She was kneeling, tending to her beach roses. The rain had cleared and the sun was bright. There was hardly a cloud above, and the surf was low. It was a truly beautiful day, and I would have felt as clear and joyful as the sky if the woman I truly loved—

As I grew close, Morgan heard me and looked back, smiling. She was having a good day.

Her father must be faring much better, ran through my mind.

"They get prettier every day, I swear," I said cheerfully.

"Thank you, Ethan." She smiled shyly.

Morgan stopped what she was doing and turned her fragile body toward me, her garden-gloved hands on her thighs now, hiding the pale flesh sprawling out of her faded khaki skirt. She looked up at me, sort of sheepishly, her eyes almost child-like.

"I take it your father's feeling better today?"

"He's already gone in—trying to catch up on office work."

"Sure is a beautiful day."

"You can say that again."

"Sure is a beautiful day."

"Why do I keep setting myself up for that?" Morgan chuckled breathily: "Hee, hee."

"I bet you can see those gravestones pretty clearly today."

"Oh no, Ethan. Don't you even think about it!"

"Why not? I mean, what if his name's down there? Wouldn't you want to know?"

"You mean his last name, right?"

"Well—"

"Ethan! There's no way that Captain Shelby's that old! I swear, you writers and your colossal imaginations. At least us librarians are literary creatures with our feet planted on the earth. That's where life is, Ethan, on the earth."

"Whatever you say. Did you find out anything from Minister Billingsley?"

Morgan suddenly stood up, her face betraying a muted graveness.

"Captain Shelby has no wife or son."

"I know."

"How?"

"Sidney told me."

"Oh."

"What else?"

"He says that Captain Shelby's lived in Pelican Bay for as long as he can remember, and, you know, Minister Billingsley's almost eighty years old. He said that Captain Shelby's always been a commercial fisherman, and used to sell fish to our town. He's never had a cottage here, but used to come to shore for fishing supplies."

"Did Captain Shelby ever to go church?"

"Many, many years ago."

"Why did he stop going?"

"No one knows. But it was sometime in the late seventies."

"That's around the time my parents died."

Morgan looked down and did not say anything. A few moments passed.

"Morgan?"

She did not answer.

"There's something you're not telling me. Something the minister said."

"Well—"

"Morgan, please, you have to tell me. I thought we were in this together."

"It's about your parents."

"My parents?"

"Mainly your mother."

More silence.

"Morgan!"

"Minister Billingsley said that your mother was part of the Pelican Bay Church charity group and was very active in helping people fix up and rebuild their cottages after big storms."

"Yeah, Sidney's told me stories about my mother and how avid she was about charity. But what does this have to do with Captain Shelby?"

"She was building a cottage for him before she died."

"You're kidding."

"Not at all. He said no one knew why, but your mother believed that Captain Shelby was an integral part of Pelican Bay and that it was our fault he was such a hermit. You should ask Sidney about it."

"I definitely will. I'm surprised she never told me about that. You know, Morgan, I asked Sidney what Captain Shelby looked like when she was a kid. Do you know what she said?"

"Oh no. Here we go."

"She said that he looked *old*, that he's always looked *old.*"

"Stop it, Ethan. I'm not going to listen to this!"

"I bet there's at least one librarian in the world that believes in ghosts."

"Not this one. Look, Ethan, let's suppose that Captain Shelby's a ghost. Why would he be a fisherman, of all things?" Morgan laughed a little louder here. It was quite a rarity to hear her louder laugh, laughed only when she was either nervous or afraid. "Let's be sensible, shall we? You've known him for years. He has a solid form, doesn't he?"

"Why do ghosts always have to be apparitions? Whoever said that?"

"It's just that classic literature—"

"Ghost story tellers don't know it all, anyway. Besides, have you ever seen a ghost?"

"You know the answer to that, Ethan!"

"I guess I do."

"Have you ever touched him?"

I had to think rather hard here. A few minutes of silence went by. The Pelican Bay sun was well perched over the horizon now, smiling at us vehemently, letting us know that is was going to become hotter and hotter the more that we dug for the secrets of the town that she watched over.

"I've handed him things and taken things from him. But I've never touched him, I guess."

"I can't believe I'm having this conversation with you. This is ridiculous—utterly ridiculous."

"Hey, you're the one that started this whole research project in the first place."

"I'm engaged in the search of a logical solution to an interesting historical puzzle, one that speaks to the very fabric of our town's genealogy. That is quite different from a ghost hunt."

"I think he disappeared last night."

Morgan's eyes became more focused suddenly and her lips puckered. She crossed her arms, as if picking up a chill, as if the winter were only announcing the news of its unusually early arrival to her and her alone. I knew that she had goose bumps, for her forearms appeared beady, and their almost invisible little blonde hairs were standing up.

"I didn't mean to scare you, Morgan. I'm just telling you the truth."

"You're absolutely impossible. What do you mean, *disappeared*?"

"Well, I told him that there are no records of him in town. We were talking about his age and it just sort of slipped out."

"Very tactful."

"I know." I looked down at the ground. "But he wouldn't tell me his age. I guess maybe I was trying to squeeze it out of him a little bit. Anyway, he became pretty angry. He started raving about people sticking their noses into other people's business, and some things being better left alone, and so on and so forth. It was getting really dark and I knew I had offended him, so I left. When I turned back, about halfway to shore, there was nothing there, Morgan—nothing but darkness. I swear it."

Morgan was looking at her beach rose garden again. Her lips were scrunched now and her pale blue eyes squinted.

"Sidney said that when she was a kid, Captain Shelby *flew* at this young boy and he fell and hit his head and drowned," I added. "She also thinks that he purposely collided his boat with my parent's skiff to protect what old wives of Pelican Bay believed to be his fountain of youth, killing them in the process."

"All right, that's it! I won't hear another word of this nonsense! I have better things to do."

"So I guess going to the beach with me after you close up the library's out of the question, huh?"

Morgan huffed.

"You can dive and daydream and tell ghost stories all day, if you want. I'm going to do something useful. I'm going to talk to the librarians in Gull Bay and Lighthouse Point. They have much more sophisticated record-keeping systems than we do. I'm going to put an end to all this preposterousness once and for all."

"Okay, Morgan. Hey, about the other day—"

"Forget about it."

"It's just that—"

"Please don't say it! I've told you not to say it!"

CHAPTER TWELVE

The sun was at the midpoint between its bed and high noon. The ocean was the clearest that I had ever seen it. You could make out the shelf, and the gravestones were quite visible. They looked like a scattered, black Stonehenge. But they appeared to have sunken a little more.

Time was running out.

The ocean felt so good against my skin, an omnipresent lover. As I swam out to the shelf, the deep, sudden drop-off into the town under our town, I looked out toward the horizon and the silhouette of a passing freighter, thick and long, like a bolded sentence, was underlined by the sea.

I put on my mask and snorkel and searched the bottom. My face submerged beneath the sea and I pictured it as part of the bottom of a buoy that had sprung bulging eyes.

I began to breathe deeply, preparing to fill my lungs for my first dive.

Most of the gravestones were tall, and I could not help but wonder if their tallness embodied how their dead lived their lives. These souls lived so long ago, the first English settlers to try a life in Pelican Bay. How could they know that they would be pulverized by formidable storms raging upon the sea, perhaps as hostile as the Native Americans who deeply resented their presence, incessantly attacking Pelican Bay, as if in cahoots with the hurricanes?

I tried to imagine the raw severity of such pioneer life. Washing clothes by hand, hunting the forest and the sea for game, all nightly affairs transpiring by candlelight, always by candlelight, loved ones missed back home in England, hopelessly separated by a vast ocean, famine in the winter, various plagues hunting them like amphibious sea scorpions. But our ancient ancestors lived and loved the same as we do now. They yearned for and relished the same things—freedom, adventure, and peace.

Searching the graves under the ocean was like diving for black, petrified tongues, as if Pelican Bay's floor were composed of a thousand sandy faces, ridiculing the sky.

On each dive, I tried to remember the names that I saw, for I knew that Morgan would want to research them. On some gravestones I could make out first names, and on others I could not. I could not see any dates, for they were inundated by the greedy sand of the gray ocean floor.

I was able to remember but a few:

Edmund J. Bigsley
Billingsley
Carlisle
Elinor R. Dustby
Farindine
Andrew F. Hodges (my last name)
Langstone
Charity E. Mortimers
Anne J. Olinsworth (Morgan's last name)
William P. Sherman
Shaw
Winstone

It was hard to tell how big the undersea graveyard really was. Many of the stones were almost completely buried under the sand, perhaps hiding from the brutal history of Pelican Bay, and I imagine others could have been moved or flattened by rushing hurricane seas, large debris sweeping the ocean floor like iron brooms.

There were at least a dozen tombstones that were unreadable and my lungs were too tired for me to take the time to decipher them. Also, I did not have the proper tools to try and clear away the built up sea grime and barnacles. But after I swam back and sat on the beach, the cool waves lapping my tired legs, it occurred to me that the name Shelby could very well be among the unreadable gravestones.

I rushed back home to write the names down on a sheet of paper. Sidney came to the kitchen for a cup of tea and saw me writing them down. She came up and kissed me gently on the cheek, peering at my piece of paper.

"What are you writing, dear?"

"Oh, uh—"

"What's that? Does that say, "Andrew F. Hodges?""

"Yes. Let me explain. I—"

Sidney sat down so suddenly and turned as white as a ghost, covering her mouth with one delicate, softly wrinkled hand. A teardrop escaped and started down her cheek. She looked like a terribly saddened child, a naked soul.

"You see, I've been diving again and—"

"Do you know who that is, Ethan?" She was beginning to cry now.

"Well, I figure that—"

"It's your great, great, great—oh, I don't know!"

I scooted up a chair and held her. She cried for a good while.

"I'm so sorry, Sidney. I never meant to upset you."

"It's not your fault. I'll be okay. It's just that—to think he's down there under the sea."

"Would you like to go to Pelican Bay Church Cemetery and visit our relatives? Would you like that?"

"Yes." She was sniffling now. "Let me make some sandwiches to take with us."

"Okay."

The sun was starting her descending path toward the inland. She always fought tooth and nail over our town, exploding pink and peach hues across the sky, summer firecrackers of our youth, slowly staining the view above Pelican Bay.

We cruised Pelican Bay Street together. Sidney never hung on to my arm, unless we were negotiating tricky terrain. She was as mobile as a veteran seagull, still chasing the retreating sea, or running away from a territorial pelican.

"Sidney?"

"Yes, dear."

"How come you never told me about my mother trying to help Captain Shelby?"

Sidney was quiet, flushed. She looked out to sea. "To protect you, dear," she finally said.

"Captain Shelby is a good man."

"You're so young, dear. So naïve."

"If the captain's not a good man, why was my mother trying so hard to help him?"

We walked in thick silence that cowered over us like the large oaks of Pelican Bay.

"Oh dear, dear. My, my. All this research is going to lead to ruin, Ethan. You hear me? Ruin."

"Sidney, this is important to me."

"Your mother was idealistic and so naïve. Just like you. She said that she felt tied to Captain Shelby in a way that she couldn't fully explain, or that I never understood." Sidney shook her head slowly and exhaled with a gentle wornness. "Ethan, dear, she believed that incorporating him was the key to the salvation of the souls of Pelican Bay."

"Really?"

"Perhaps I've held this from you for too long, dear, but your mother was not altogether well."

"What do you mean?"

"I think that if she had lived any longer she would have suffered from some kind of mental illness. I worry so much about you too, dear. Sometimes the things you say—"

"What?"

"—are just so like her. And with this dreadful investigation all of you are involved in now—oh, my, my—I'm so afraid for you, dear."

Sidney stopped and hugged me. She was mildly shaking.

"Sidney, you're very sweet, and I know how much you love me, but you worry way too much. Really. There is nothing wrong with me at all."

"Oh dear, dear."

"There's still something I just can't figure out."

"Dear Lord, please release this young man's mind from this dark pursuit and grant him the will to move to Gull Bay and find a healthy woman to love."

"Sidney! Stop that!"

"I'm always praying for you, dear."

"What I want to know is why you think Captain Shelby would kill my mother and father if they were trying to help him?"

There was a long silence.

"That old man doesn't follow the laws of humans, sweetie. I've said it before, and I'll keep saying it, there's something not right about him."

Soon we passed Pelican Bay Library. You could see Morgan inside, her hair tightly drawn back, hunched over a book, its pages appearing exhaled from her nose. Sidney saw me looking in her direction and huffed softy, sardonically, shaking her head.

"Ethan, my poor boy," she said sagaciously, her voice starting on a high pitch, "have you ever thought of just telling her how you feel? I mean, if you must insist on torturing yourself with this illusion of love, you might as well at least get a little more out of it."

I gave Sidney a hard look. "She won't let me," I said.

"I don't understand. Why, this is America."

"She just somehow knows when I'm about to say it and stops me."

"I'd sure like to shake that girl up," Sidney said petulantly. "I'd like to sit with her over tea sometime and speak my mind."

"Sidney, please. You promised me, remember? Besides, we're just friends—that's all."

"Okay, dear, okay. Well, at least the cemetery has dried up."

"Yes."

There were many tombstones with the name Hodges on them: fathers of fathers, mothers of mothers, cousins of cousins, and so on and so forth. We only visited my grandfather's grave, James E. Hodges, and my parents, Anthony and Jessica Hodges. We did not say anything at all, not outwardly anyway.

When I looked at Sidney standing before my grandfather's grave, she cried silently, smiling feebly at me.

Afterward we sat on a picnic table under a tree only twenty paces or so from the church and ate the sandwiches that she had made for us. Before long, Minister Billingsley spotted us and came outside.

"Beautiful day, wouldn't you say, Sidney?"

Minister Billingsley had always had a crush on Sidney, although he would never admit it to her. He was a longtime widower, just as Sidney was a longtime widow. He was quite tall, almost cadaverous on account of his long face and advanced age. However, he could charm a rattler, calm a crying baby when even the gentlest mother failed, and his eyes, almost an emerald green peering out of a kind face wrapped in a full head of strategically disheveled gray hair, lent him the appearance of a retired famous film actor, one of those types that you might see cast as a U-boat commander in a black and white World War II film.

"Would you like a sandwich Minister Billingsley? They're fresh."

"I already had lunch, but thank you kindly anyway."

He smiled his easy smile at Sidney, and she looked away almost immediately, blushing.

"I saw your girlfriend the other day, Ethan," the minister said, turning his magnetic gaze upon me now. His voice always imperceptibly trembled when he spoke, as if the silent opera of a dormant volcano. It was hypnotic. Everyone loved to listen to him talk, in or out of church.

"Actually we're just friends."

"Whatever you say, Ethan. By the way, I heard that you and Morgan are investigating the sea graveyard."

"Minister Billingsley," Sidney blurted out with the excitement of a child, her voice quivering. "Today Ethan found a sunken headstone with the name Andrew F. Hodges on it."

"Remarkable," the minister said, matching Sidney's enthusiasm. "Doubtless a very, very, very great grandfather, correct?"

"We think so," Sidney added fervently.

"I also saw a grave with the last name Billingsley," I said. "But I couldn't read any first name."

A placid smile overtook the minister's face.

"Yes, the Billingsleys go way back, way back," he said, nodding his head firmly. He appeared to beam with happy pride.

A brief moment of silence passed.

"Did you find a gravestone marked Shelby, Ethan?" Minister Billingsley asked the question almost defiantly, a hidden wild gloss in his eyes.

"No, but there are at least a dozen unreadable stones. I need to try again with a friend and the right tools, maybe even scuba gear, if we can rent it from Gull Bay."

"I don't see the point in it," the minister said, almost haughtily. "Since Shelby is not a name in our cemetery, it is quite unlikely that the name would appear out there." Minister Billingsley gave a chuckle, but it was largely a nervous one.

"But you told Morgan that Captain Shelby's always lived here, as long as you can remember."

"That's true, Ethan, but there's always an explanation for these sorts of things."

Sidney turned very serious eyes upon me, as if to say, "Don't go there, dear, don't go there. Please."

But you know I did anyway.

"Do you believe in ghosts, Minister Billingsley?"

He cleared his throat, uncomfortably. Sidney took a big bite out of her sandwich.

"Why, what a strange question, Ethan." He was quiet for a moment or so, rubbing his chin. "I believe in the Holy Ghost."

"That's not exactly what I mean. Do you believe that people who don't know they're dead can linger and haunt the earth?"

"Ethan!" Sidney blurted out. "What has gotten into you?!"

"That is quite all right, Sidney. I am trained to answer any question regarding the mysteries of God's creation." The minister turned and looked directly at me, his eyes widening, shining with a healthy focus of curiosity. "Why, that is quite a question, Ethan. Many believe in a purgatory, which has different names and different concepts in various religions. However, it is not a place that is discernible by the living."

"No, I don't mean that. I mean the spirit of a dead person who has not left our earthly plane yet, who is trapped between our world and the next."

"I see, I see. I'm afraid, my dear boy, that I cannot speak to such matters with any informed opinion. I've spent my life educating myself in theology and theosophy, on religious matters and interpretations of the Bible. I suppose I would have to say that this sort of conjecturing occupies itself primarily with those minds who dismiss the immediate crossing of a departed soul into the Sphere of God—perhaps with minds that want to hang on to the physical part of existence and so create paranormal fantasies in order to do so. I think that Captain Shelby, empirically speaking, and, in the tradition of practical common sense, is a soul in a physical body, still quite alive, I should say. And if you want to continue with a practical investigation, I would start checking other nearby coastal towns to ascertain Captain Shelby's origin. He may just be a very, very old man, or, we must suffice ourselves with the virtually impossible reality that he is immortal!"

The minister chuckled heartily, quite satisfied with his harangue, and looked at Sidney, who, rather embarrassed, could not seem to accept his gaze.

"Thank you, Minister Billingsley. That seems to make a lot of sense. I guess what still bothers me though is that Sidney remembers Captain Shelby being very old even when she was a kid, and so far, no human being has ever been reported living past 115 years old."

My thought hung in the air like a malingering chord progression, and an afternoon shadow began to creep its way across the cemetery, longing to resolve it.

We all sat in silence under the musty coolness of the archaic, colossal oaks, sprawling their thick, moss-covered arms over us—the arms of our forefathers.

CHAPTER THIRTEEN

That night I had a most curious dream. It was one of those dreams that you never really wake from, one of those dreams that you carry with you like a soldier a memory of battle, one of those dreams that gives you answers that you are not prepared for because you do not yet know the right questions to ask.

I was on the beach of our tiny town, standing atop a dune and looking out to sea. Somehow in the dream I just know that I am in Pelican Bay, even though none of the buildings look familiar at all, and the town seems completely deserted. I keep scanning what looks like huts made of wood and beach mud. I feel a wistful longing for the cottages of my era, a longing that herds my cells like old cowboys wild buffalo, a deep sort of dread in the pit of my stomach, that sort of dread that starts like a faraway voice on the horizon of the psyche and grows increasingly closer and louder, a voice that says, "My God, I hope this is not real."

As I peer back out to sea, the captain's boat is anchored near shore, deserted. There are no docks at all, and I think to myself, *Boy do I miss them, even more than the cottages.*

Just on the edge of the town I can see a dark gathering of stones, and I quickly realize that it is what will be the underwater cemetery. Without even thinking about it, I begin to walk toward it.

As I walk into town, negotiating the dunes, wider and taller than I can ever remember them being, I feel a mighty presence next to me and a stench that is dizzying yet beautiful somehow. I know that it is the old man, but for some reason I do not turn my head. I do not look at him, and I am not sure whether it is out of fear, or some inability in the dream to be able to see him.

"What are ye at, me Son?"

"I don't know. Walking into town."

"What are ye after?" His voice is not coarse or jarring or roaring at all in the dream. It sounds young and beautiful and velvety and I take great solace in it.

"I'm going to see the cemetery. I guess you're coming with me?"

"Eh boy."

"Where is everyone?"

"All dead, me Son. Either cholera or the Indians got 'em."

"Not the Great Hurricane?"

"Thee be talkin' bout things that aren't been yet, I say."

"Am I dreaming?"

"Go on boy! Ye may, ye may! Ha! Can't be right sure."

"Am I dead? Is this heaven?"

"Ha! No, me Son. Thee be alive as I be."

"Why am I here, Captain?"

"Now yer on the go! That's me sharp scopie!"

"To go to the cemetery?"

"Eh. Want ye to see somethin' there."

"Okay Captain."

The dunes end and I am finally able to turn my head now and see his face. He looks to be in his prime, a strong man, bronzed skin, with black playful hair and sad eyes that resemble so much my own that I begin to cry.

"Easy me Son. Mind ye that crooked things always straighten themselves out. Look, we be not far now."

We are well out of the dunes and passing the houses, their mangy old logs and trickling mud like the decay that stole their inhabitants.

"Did you try to save them, Captain?"

He looks at me peculiarly, wistfully, a twinge of defensiveness coloring his aura.

"Eh, but there be things I can't stop. I killed some a them Indians, but they just keep a comin' and a comin', like the sea eatin' the shore."

We are now upon the cemetery.

"Captain, what year is it?"

"Truth be told, the years are always after gettin' away from me like them gulls with me bait. Seems like just yesterday we came down here from the first big settlement up north, see?"

"Is this Pelican Bay?"

"Pelican Bay? Mind yer talkin' ahead all crooked-like, me Son."

"Sorry, sir."

"Don't be sorry, me Son. I'm not sure what they be callin' this town in the here and now. There was many fine Newfoundland folk here though, and more English folk'll be after settlin' here soon for the fishin', I say. God willin' them Indians'll stay away for a while now. Look, over here—what I be after ye seein'."

He pointed me to a gravestone, his tender, sad eyes crying now. Unmistakably crying.

LAURA H SHELBY
1518-1551
God rest thee
in the sea barley

"What does the 'H' stand for, Captain?"
"Hodges."

CHAPTER FOURTEEN

Morgan found no word of a Shelby from her fellow record keepers in Gull Bay or Lighthouse Point. The mystery of Captain Shelby grew more eerie as fall began to touch Pelican Bay. My restless nights were becoming more frequent and more unsettling with every creepy clue that we unearthed. My dreams seemed to turn the fall leaves prematurely with fright. Soon the sea cemetery, possibly the only chance to solve our mystery, would be buried beneath the ocean floor once again.

Maybe gone forever this time.

I needed to rent scuba gear from Gull Bay. I had talked Morgan into coming with me, promising her that we could visit the cemetery there, and if necessary, visit the one up north in Lighthouse Point.

It was Sunday morning when Morgan and I headed south for Gull Bay. Sidney let us borrow her old white Monte Carlo with the black roof, a dilapidated but charming car that she let me take on trips to Gull Bay for special supplies, a car that she barely drove anymore. And she gave me special instructions regarding Morgan, instructions that I did not want to follow.

Morgan's eyes, set against the dingy white Monte Carlo and the blinding blue sky just beyond her, were more the eyes of the Caribbean Ocean than the Atlantic Ocean.

We were following the coastal highway, which departed south out of Pelican Bay, a terribly winding, poorly paved road, its crookedness a subtle warning. The beach, modeling modest surf, occasional wind-swept, fetid marsh, and wandering dunes, sat beneath a sky that was lonesome for clouds.

But all that *I* could see was her, and I think that she knew it.

"Here's something else for your research," I said, slipping Morgan the list of undersea headstone names. She knew what it was instantaneously, and stared at it blank-faced. She was quite still.

"This is fascinating," she finally said. "Utterly fascinating. Many of these names came up in my research of Pelican Bay's forefathers except, well, I don't know what to say about this one."

She suddenly closed her eyes and held the small piece of paper to her chest.

"Are you okay, Morgan?"

"Yes," she said, almost inaudibly.

"Are you sure?"

Morgan's body was softly trembling, and I saw tears rolling down her cheeks. They just streamed out of her closed eyes, so slowly, so consistently, but she never made a sound. I had never seen anyone cry like that before. Her face was soon soaked with two paths of tears. Her still-shut eyes could have been obstinate patches of snow perched upon a mountain side on a spring day.

I wanted so much to reach over and stanch her tears, but I dared not. I just let the miles gather her.

Finally, she spoke again. "Ethan, I have never felt so grounded before in all my life—all my life. Whomever Anne is, whether an unaccountable great grandmother or aunt, she is likely the oldest relative of my heritage. I don't know how to feel this feeling."

"It's okay, Morgan. You don't have to explain anything."

I reached for her hand, very slowly, and she let me hold it for a moment or so, freeing it stealthily to retrieve a Kleenex from the glove box.

But that moment might as well have been an eternity for me. I had not felt the fateful lull of her hand for that long since high school.

"This is all so incredible, just so incredible, Ethan." Her unassuming eyes were open again, indigo blue mascara faintly running away just underneath them, oceanic planets leaking into white outer spaces. She finally looked my way, but more at the passing beach pines beyond.

"I know. But we still have one mystery to unravel," I said.

"Captain Shelby."

"Yes."

The miles passed too quickly. It was still early morning when we saw a faded sign looming.

Gull Bay 7 miles

"Can we visit the cemetery first?" Morgan asked.

"Sure, sweetie, uh, I mean sure."

Morgan shot me a quick look, but it was more one of playful annoyance.

"Look, I didn't mean—"

"It's okay. Just drop it, sweetie."

I smiled a giant smile, a smile that only the sun could have matched that day, and I looked at her like a greedy child. She peered out at the passing ocean, shaking her head. There were no gravestones out there, beyond the shelf, only coastline, but I could not help wondering if Gull Bay had an undersea cemetery too. An undersea town.

Gull Bay was a much bigger town. Fast food restaurants, two gas stations, a modern, large bank, a slightly bigger post office, an immense library connected to their only school, which was twice the size of ours, two hotels and churches, and, of course, the Gull Bay Courthouse, passing on the right now. Being in Gull Bay made us feel even smaller than we already did.

"You know, Morgan, a lot of Pelican Bay couples have gotten married at that old courthouse."

Morgan did not look my way at all.

The main cemetery was at the southern end of Gull Bay. It was not as old as Pelican Bay's cemetery. Pelican Bay, due to its fruitful fishing, was the first coastal town to be established in the area, a fact we loved to boast of, a fact that made us feel less forgotten.

We pulled in and parked behind the church next to the cemetery. I turned off the engine. It jumped and burped. Morgan looked at me and surrendered her signature, murmuring giggle.

"This one's going to take a lot longer," I said, exhaling slowly for emphasis.

"Not if you're a librarian. You go ahead and get started. I'm going to talk to the minister inside."

"Okay."

The morning was cool, but it would not last long.

The graves were much more orderly, and there were more vertical than horizontal headstones, which would make things easier. The cemetery did not have the bleak look of Pelican Bay's, nor was it as ancient in appearance. The stones were generally more legible. I started scanning them.

I was surprised to see some familiar names, and I wondered how many cousins, aunts and uncles, etc, of Pelican Bay might live here. I saw Sherman and Carlisle, even Bigsley, which made me laugh to myself.

Before long, I saw Morgan walking toward me in the distance, briskly, awkwardly, and for a fleeting moment it occurred to me that I would never fully understand the enormity of my love for her.

"I talked to the minister," Morgan said, "and he doesn't think there's any Shelby here. He said he could check cemetery records but they get pretty hazy once you get into the 1700's. It could take a while. He did say the oldest graves here are in the northwest corner, under that big elm tree over there, and that we may want to start looking there."

I followed Morgan's eyes over to the elm tree, an old grandfather dressed in moss like a camouflaged Confederate Civil War soldier. The shaded gravestones stood erect still, defiantly against the gnawing teeth of time, and the tiny cemetery within a cemetery somehow exuded a colonial smile, as if always hiding some inestimable treasure from the hands of Atlantic pirates.

"Okay. By the way, I'm proud of you."

"What? Why?"

"I've never seen you this calm in a cemetery before."

"Well, don't get used to it. It's only ten in the morning and you're with me. I certainly don't want to dillydally, okay?"

"Okay. Let's go."

We searched the northwest corner, as well as all the older graves nearby. Nothing. Frustration seemed to now fill the air in the form of pressing heat. Over an hour had passed.

"Morgan, I told Rich I would meet him at his boat to pick up the scuba gear before noon. Why don't I go get it and come right back. You could look by yourself a little longer."

I turned and started to walk away. Suddenly Morgan came running up behind me as fast as she could and hung on to me.

It felt good, and I laughed out loud.

We picked up the scuba gear and then checked the other small cemetery in Gull Bay by the Episcopalian church. There were also no gravestones with Shelby on them, so we picked up a few hamburgers and sodas at the Burger House drive thru and started our way back up north on the coastal highway toward Lighthouse Point, a final bastion of hope granting us a second wind.

"Morgan, maybe we're going about this thing all wrong."

"What do you mean?"

"Well, this *is* the Computer Age, after all, right?"

"Yeah."

"I think we need to broaden our search."

"I've already checked all vital records in all the major cities up and down the east coast. I found no last name Shelby, or any similar spelling. I was just hoping that an old gravestone, given the poorer record keeping centuries ago, might turn up something."

"Geez."

Silence.

"I was thinking," I said, "if he's a fisherman, we need to check fishing towns at least a hundred miles in each direction. I mean, somebody's got to know something, right?"

"That's not a bad idea. I suppose I could check fish delivery and purchase records of canneries and commercial buyers up and down the coast. Something's got to turn up."

"That would be great. You could do that while I take one more dive and try to clean off some of those other gravestones. Do you think we'll ever figure this out, Morgan?"

"Never underestimate a librarian."

The Lighthouse Point Cemetery revealed nothing either. We drove to the fishing docks and walked around a bit, hoping to dig up something there, but all the fishing boats appeared to be deserted. It was already after three o'clock in the afternoon, and our hopes seemed to now set with the sun.

"Look, Ethan, at the end of the dock, there's a man washing his deck. Go talk to him." Morgan nudged me excitedly.

"Why me? What, are you afraid he's a ghost, too?"

"That's not funny, Ethan. You know how shy I am. You go. Hurry! Before he leaves!"

"All right, all right. Good grief."

I walked to the end of the dock, Morgan following sluggishly behind.

"Uh, excuse me, sir?" I yelled out.

He turned and looked at me with an open, inquisitive face. He was a generally handsome man, tall, tanned, young, his beard the color of late fall, his long hair a sandy, incongruous offshoot.

Morgan stopped a few feet behind me, looking away.

"You must be looking for my father, Captain Langsley, right?"

"I'm sorry?"

We drew up close to the boat now. The man still appeared young but his long face was weathered, like a buoy. His eyebrows were disturbingly thick, as if grown of coconut hair.

"They only call my father, 'Sir'." He provided a full grin, looking toward Morgan now, whose eyes were scavenging the dock.

"Oh. No, actually we were hoping that you might be able to give us some information on a Captain Shelby."

"Captain Shelby?" he asked, scratching his long, dirtied, carpet-like hair. "That name sounds sort of familiar. Is he a fisherman?"

"Yes. A very, very old fisherman."

The young man tilted his head and lowered his brows. Suddenly an older man came out of the main cabin door of the boat. He looked much like the younger man but with a face even more weathered, much resembling pecan-colored rawhide. He had brazen, piercing blue eyes, and very little hair falling out of his captain's hat, leftover white gravy dripping from an overturned iron white pot. He seemed to hobble slightly and I chose to keep my attention on his face.

"What do you want?"

"They're trying to get information on some old fisherman with the name Captain Shelby," his son said.

"What do you want to know about him?!"

Captain Langsley was staring right at us. His eyes were like two ocean-colored jewels jammed into the face of a worn saddlebag, gazing out hungrily, almost hypnotically. I was looking at Morgan who was still looking down, fidgeting furiously. His voice was so abrasive that we both jumped a little.

"I take it you know him, sir?" I asked.

"Know him? That crazy old man's been fishing these bays since I was just a boy. They say he killed a little kid in 1931. That's right. Used him for bait. They also say he crashed another fishing boat in 1945. They were hoarding in on the old man's secret fishing spot, or so he claims, which don't exist if you ask me. Anyway, he shoved that other boat right into some tough rocks right before a mother of a storm took the coast. Every man was lost, never found a single one, they say. Why are you asking, anyway? You a cop or something? What's that old geezer done now? Lord, he should be fish bait after all this time. That old fool."

"I'm a writer."

"A what? Speak up, boy!"

"I'm writing a story about Captain Shelby."

Captain Langsley fell silent for a moment. His eyes drifted over to Morgan. Before long he was staring right at her bosom. Now both he and his son were staring a hole through her chest.

"That girlfriend of yours, she don't say much, does she?" Captain Langsley asked, laughing, as if a spasmodic cough.

Morgan took my arm, now staring at a neighboring boat, as if studying it for purchase.

"Do you know how old Captain Shelby is?" I asked.

"Old enough to be dead!"

"I mean, if you had to guess, sir, how old would you say he is?"

"You sure ask a lot of questions, son. You sure you ain't a cop?"

"No, sir. Like I said, I'm a writer doing a story."

"The last time I saw him up close was in 1953, I think, and he looked like he had both feet in the grave then, if you ask me. I still see his creaky old boat sometimes peddling for fish, but hell, I thought it was someone else bought his boat or something. Are you saying he's still alive?"

Morgan lanced me with her elbow.

"Uh, well, we don't know. That's what I'm trying to find out, sir. Do you know where he's from?"

"Pelican Bay. Why, everyone knows that. If you ask me, that's where you should be asking these questions." Captain Langsley fixed a suspicious, almost scowling stare on us now, his son joining in. "Where you folks from, anyway?"

"Uh, we came down from up north, Rocky Island, just today, sir. I found an old article about the little boy in 1931. Seemed interesting. We're making our way down to Pelican Bay next. Can I ask you one more thing, sir?"

"You've already asked me a hundred questions, son. I don't see how one more's going to matter."

His son poorly smothered a laugh.

"We haven't been able to find any record of a Captain Shelby anywhere. I was just wondering if you knew someone else in our coastal area that might know about his family."

"I told you, he's from Pelican Bay. That man's older than records, that's all."

"You sure are pretty," his son said to Morgan. "Does she talk?"

"Thank you for your time, sir. We need to be going now, but we're very appreciative," I said.

"Yeah, good luck with your 'little story' or whatever the hell it is you're doing," Captain Langsley said.

His son laughed louder now.

I took Morgan's hand firmly and led her rapidly back down the dock. She let me hold her hand the entire way.

I'll never forget this.

I thought that Morgan would want to talk about the strange fishermen and what they had said about Captain Shelby, but she was utterly quiet. I thought that she might leave her exquisite hand out next to her while she watched the dunes hump by, but she did not. This is the life you choose when you love a librarian. When you think you have come the closest, you may be the farthest away.

"Morgan?"

"What."

"Are you upset about the way those fishermen were staring at you?"

"No. They can't help themselves."

"Are you upset with me?"

"No, Ethan. Just frustrated."

"I know. Look, I have something strange to tell you and I'm not sure how to say it."

Morgan darted me a look painted with incipient panic.

"I had this dream," I said. "And—"

"Oh no. Here we go."

"I think that Captain Shelby had a wife."

"And how exactly do you know that? Dreams aren't real. They're just your subconscious mind playing games with you."

"I thought you'd say that. I've had lots of dreams about the old man, but this one was *so real*."

Morgan looked at me quickly and then back out at the dunes that intermittently showed wild grass patches like white witches' hairy warts.

"I was in Pelican Bay," I went on, "only it wasn't Pelican Bay, but some old version of our town. *Really old*."

"It's just all the things we've been talking about writing a novel in your subconscious while you sleep. That's all."

"Maybe so, but I saw the underwater cemetery only it wasn't under the sea."

Morgan gave me a haunted look.

"In the dream Captain Shelby walked with me over to it, saying he wanted to show me something. There was no one in the town. Everyone was killed by cholera or Native Americans."

Morgan chuckled. "You really live in your own creative space, Ethan."

"He took me over to a grave that said Laura H. Shelby on it."

"Laura H. Shelby?"

"Yeah. And he said the 'H' stood for Hodges."

"Hodges is your last name."

"Yes. And then I woke up."

"I have to admit, even for you, that's a little strange."

"I know. Could that name help you in your research maybe?"

"I research facts, not dream material."

"Oh come on, Morgan. What have you got to lose?"

"All right. I'll check it out."

"You will?"

"Yeah, but don't get your hopes up. Even if Laura's some vastly distant relative, it's just a coincidence, and besides, I don't see what it would prove. "

"In the dream Captain Shelby was crying when he pointed to her grave."

"Oh Lord."

"Thanks, Morgan."

I reached for her hand but she moved it away.

As we rolled into Pelican Bay, the sun was nearing the horizon, arguing its case against a few hovering clouds, spraying rays of light from behind them all over the sky, thick, laser-like, pale tentacles burning bright in all directions, as if it were the day that God had decided to show his face in the setting sun and the clouds were sheltering our feeble human eyes from His unfathomable beauty.

Standing quite still, like a sleeping pelican, we saw a man-like figure on the beach gazing out at the undersea gravestones.

"Do you see that, Morgan?"

"Yes."

"He's back."

"How do you know?"

"I don't know. I just do. Let's be sure though."

I slowed down and started to pull off the road.

"What are you doing?"

"I just want to be sure. We can hide behind that big dune right there."

"Ethan! Take me home!"

"Calm down. You said he's just a man, and there's a logical explanation for it all, right? So what's the big deal?"

"I don't like it. I'm scared, Ethan. Please!"

Morgan was grabbing my arm, her importunate eyes gleaming with fright.

"Morgan, look, you can stay in the car and lock the doors if you want, all right? I just want to make sure it's him. I'll be right back. I promise."

"Ethan, please don't go."

I parked behind the dune from which thick wild grass protruded, a sparsely bearded, inflated cheek of the beach. I closed my door quietly and communicated with my right hand to Morgan to lock both doors. She did.

I crept over, crouched down, and glanced over the dune. About fifty feet away, a short man stood there facing the sea cemetery just beyond the surf's reach, practically a black silhouette against the reclining afternoon sun, so still, statuesque. It chilled my blood. The only things in motion about him, undulated by a light ocean wind lullabying Pelican Bay, were the dingy, navy blue wings of a moth-eaten fisherman's coat, silky strands of white hair about the sides of his head and ears, tiny fingers casting a spell, and sail-like bilges of pants weathered to the point of oily colorlessness, folding about his skinny legs, miniature flags of surrender. The man wore no hat, and I imagined that he held it in his hands giving a eulogy to our submerged forefathers.

There was no doubt.

It was Captain Shelby.

He had come back.

Suddenly a seagull landed on top of the dune. Then another. And another. They began squawking at me bellicosely.

"What are ye at there?"

The wind carried his voice over the dune toward Pelican Bay, and I fancied that all the townspeople could hear it. How he made it near the dune so quickly will always baffle me. My blood froze. I ducked down and closed my eyes, wishing that I could disappear at will, like a just-discovered child playing hide and seek.

"I said what are ye at there?"

I ran around to the driver's side of the car, furiously displaying a "thumbs-up" signal for Morgan to unlock my door. She must have seen Captain Shelby coming toward us. He seemed to move so quickly across the sand. She now had her hands over her eyes and her head in her lap. Her muffled screams were like an alarm sounding beneath the sea.

I fiddled for my keys.

Finally, I opened the door, got into the Monte Carlo, and started it up.

As I was putting the car into gear, there was a thunderous sound on the passenger window.

I floored the accelerator, the V8 making our tires squeal, the car fishtailing back onto the road.

"Oh my God! Was that him?" Morgan screamed.

"Yes."

After we had traveled not fifty feet, I looked in the rear view mirror and he was gone.

CHAPTER FIFTEEN

Sidney awoke the next morning, just before the sun, and went about her morning rituals. These included, while water was boiling for tea, brushing her teeth, looking for the young English woman she once knew in her simple oval bathroom mirror, and sneaking into my room while I slept to pick up dirty laundry I always left on the floor.

She liked to watch me for a few minutes while I slept. I did not know this for years until I caught her one morning and pretended to be asleep. I could hear her regal hands sweeping the floor for loose clothes, the sound of a guardian angel's wings settling. She sighed rather softly, that same angel exhaling just so much as to indicate her dissatisfaction with my youthful state of disorganization. Before she left she said something, a whisper. To this day I believe it was, "I love you, Ethan," though my heart heard it more than my ears.

And ever since that day, I have always felt like the safest boy in Pelican Bay.

Sidney sat at our little breakfast table near a large window that overlooked the bay. On a clear day, one could see all the way to the sea over the dunes, the humps of great white sleeping camels collapsed for having confused, out of feverish thirst, seawater for fresh. The dunes' grassy patches in the distance might have been Pelican Bay settlers rooting themselves in a place where perhaps they never truly belonged, grass transplanted from England and for all I knew from mighty Newfoundland, grass in a place not meant to grow.

Sidney sipped her Earl Gray and nibbled on her burnt-looking toast, which she always insisted was perfect, just as she always insisted that I was the perfect boy.

A knock on the side door entering our little kitchen came that should have awoken me, would have awoken a great king after years of battle. It rattled our beaten cottage.

"Oh dear. Now who on earth could that be so early?" Sidney muttered aloud. And this was an excellent question. The sun had barely risen, and the visitor knew to go right to the kitchen door, a door we rarely used.

She rose anxiously and shuffled reluctantly to the door.

"Oh dear."

When she opened it, a leathery face with eyes, oh those ancient Atlantic eyes, brilliant mood gems dragged from the deep, greeted her. That face was all that she could see, all that she could fathom in that awkward moment.

"Laura, me Ducky, 'tis me!"

At first Sidney could not speak. She just stood there, her eyes broad and darting. It was a contest between the sky and the sea, those two sets of eyes warring in the doorway.

"I'm afraid you have me confused with someone else. And I've told you never to come here."

"Don't ye know me, Laura?"

"You're a crazy old man. Oh my dear." She began to experience vertigo. Standing there in the old fisherman's undertow.

"Don't get so crooked now, me Laura."

"I told you not to call me that!" Sidney cried.

"Take a rúm then. Why don't ye take a rúm."

"Oh dear, dear," Sidney mumbled.

"Well are ye after lettin' me in? Or will ye curse an old mate with standin' here in this doorway forevermore?"

"I'm not your friend. And don't you try to charm me. I know who you are," Sidney said.

"And who might that be?"

"You're not human." Sidney's voice broke and she stepped back.

The old man crossed the threshold and removed his captain's hat that was faded beyond recognition. Sidney took a few more steps backward.

"Go on now! Then what I be Laura?"

"Oh Lord. I don't know! And if you call me Laura one more time, I'll—"

"Ha! You'll what?" Captain Shelby summoned his belly laugh and the salt and pepper shakers and silverware and little English tea cups and saucers all danced in their places on the breakfast table.

"Oh my. Oh dear," Sidney said as she almost collapsed into the same chair in which she had been enjoying her tea only moments ago. She looked as if she might faint at any moment.

Captain Shelby helped himself to an opposite chair, which Sidney was afraid would break. She cringed. But underneath all the old man's globs of moth-eaten clothing, under his face that was as big as a crooked sky, beneath his eyes that lassoed the world about him, was a man of only moderate height and weight. He seemed to have a belly sometimes and not others, but was not a large man by any means.

It was only after Sidney could gather herself, wrestle her consciousness away from the captain's face, that she noticed the stench. I'll never forget how she described it to me one time during a storm wailing in the distance—always a damned storm in the distance.

She said you would have to bathe for hours in the first ocean of the primeval earth, breathing the sea foam into your nostrils, into your soul, to understand the glorious pungency. Were the captain a gardener, there would be so many roses to smell that you would succumb to death by roses.

Now Sidney was sure that she would faint, until the old man barked at her again.

"Where me boy be at this morn?"

"None of your business," Sidney said, staring at her cup of Earl Gray.

"He's been actin' right crooked. Saw him near the dunes yesterday and tried to talk to him, but his girlfriend screamed in the car and they skidded off leavin' tire marks. What sagas ye been puttin' in me boy's head?"

"Would you like some tea?"

The old fisherman cleared his throat in his sea rover way and Sidney jumped. His surreal eyes darted about and seemed to look through the walls.

"Ye can keep yer English tea for yerself."

"I could make some strong black coffee. Maybe it would help your manners."

Captain Shelby's face relaxed suddenly. Sidney shuddered. Then the old man smiled, his awesome wrinkles deepening like an opened crumpled piece of yellow parchment paper being re-crumpled. "Ha! Ye got the fire below just like me Laura!"

"I don't want you around Ethan. I've told you that."

"Now yer testin' me, Ducky. He's a full-grown sailor and can set his own mind. A young man's will is the will of the wind."

"I don't want you hurting him like the others."

"What ye know bout hurtin'? I'll show ye some hurtin'!"

The old man stood up. A perfectly good dawn sky rumbled in the distance. Sidney began staring at her lap and praying.

"I've never done nothin' for all ye fools but try to save ye. Why ye got the contrary nerve, I say! I'm here to tell ye I be done with it all! Ye can save yerselves from them crooked storms and the doom that lyeth ahead!"

A bigger rumbling in the distance now.

"This town doesn't need you. We never did."

Black clouds swallowed the sun and the breakfast room darkened.

"Have me cursed thee in another life?"

"You don't belong here. You're an abomination under the eyes of God."

"If memory be after servin' me, yer little ducky felt different."

"She didn't know any better. And look what fate befell her!"

"I tried to save 'em!"

The thunder became deeply explosive, distant cannon balls striking some forgotten battlefield.

"You killed them!" Sidney cried, covering her eyes and crying now.

"I'd guard the Hodges with me life. I'd never harm ye."

Sidney betook the old fisherman with ample, wet eyes.

"That's right. Look within yer soul, Laura. Look deep within' and I be there."

Sidney wiped away her tears and her face filled with wonder. She felt something in that moment that she would not dare describe, similar to a child beauty being mollified by some beast roaming the countryside.

"Ye see? 'Tis only me, Laura. 'Tis only me, yer wild rose."

Sidney suddenly managed to gather herself. "Please stop! You're upsetting me. I want you to leave before I—"

"That won't be fit, me Ducky. I was not after makin' ye crooked. Was just after findin' me boy. I'll leave ye in peace now."

"He's not your boy!"

Captain Shelby walked past the breakfast table and sailed for the door. A piece of ancient folded yellow paper flew from his side, making a chafing wisp across the center of the table.

Sidney did not move or say anything.

A few minutes after the captain and his glorious stench had departed, the sun returned and quieted the sky.

CHAPTER SIXTEEN

The night after Morgan and I returned from our road trip, I dreamed that Captain Shelby stood like a zombie ambassador before the undersea graves. Our forefathers, barnacle-ridden, slimy, skeletal, eyes glowing, walked clumsily toward the shore as he waved them on. I woke up shivering, giving obeisance to the mundane reality of my room about me.

"Aren't you going to have some breakfast, dear?" Sidney asked.

"I don't think so. I'm not really hungry."

"Are you okay, Ethan? You rarely sleep this late, but I was afraid to wake you earlier because you've been looking a bit pale lately."

"I'm okay. I had a nightmare, that's all."

"Would you like to talk about it, dear?"

I was silent.

"Is it about Captain Shelby?"

I still said nothing, avoiding Sidney's tender gaze.

"I knew it. It might help to talk about it, Ethan."

"The one I had last night jolted me a little bit, but it's not the one that's really bothering me."

"No, dear?"

"I had one recently where he showed me one of the underwater gravestones, only it wasn't under the water in the dream. It was part of the cemetery from a much older version of our town."

"Hmm," she said.

"It looked to be the first town ever settled here."

"Oh my, Ethan. Oh my. What a dream."

"Yeah. And you won't believe what the name on the gravestone was."

"Do I want to know?"

"Laura H. Shelby. The 'H' stood for Hodges."

A chill seemed to take the air, not just in our cottage, but everywhere.

"Sidney, do you know who that is? Could she be related to us?"

Sidney would not look at me.

"Sidney, please, if you—"

"Laura Hodges is a distant grandmother of yours," she said faintly, her voice shuddering.

"Wow," I said. "So the Laura on the gravestone could be—"

"I don't know."

Enduring silence.

"Sweetie, this is all getting way too creepy, and I'm worried about you, dear, what with all these dreams—and then what happened yesterday. I should have never told you those ghost stories.

"What happened yesterday?"

"You know what, dear. What were you doing with Morgan at the beach yesterday?"

I turned suddenly and looked at Sidney, almost gravely.

"Who told you that?"

"Captain Shelby."

"What?"

"Why are you shouting, dear? He stopped by this morning and left you a note."

"You talked to him? This morning?"

"Yes. What's the big deal?"

"He came here?"

"Yes, dear. He was trying to be charming, but I spoke my mind."

"Charming?"

"Yes, well, we didn't talk for very long. He was looking for you. He said that he saw you and Morgan in the Monte Carlo by the beach yesterday afternoon. He tried to come up and talk to you and he said the two of you skidded away, leaving tire marks. That doesn't sound like you, Ethan—not at all. He also said that Morgan was screaming at the top of her lungs inside the car. What in God's name were the two of you doing?" Sidney's cheeks were becoming flushed and her eyes narrowed.

"Sidney, it's not what you think. Look, I have to go."

"Go? Where?"

"I just have to go."

"Ethan, you're acting very peculiar. Ever since those undersea gravestones appeared, you and Morgan—"

"I love you, Sidney. I'll explain everything later. I just have to go."

I kissed her on her cheek.

"Wait! Captain Shelby's note."

Sidney handed me a folded piece of paper that looked like a piece of an ancient treasure map. I looked at it, open-eyed.

"Thanks."

"Aren't you going to take something to eat with you?"

"Don't worry. I'll pick up something later in town."

"Promise me you'll stay away from those gravestones!" she yelled after me. But I did not turn back.

The porch screen door slammed behind me like a big exclamation mark.

"Oh dear, dear," Sidney said to herself, sipping her tea and shaking her head. "Oh, dear, dear."

I was on my way to Pete's house. We were going to scuba dive to clean off the unreadable gravestones under the sea.

Pete was an old school buddy. We were not that close, but he was my only other friend, really, except for Morgan—my only other friend my age, that is. In Pelican Bay, casual friends were close friends.

Pete was tall, athletic, friendly, and pleasant-faced with blondish hair and light brown eyes. We became friends on All Team together. All Team was the Pelican Bay School team for anyone that was interested in sports. Our town was so small that we kept the same team all year round. There were not many sports offered, mainly because no one would have gone out for them. The only sport that we actually practiced in Pelican Bay was track and field, only there was no track, and no field, unless you counted the almost endless stretch of coastline to run on, which is where we trained. For basketball we had to go to Gull Bay to practice and play games, borrowing their gym, usually quite early in the morning, when Gull Bay High School was not using it. All Team started in 9th grade and went until 12th grade. There were never more than six town denizens at one time on All Team that I can remember. Pretty pathetic. We could not have our own football team, of course, not enough players, and instead had to play on Gull Bay's football team, always guaranteed to be a bench-warming experience, except in practice, of course, where we were used as trauma dummies.

Pete and I always played football and surfed together growing up. I was about the same height and athletic build as Pete, six feet roughly, only I had dark hair and brown eyes several shades darker than his, and my face was not as friendly, often sunken and sometimes too pensive and even saturnine. But Morgan always said that when I finally took to smiling that I could light up a whole room. Maybe this is why I was always trying to smile at Morgan, every chance that I had.

But it never seemed to help that much.

I had put Captain Shelby's note in my shirt pocket and it seemed to stare at me the whole way to Pete's house. I finally had to just pull over and read it.

How ye getin on me son Im sorry I was crookid the other day I like to keep me bisnes to me self I hope ye understan I bin woreed about ye Morgin to she was screemin yesderday pleese come see me be after takin ye fishin

Captin Shelbee

I refolded the note and put it back in my shirt pocket. As I sat there in the Monte Carlo, a bright blue sky of late August grinning at me, my mind was racing.

Is this all just a bizarre case of imagination gone wild? I've known Captain Shelby since I was a kid. And now the poor old man's worried, and he says he's sorry! Maybe we're just suffering from some kind of small town fever. This has got to stop. Now.

I turned the car around and headed back home to get Captain Shelby's flashlight.

"That sure was a fast trip," Sidney said. "What happened? You had me worried, dear."

"I'm sorry Sidney. To tell you the truth, I was going to pick up Pete to make another dive with the scuba gear I rented from Gull Bay."

"Scuba gear?"

"I just didn't want you to worry."

"What has gotten into you, Ethan?"

"It's all over, Sidney. You heard me say it, right? We've really gone overboard with this whole thing and it stops right now!"

Sidney's face appeared lightly rustled by incredulity.

"I read Captain Shelby's note," I added.

"I read it too, dear. I think he's just lonely. You're all he's got."

"You know what Captain Shelby's always telling me?"

"What, dear?"

"Some things are better left alone."

"Well—that's true."

"I'm leaving this alone now. He's my friend."

"Listen dear, something strange happened this morning that I've got to tell you about."

"What?"

"Well—"

"You can tell me anything, Sidney."

"Okay. Captain Shelby smells like the sea."

"What?"

"You heard me, dear."

I looked at the ground and shook my head slowly, a faint smile raising the corners of my mouth.

"Of course, the old man practically sleeps in it," I said.

"That's not what I mean. It's like he *is* the sea. It felt like I was wading in the ocean when he was in the kitchen."

"Not you now! Not you, Sidney!"

"Dear, I don't want to cause any stir, please know that. I think this is better left alone, and I'm sorry if I've been a bit superstitious or fancy-minded about that strange old man, but he's not *human*."

"Sidney!"

"Ethan, I'm sorry, but he was right at the door and I couldn't smell anything but the sea."

"That's ridiculous!"

"A man like that ought to smell something fierce. I mean, he probably bathes very infrequently, if at all. But he had no body odor, only the smell of the ocean."

"Stop it, Sidney. Really. That's it. I've heard enough. If anyone was going to be sensible, I really thought it was going to be you. You're not helping things at all. Did you ever think that maybe he bathes in the sea?"

"Yes, but he would still have body odor. I'm sorry, Ethan, I'm just being honest. I really don't want you around him anymore. Something's wrong with him."

"I can't believe this. Are you listening to yourself?"

Sidney chuckled perfunctorily, a tad uneasily.

"I'm going to call Pete and tell him there's no diving today. As soon as I find that flashlight. And if Morgan calls with any new research data, you can tell her that Captain Shelby and I went fishing and you don't know when I'll be back."

"Ethan!" Sidney covered her mouth with her hand and inhaled a woeful sigh of disbelief.

"I don't want to hear anything else about this. You hear me?"

"Oh, Ethan! Please at least let me make you and Captain Shelby some sandwiches. Oh my! Oh, my, my! Please be careful! Please! Oh dear, dear."

CHAPTER SEVENTEEN

It was only the second time that the old man and I had gone fishing together that summer. The sun was taking her time climbing the sky. She glistened on the shiny backs of the greedy gulls that haunted our boat all that morning. The sea was steady and calm and broke on our bow like a loving woman willfully giving way to a man.

Captain Shelby's boat was old, as old and creaky as he. But he had built her to last, and so she knew a life inestimably longer than her jealous cousins adrift in the nearby bays that formed the old man's nostalgic hunting ground.

Long planks of dark, solid oak that appeared fossilized by both ocean and time formed the hull and keel. A sturdy, wrinkled and pocked pine, the color of the captain's face before the Atlantic sun had permanently baked it, made up the bridge. An ancient, belching one-lunger marine engine, painting the old man's wake with miniature storm clouds, incessantly spat upon and glued by his ageless wisdom, fashioned the meager propulsion system.

Oh but she was loved and true, no more than fifty feet, painted white every summer along her sides to hide the wear of the sea, as if given new life, new skin, but like a legendary warrior's face under battle paint, her scars showed through. Her nets were mended more times than the old man could count, but still passed the test of a weighty bounty of fish. Four thick, heavy-reeled deep sea fishing rods always protruded from the stern of his boat, too, so that an onlooker from reasonably far off might assume that the old man always had a line in the water—and this was not too far from the truth.

Just behind the bow, up on both sides, the boat's name was freshly painted in large black letters: *The Grate Hurican*

"Where are we going fishing today, Captain?"

"Me Secret Spot. It's time for ye to see it."

"Secret Spot? Is it far?"

"It's just a few miles off Oyster Cove. All them deeper bottom boats can't go where we be goin'. They're built to get stuck. Lots a nasty rocks in there. Are ye mad at me, me Son?"

"No. I thought you might be mad at *me*. I've been acting like a real fool lately."

"Listen, me Son, that's why I don't have any friends, save for thee. People get to bein' nosy and they bring all sorts a trouble, see? Like me said, some things are better left alone."

"Yes."

"How Morgan be gettin' on?"

I chuckled and the waves chuckled back.

"She's just fine. Just your typical, nosy, squeamish librarian, that's all."

We both chuckled now. It felt good.

"I wasn't after scarin' nobody," the old man softly bellowed.

The wind was starting to pick up. We were slowing down, and I figured that the Secret Spot was not far.

"How come you've never wanted a cottage in town?"

"I was after that once, more years ago than I can remember."

"May I ask what happened?"

"Folks were after askin' too many questions. Always happens. People start askin' me age and why I smell the way I do, and before ye know it people start investigatin' and trouble comes. Got right crooked with it all. Just want to be left in peace to do me fishin', that's all. Don't want no trouble."

"I guess I never noticed. I mean, about you smelling like the sea. I guess I've never really spent any time with you on land."

"Seems everyone's got a bone to pick with a man bein' different. Just can't leave things be. I suppose I was born with this here sea in me veins. The duckies seem to notice it more than the scopies."

"Do you think woman are more sensitive to scent than men?"

"Go on boy! God only knows, me Son. God only knows."

We entered a little shallow channel with large, jagged rocks on each side, festooned with tuxedo seagulls and a few rusty, proud pelicans. I noticed that the pelicans and the seagulls did not share the same rocks, and I don't remember ever seeing a pelican and a seagull sitting near each other. But I was young, and youth has a way of making the wrong conclusion often seem irresistible.

Up ahead a small island loomed with rocky shoreline, but thick with foliage at its center.

"Ye see that little island up ahead, me Son?"

"Yes."

"That there be Fisherman's Island. That's what I call it. No one dares take their boat through this shallow, rocky channel cause they'd get stuck. The current can be wicked, too. Grab this wheel for a second. Ye see how she's fightin' ye? But up ahead the sea's calm, always calm, and deeper than any anchor or fishin' line can go. 'Tis me Secret Spot. Why, I've caught fish there even seasoned townsfolk couldn't recognize."

"Wow."

"Start preppin' the lines and cuttin' the bait, me Son."

"Okay. You got it."

Captain Shelby was right. Just beyond the toothed pass it was as though we had entered a brand new sea, gone from the Atlantic into some unchartered small ocean. It was so calm, almost still. The horizon seemed immeasurably farther away now. There was not a cloud in the sky to be found. Everything was so bright, almost blindingly so, and clear, and the color of the sea was even different, the same color as the old man's eyes. And the smell of this new sea was so pungent, but not in a salty way, in a poetical way.

"Ye got them lines ready, me Son?"

"Yeah. I used the biggest hooks you have."

"That's me boy! We're goin' to fish them lines deep, and say us a special prayer our bait reaches as far as them spools will go without bein' eatin' first."

It was so exciting, as I remember it. I had never fished a spot so dark, so deep. Just thinking of what sea monsters may lurk down there sent big goose bumps all up and down my arms, as if big chunks of salt from the new ocean were jumping out of the sea and swimming in through my fingers and up my forearms.

"Why is it so deep here, Captain?"

"God only knows, me Son. God only knows. Ye have to drift to fish, and I've never had a line hit bottom. I've tried spools on top of spools."

"It must be a trench, you know, like the Mariana Trench, only not as deep, I'm sure."

"Go on boy! But the fishin' here's the best in these parts, I say."

Our fishing lines seemed to drop endlessly, like the expanse of sea before the blurry horizon. The gulls had given up on our boat, and you could hear their squawking off in the distance, down along in the rocky channel.

"Okay, stop it there, me Son. Ye need to protect some fightin' line."

"All right."

The sun was high up in the sky now, making her presence known, but it was not hot.

At least an hour must have passed with the old man and I saying little if anything. From him I had learned patience, among many things. Sometimes it could take hours to get a bite, but those hours could be the greatest investment of your life. Captain Shelby said that God gave us hours so that we could pass the hours, and we passed the hours that afternoon with a beautiful serenity.

I made it a point that day not to stare at Captain Shelby, not to be hypnotized by his brilliant eyes, not to ponder his wrinkles. I wanted to put all that ridiculousness behind me.

Yet I could not help but wonder if Morgan was researching the mystery of the old man as we sat there. I could picture her wearing her glasses at the library checkout counter, the tip of her striking nose dusting a tiny spot on an old computer screen, or on the phone, talking to countless people in what I called her "411 voice." She could be so efficient, polite, and proper, that information would seem to leap onto her lap at her very command.

Just then, as if reading my mind, the old man said, "Well, me Son, I'm after givin' ye an answer." He was staring vaguely at the place where one's fishing line disappears into the water.

"About what?"

"Ye asked how old I be."

"You know, I don't really care about that anymore."

"No, me Son, a question deserves an answer. I guess I was just afraid of ye actin' like all them other land folks. Can ye keep a secret, me Son?"

"Sure."

I was afraid.

I could feel my body shuddering slightly. I do not remember ever being in such a state of suspense. I almost felt sick.

Suddenly there was a yanking thump in my line, almost pulling my fishing pole out of my hands.

"Hang on, me Son! Get on the go!"

My heavy reel started to zing, its old drag louder than excitement. I remember thinking how glad I was that I had taken the old man's advice and protected some fighting line.

"Look! There she goes! There she goes!"

I hung on to my fishing pole for dear life, as the sea creature took much line into the sea. Thank God I had 50-pound test. The only thing that I was afraid of was my line running out.

"Ye have to tighten yer drag, me Son. Don't be afraid. Just a little, just a little."

I tightened the drag and my pole bent almost to its full tension point.

"Look! Go on boy! She be a monster!" the old man roared, exhibiting the excitement of a boy's first catch. I loved him in that moment, like a grandfather. But now I realize that I always loved him.

The sea monster was still taking line, line that I no longer had to give, like some tragic disease taking my life before I was ready.

I tightened the drag just a tad more.

"Look! She be hardly tirin'!" the old man growled. "Whatever she is, we may have to cut her loose."

"No!"

"She'll take me pole, and pull ye down with her."

Suddenly the line stopped going out.

"Today's yer lucky day, me Son! She's changin' direction! Take up that slack while ye can! While ye can!"

I was able to recover a lot of my lost line. It almost felt as though I had lost the fish, but then she ran away from us, and the drag sang an even louder opera of her aged, tarnished, clicking moan: "Rat, tat, tat, tat, tat, tat, tat—"

"There she goes again!" I yelled.

After about forty-five minutes, my arms feeling like hot lead, she finally began to tire. I began to have my way with her.

"She's yers, me Son! Don't give up now!"

"I got her."

After another thirty minutes she was nearing the surface. I have never been a father, but I imagine that the raw excitement that I felt must have been akin to watching one's baby being delivered, not knowing the sex ahead of time.

Suddenly she made a spectacular jump, almost ten feet high, as if wishing to skip the catch and go right to heaven. She twirled and gleamed in the afternoon sun like a silver wind chime.

The old man finally helped me gaff and board her. She was a tarpon, a 117-pound tarpon, the biggest fish that I had ever caught, and ever would.

CHAPTER EIGHTEEN

When I awoke the next morning, the sky was growling, bent on blackening yet another Tuesday. It was not even eight in the morning as I lay lazily in bed, my body still sore from my bout with the big girl the day before, the tarpon. I could still see her thick, torpedo-shaped body taking a final dive, just when we thought that we had landed her, a third wind that likely even she did not know that she possessed.

Captain Shelby asked me if I wanted to stuff the fish to mount it on my wall. I said no. There is something immensely creepy about taxidermy. Why not mount a human on the wall instead? Would my tarpon mount me proudly on her wall if she had caught me? Would she put me in her entertainment room in her beautiful basement under the sea, along with her other land creature trophies, each spurring little stories, as if they could come alive to regale other fish with tales of their captures?

Taxidermy is just so unsettling. A gloss of death, a dumbfoundedness, seems to remain in the eyes of all stuffed animals, their final struggle with inevitability recorded eternally in their stares from their mountings, even in the smallest of creatures. The eyes of a stuffed sparrow can haunt your soul and render even the nicest living room quite dreary.

"Can we sell her?" I asked.

"Them tarpon aren't commercial fiskr, me Son. Too many bones."

"Is she a record?"

"She be a monster. But I've seen bigger. No sense keepin' her for proof. Let her go so she can live to fight another day. A cleaved head no longer plots."

I just lay in bed. It was the perfect day for it. But I had work to do. There was a 1000-word article that I was finishing for the Gull Bay Post.

Suddenly the phone rang, near deafening against my thoughts.

Sidney must be out.

"Hello?"

"Ethan?"

It was Morgan. She never called me on the phone.

"Yeah," I got out, rather sleepily.

"You're not going to believe it."

"Are you at the library?"

"Yes. Guess what?"

"What?"

"I found out Captain Shelby's full name."

"Really?"

"Yeah. I got it from the old purchasing records of a cannery just south of Gull Bay."

"I give."

"Nereus H. Shelby."

"*Nereus?*"

"That's right. Guess what the date was?"

"1750?"

"Very funny. It was 1912."

We were both silent for a moment.

"Listen, Morgan, there's something I've been wanting to tell you."

"Yes?"

"Some things are better left alone."

"What? Oh. I see. Look, Ethan, we're so close on this."

"I just want to leave the poor old man alone."

Silence.

"You're the one that started this whole thing, and now you just want to quit right when we're getting close? How typical."

"Look, Morgan, I went fishing with him yesterday and caught a 117-pound tarpon."

"That's just great, Ethan. Good for you."

"I had a great time. I really love the old man. All he wants is to be left alone. He said that he lives out there on his boat because of people like you and me, always causing trouble for him."

"Typical. You're always going with your heart, Ethan. That old man's got you brainwashed. What if he really is crazy? What if he murdered that boy and killed those fishermen? What if he was responsible even indirectly for your parent's accident at sea?"

"The only thing that old man's guilty of is being different. And the only things he's ever killed are fish."

"I think you're letting your feelings bar your reason here. Something just isn't right."

"You're starting to sound just like Sidney. I can't believe this."

"Well, maybe you should start listening to your grandmother."

"I have something I want to show you, Morgan. I think it'll change your mind about this whole thing."

"What is it?"

"You'll see. Can I come to the library during your lunch hour?"

"Okay. Just be careful, it's really starting to blow and thunder out there."

"See you soon. Bye."

"Bye."

Sitting down at my desk in my room, I tried to put it all out of my mind, but my thoughts soon turned to the undersea cemetery.

What if the old man's name is down there, after all? Wouldn't I regret not knowing?

I listened to the thunder in the distance, perhaps echoes of the old man's scraggly voice, and his answer came as though on the cool wind, prologue to a big storm.

"Some things are better left alone."

I wondered if the new storm would cover up the tombstones for good, and I thought about the scuba gear in the trunk of Sidney's Monte Carlo. *I'm sure I could call Joe to get a few more days. After all, it's not like he's going to be using it.*

More thunder, now growing closer, gave the old man's answer again.

My mind was under the spell of its own storm, a warm front carrying the desire to know the truth, almost a burning heat wave of curiosity, facing a cold front bringing soft snowflakes of peaceful release, the breezy serenity of letting go, of fully accepting another.

I went to the kitchen to look for something to eat, realizing in that moment that a storm still raged in my mind because the old man had not shared his secret yesterday. With all the excitement of the tarpon, getting her aboard, and then negotiating the rocky channel back home, he never offered it again. And it just felt wrong to keep bringing it up.

There were never many people in the Pelican Bay Library, and I think that Morgan preferred it that way. Occasionally, a small school group might come in, and there was always the spattering of very old senior citizens loafing about like lovable sea creatures, seeking solace from the usual onslaught of Pelican Bay storms, thumbing through the

New York Times or reading old books, usually with a respectable dose of sea imagery, books the likes of London or Melville or Hemingway.

Sometimes Morgan would give a short lecture on a new author, but I never attended because I just seemed incapable of visualizing her possessing the outward persona of a speaker or of a teacher.

It was raining hard now, and Pelican Bay Street was already blemished with formidable puddles of rain water, black lakes on a sullen map. I was only wearing a hooded windbreaker and I watched the rain splatter and soak my legs as I ran for the Pelican Bay Diner to fetch a chicken salad that was Morgan's favorite. It was a probable certainty that she had brought no lunch.

When I finally entered the library, Morgan was crouched over a book. She saw me coming and closed it quickly. She appeared somewhat disheveled, no makeup, her skinny metal-framed glasses on the verge of fogging up, her hair quickly put up in a ponytail, and wearing a cotton blouse and denim skirt that were haggard and unironed.

"Make sure you stomp your feet really well, and dry off as much as you can. I don't want to make this old library any mustier than it already is."

"Yes, Miss Olinsworth."

"Very funny."

"I have your favorite: chicken salad."

"That's sweet, Ethan." She smiled at me sincerely.

"What are you reading there?"

"Oh, nothing, really."

Morgan's cheeks became flushed. I walked over to her and moved some newspapers out of the way.

"Ethan, don't!"

"*Ghosts of the Sea?*"

"I was just thumbing through it for fun, that's all. I saw it with some old books in the back, and—"

"This is from the Gull Bay library!"

"Well, I—"

"We need to talk, Morgan. This has gone way too far."

"Okay, talk then," she said.

"I want you to read this note."

I took Captain Shelby's note out of my pocket and handed it to her. She read it quickly.

"What's this supposed to prove?"

"He's just a man, an old man that doesn't mean any harm and who wants to be left in peace."

"He's got you wrapped around his old salty thumb, that's what that proves. It also indicates that the poor old man is borderline illiterate."

"For God's sake, Morgan, he's a fisherman. That's what he does.

That's *all* he does."

"Ethan," Morgan said, suddenly offering soft eye contact with me, "there's something else that I haven't told you, something I found out yesterday. You might want to sit down."

"I can't wait to hear this," I said, with just enough sarcasm to earn a lip-curled, squinty-eyed expression from Morgan.

"I did a lot of checking on different variations of the last name Shelby and I learned that it's a remnant of Old Norse, the language used by the Vikings."

"Yes, Sidney mentioned something about that."

"I also found a journal passage that's very, very old."

Morgan ran to her computer and came back with a printed piece of paper, reading a passage from it out loud.

> *"Seeking freedom from oppression*
> *and tyranny, we placed our faith in*
> *Captain Selby, a most agreeable*
> *man whose life depends upon the sea,*
> *to find us a new home across*
> *the great ocean—a place to finally*
> *call home and start anew."*

From the *Journal of William Brockleby*
11 April 1535

"I'm impressed, but I'm not sure what that proves. The last name is similar, but not the same, really."

"The name Selby is believed to be the origin of the name Shelby," Morgan said enthusiastically.

"So what?"

"I think somebody needs to brush up on his early American history."

"Okay. I'll bite."

"Based on the best archeological evidence available, the Vikings are considered to be the first settlers in America—Newfoundland, to be exact. Around that same time they invaded and ruled England, many centuries before this journal entry was ever written. At the start of the 16th century, there was a good deal of migration from England to Newfoundland, where I believe William Brockleby and his settlers were heading. Jamestown was not until almost a century later."

"So what are you saying?"

"Since I haven't been able to find any vital records on the east coast, from Florida on up to Newfoundland, of any variation of the spelling of a fisherman or captain with the name Shelby, especially first name, Nereus, or first initial, N., only two likely alternatives remain."

"This is going to be good."

"Either he's not from the east coast of our continent, or he's that same Captain Selby from the passage, a man of Viking ancestry. It seems unlikely that a fisherman would come all the way from the Caribbean just to fish Pelican Bay, so—"

"Listen to yourself! Don't even say it!"

"Captain Selby and Captain Shelby are the same man."

I applauded and smiled sarcastically. Morgan scowled at me.

"Ethan, when the best explanations have been exhausted, whatever remains, even the remote, must be plausible."

"Now whose imagination is running wild? As soon as the storm clears, I'm going to get one more look at those gravestones."

"I don't see how that's going to prove anything."

"It's simple, really. Assuming he's just a very old man and not a ghost or an immortal, either his ancestors are down there, which proves librarians don't know everything and some people don't have records or marked graves, or I find no evidence down there, which proves librarians don't know everything and some people don't have records or marked graves."

"Oh, that's a riot, Ethan. You're a hoot."

"At least one more dive gives us a chance to put all this nonsense behind us and leave the old man in peace."

"What about the stories we've heard, from reliable locals?"

"People love stories, Morgan. You know that." I chuckled. "I swear, you and Sidney could write a book together! She actually told me yesterday that Captain Shelby s*melled like the sea.*"

"What did you just say?"

"That he smelled like the sea. Why?"

"Oh my God! Ethan, look!"

> *"We were afraid to face the vast ocean, fearing our lives might be lost to a storm, famine, or disease, but how could we not trust a man who smells like the sea?"*
>
> From the *Journal of William Brockleby*
> 11 April 1535

"That's it. I'm going home."

"Ethan! Don't! Please! There's one more thing you're not going to believe."

"That's probably right."

"The journal included a passenger manifest. You'll never guess who one of the other passengers was."

"Eric the Red?"

"No, smarty pants. Laura Hodges."

I just stood there silent for the longest time.

I felt dizzy suddenly.

"Ethan? Are you okay?"

"Yeah—I just—"

"Will you stay till the library closes and walk me home? I'm really scared."

Her eyes were so soft when she asked me, and she reached for my hand.

"Okay. Okay."

"By the way, guess what Nereus means?" she asked.

"What?"

"He's the Greek god known as 'the old man of the sea.'"

CHAPTER NINETEEN

Everything was eerily calm after the storm departed Pelican Bay. All that I could think about was getting to the beach to see if the gravestones were still visible under the ocean.

I hurried out of the house, without even eating breakfast, and headed down the worn foot path through the wild grass. At the bottom of the path I could see the harbor clearly, the old man's boat sitting almost still on the tranquil bay, reclining in its common place. My heart fluttered, but he was not about the deck, as usual, mending nets and prepping tackle. His boat seemed deserted.

I walked briskly down the beach and I saw a tall, sleek figure in the distance. Pete. He had equipment all about him like an amateur Jacque Cousteau preparing to prove the existence of a possible sea creature: scuba tanks, wetsuits, dive masks, flippers, and thick steel putty knives.

As I came closer to Pete, I saw the ominous-looking gravestones, as if a prehistoric underwater footpath leading off to Atlantis. Seeing the immersed cemetery always beaded my flesh, and that day was no exception.

There appeared to be fewer visible tombstones than the last time.

"Hi, Pete," I said.

"Hey, Buddy. The water's pretty clear today and nice and calm. That'll help things."

"Yeah."

"So what are we looking for again?"

"Anything with the name Shelby on it or any variation of that name, such as Selby. But as you clean off the gravestones, try to remember all the names that you see. It'll score huge brownie points for me with you-know-who."

"Your girlfriend, Morgan?"

"She's not my girlfriend."

"Whatever you say, Buddy. So you're investigating that old crazy man, eh?"

"It's kind of a long story."

"My dad's told me some strange things about him."

"How come you never talked about it?"

"I don't know. It just never came up, I guess."

"What do you remember?" I asked.

"When I was just a little kid, I overheard my dad talking to a neighbor about his age. They said that the sea made him immortal somehow."

I surrendered a jittery laugh. "That's all just a myth. I assure you, he's quite mortal. I just went fishing with him. Caught a 117-pound tarpon."

"117 pounds?! Isn't that a record or something?"

"No."

"Oh." Pete frowned. "What are you doing fishing with that old crazy geezer, anyway?"

"I like him. I don't think he's crazy—just different, that's all."

"Well why do you want to see if his last name's down there?"

"I really care about the old man and I want to put an end to all these rumors. He really just wants to be left in peace. A lot of research we've done points to him being from here. It's pretty certain he is."

"Dude, what if his exact name's down there?" Pete asked, giving me a rather creepy, broad-eyed look that made my flesh crawl.

"Don't be stupid."

Pete gave me a sheepish smile. "What's his full name, anyway?"

"Nereus H. Shelby."

"*Nereus*? Weird name."

"Nereus is the Greek god known as the 'old man of the sea.'"

Pete stared at me vacantly.

"Well, we're not diving too deep," Pete said, "so not a lot to worry about—almost like scuba diving in a pool, just a little deeper. Just be sure to keep an eye on your oxygen gauge. I have a dive watch, so I'll be our backup. Also, let's stay in eyeshot of each other, all right?"

"All right. Remember to try and memorize any names that you can read."

"Okay," Pete said with feigned enthusiasm.

The sea felt a few degrees cooler, perhaps the recent storm having taken some heat from out of the air as an Atlantic souvenir, stealing the hot breath out of the iron lungs of our pelicans, Pelican Bay's original inhabitants.

We swam out just beyond the shelf, gave each other an official, confirming nod, and then dived down to the ocean floor.

The work was tedious and the morning seemed to quickly blend with the afternoon. The undersea, riddled with occasional small fish, either loafing about the graves or darting away at the perfunctory motion of a diver's arm or fin, regarded our comings and goings as unclassifiable but quickly forgiven intrusions.

The first few headstones only revealed names that I had already seen, perhaps brothers, sisters, aunts, uncles, and so forth, ancestral tentacles of a miniscule beach town.

Finally, the unthinkable happened.

I had chiseled away the last name, "SHELBY" on the face of a gravestone. I felt immediately dizzy. I looked up at the surface, rays of sunlight, as if long arms of incredulity piercing the sea and poking my soul. I began to shudder all over, but my hand continued scraping as though with a will all its own.

Suddenly the middle initial, "H" appeared.

Everything felt dauntingly peculiar, the tiny particles and sea life about me seeming to slow down, almost to suspend their motion. I looked over to my right and saw Pete grating away at a tombstone with his steel putty knife, oblivious to the reckoning with surrealism with which I was now faced. He was like a lucky child too young to view an open casket and taken away with his mom to a room with waiting cookies and punch.

I continued scratching leftward with my putty knife and the letters, "US" materialized. My vision was becoming blurry now and it felt harder to breathe with every passing second. I paused for a moment, just trying to concentrate on simply filling my lungs with air. As my scraping reached its end, I did not want to see what was before me:

NEREUS H SHELBY

LOST AT SEA
JUNE 1721

I could no longer breathe. My body began to convulse violently as I coughed and swatted the oxygen mask away from my face. I struggled and writhed, my lungs aching like never before, and it seemed as though the sky were falling through the top of the sea, reaching down to cradle me.

Suddenly, everything went black.

The next thing that I remember I was lying on my back on the shore, waves lapping my legs, as if I were at the shallow end of God's Pool and He were making submarine waves in jest. I spit water back in playful retaliation.

"Ethan! Good to have you back!"

"Uh—what? Where am I?" I coughed out pathetically, seawater thickly seeping from the sides of my mouth.

"You're here on Pelican Bay Beach. You're lucky to be alive! Something went wrong with your oxygen regulator, I think."

"I—saw something. I think—I—"

"Just take it easy, Buddy. Take it easy now."

"No, no, please. I want you to go back in for me. I need you to verify something. Please!"

"Just relax, okay? Take it easy, fellow."

"Please, dive again, just to the left, about thirty feet down." I coughed again, wincing and holding my chest, spitting up more sea.

"Don't you worry about that right now, Buddy."

"No! You have to go before it's too late. Before—"

The piercing, forlorn, antiquated sound of the Pelican Bay Volunteer Fire Department truck pulling up just beyond the beach invaded my consciousness.

"No!"

"The only place that you're going now is to the hospital."

"No!"

I lost consciousness again.

"Let him be, scopie!"

"What? Who—?"

"I said let him be there," the old fisherman snarled.

"Wait a minute, you're—"

"Eh boy, 'tis me."

"What are you doing? Don't touch him. The authorities are coming and—"

"And what? The only authority me knows is the sea."

"Look, I told you not to touch him. I'm going to—"

"Yer goin' to what? A man who has his feet hacked off cannot scurry far."

"What? I—"

The captain's face seemed to grab a ray of morning sunlight, its omniscient lines a hundred awesome cracks in an oval mirror, two blue diamonds fused into some beautifully hideous sculpture.

Pete gulped for air like a beached fish. The sea began to rise like a foamy funeral pyre. The plaintive cry of the Pelican Bay Volunteer fire truck grew nearer, a colossal gull lonely for the sea.

The old man's eyes shifted toward the bleak sound, but Pete's remained upon the sea.

"Be gone and let me tend to me boy. The sea is after thee," Captain Shelby croaked as he knelt down beside my body.

"He needs professional medical attention. He may have an air embolism. He could die."

The ocean, crashing now, was up above Pete's ankles.

The old man began to drag my body away from the vengeful surf. Pete tried to follow but realized that his feet were stuck below the ocean mud, which seemed to be sucking him under now. Tidal bed quick sand. His face must have looked quite shocked.

"The sea be all any man needs. She'll mend me boy. But she's right crooked with thee now. Look, yer sinkin' boy." The quick sand had swallowed Pete all the way up to his knees.

"Help me!" Pete yelled.

The fire truck had pulled off the road and two volunteer firemen, one with an oxygen tank on his back, the other carrying a red-and-white paramedic rescue box, both with dirty-white fire helmets and the letters, PBFD in bold red on the front of them, came running up the sand from behind the dunes.

The wind suddenly began to blow fiercely up the beach and it was becoming hard to see. Pete was inundated up to his waist now, grains of sand blasting the side of his face like a BB machine gun. "Please! Help!" he yelled.

"Well one man can't save the two of ye, can he?" the old captain yelled, beginning to lift my body now. Pete was down to his chest and his face was still laced with panic but beginning to look oddly resigned.

The firemen finally arrived on the scene, their confused faces obscured by their hands against the swirling sand, as if the somersaulting grains in the wind were rays of blinding sunlight.

"What's wrong with the boy?" yelled one of the volunteer firemen.

"Nothin' me and the sea can't mend," creaked the old fisherman. "That boy be after help. Look, he be sinkin' into the sea's grave."

"Quick sand," yelled the second fireman. "I'll get it."

"Be careful! Watch your footing!" the first fireman hollered.

"Get on the go!" Captain Shelby yelled. "That there young scopie be needin' two men. Ye better not underestimate the wrath of the sea."

The second fireman was lying on his stomach trying to pull Pete out, but Pete was not budging at all.

"Get on the go I say!" the old fisherman roared.

"This looks like a diving accident," the first fireman shouted into the sandy wind. "You're not qualified, old man."

"Old? Look again."

The fireman looked at the captain again, who now stood with my body, my legs, black with wetsuit rubber, dangling stiffly in the oaky wind, my naked feet completely coated with sand save for a few spots that spoke volumes about my humanity. He suddenly had the bronzed face of every young man who ever gazed longingly at the sea, his eyes ocean-blue oval fires.

"Well, I—"

"I need some help over here!" the second fireman yelled, unable to pull Pete out of the random quick sand. His hand was now under the shallow seawater up to his elbow.

Pete had vanished.

"It's too late! Let him go before you go under yourself!" the first fireman shouted.

"Ye can't fight the sea ye ignorant fools!"

The second fireman let go of Pete's hand and ran back over, his eyes sunken.

"That's Sidney's boy," he finally yelled at the old fisherman, his voice gray in the hurling wind. "We need to get him to the hospital, sir, unless you know how to treat an air embolism."

"He's right," the first fireman added loudly, feeling my pulse. "This boy may die without proper medical care."

"What ye know bout ailments of the sea? Her mysteries have sunk yer town and they'll do it again."

Captain Shelby's face had turned ancient again, as if speaking of the past turned him into it. The firemen looked at each other with a stare meant to confirm they were awake and not dreaming, their eyes bulging, their eyebrows tangoing with one another.

"This has gone far enough. Put him down or we'll have you arrested. We got this," the first fireman shouted, the sand now a dark writhing miniature sky about them, the sea rising at their feet.

"Go on boy! Ha!" There was thunder behind the captain's voice and the firemen could suddenly not decipher the stinging sand from drops of rain as though spit from the sea now rather than the sky.

Just then a third fireman came up behind them. "You guys all right?"

"No," the first fireman hollered. "We got a problem here."

"Diving accident?"

"Yeah. We got to get him to Pelican Bay Hospital, but this old man won't hand the boy over."

The third fireman looked at the old man detachedly for a moment. "Captain Shelby, you know the sea, but not about air embolisms. Let us save the boy."

"And who thee be to address me that way?"

"Billy Bigsley."

The old fisherman had locked eyes with the third fireman and it was as though the two of them were in some kind of trance, neither of them blinking.

The third fireman reached for my body and Captain Shelby let him take it.

CHAPTER TWENTY

The Pelican Bay Hospital insisted on keeping me overnight, as they were worried about a possible air embolism. However, after the doctor examined me, he said, "I've never seen anything like this. This boy arrived at the hospital with completely healthy lungs, as if there were never any diving accident at all. I simply can't explain it."

I awoke alone, my eyes trying to focus. I had not been in the hospital since having my tonsils removed as a teenager.

Pelican Bay Hospital had surrendered itself to the same beach wear of its neighboring buildings. The peeling walls were an unpleasant shade of green. The beds were antiquated and petulant. The clock on the wall was as big as one might picture a clock to be, perhaps made by someone overly concerned with time, maybe even obsessed with it. It made a loud clicking sound that reminded me of Captain Shelby's old deep sea fishing reels, only slowed down, as if time were some torpid fish escaping out to sea, a fish that you could never catch and which would eventually snap your fragile line of life. And there was shiny metal all about me, vague medical things, frames and rods, a rusty steel ocean.

There was the faintest knock. Morgan poked her head in the door. I smiled halfway and motioned for her to come in. She approached my bed gingerly, apprehensively, and watching her walk, her head slightly tilted down and her face betraying a tentative smile, my love for her suddenly pervaded my entire body like warm sunlight after an endless winter's eve.

Her skin and hair shone so, extensions somehow, of the hospital's metal innards. Her reticent eyes presented the color of a palest blue sky, a backdrop to the luminescent jets of hospital objects crowding the air.

"Ethan, I was really worried about you."

"I'll survive."

"They said you almost drowned. Do you remember what happened?"

"It's all pretty hazy. The last thing I really remember is a cold feeling, and the sensation of suffocating. Before that, Morgan—"

My eyes expanded and I took to staring through my feet.

"Ethan, what?"

"You're not going to believe it."

"Ethan, what is it? You can tell me."

"With the oxygen regulator malfunctioning, it could've just been—"

"Ethan, you can tell me. You know you can tell me anything, right? Was it his name?"

I looked toward the small, forlorn window that gazed upon a miniature countryside of beach pines just behind the hospital, wishing that I could be brushed by their serenity. My face revealed a strained expression.

"Ethan, it's okay," Morgan said quietly.

"Yes. I saw his name."

"His exact name?"

"Yes."

"That's hard to believe, Ethan."

"I know."

A moment of silence passed as the beach pines seemed to whisper the old man's secrets to us through the growing wind.

"Ethan, what else aren't you telling me?"

"What do you mean?"

"Come on. I know you."

"Well—"

"Ethan."

"I had this dream you won't believe and, when I woke last night, just after they brought me in, my body felt like none of it had happened at all. The diving accident I mean."

"That is strange. What dream?"

"Captain Shelby was standing, holding me in his arms on the beach. I felt like I was in the arms of a great ancestor, an ancient grandfather. Nothing mattered. Nothing at all. I wasn't afraid, either, Morgan. I felt so serene. So safe. It was incredible," I said.

"We were looking out to sea. There were all these old passenger ships, with those old canvas sails and thick ropes. I could hear the ships groaning and creaking out there and the sound on the wind was like the music of the old settlers. I looked to my right and Pelican Bay was not there. There was nothing there at all except for tents and campfire rings and strange hanging clothes."

My body gave a small, involuntary shudder.

"I looked back out to sea at the beautiful moaning ships again, some ringing loud bells that sounded like bobbing metal buoys slapping the ocean in the distance. The captain said to me, 'Here they come, me Son. Here they come! Alas! Ahoy! But yer time be not here, me Son. Ye belong to the morrow. Forget what ye saw below. 'Tis not meant to be disturbed, ye hear me? 'Tis better left alone.' That's all I remember."

Morgan's face had become pale and engrossed but she noticed that I noticed and quickly gathered herself. She said softly, "It was just a dream Ethan. Just a dream."

I must have looked rather frightened now.

Sidney suddenly came in, the wrinkles on her face seeming to have bowed to concern. I made my best effort to calm myself.

"Hello, dear. Hello, Morgan."

"Hi, Sidney," Morgan said, her eyes nervously sweeping the hospital floor.

"Are you feeling better than before? Your face looks troubled, dear."

Sidney had rushed to the hospital almost immediately. They had called my next of kin as soon as I had arrived. She had stayed with me all night and her face showed it today.

"Yes, Sidney. I'm much better. Thanks."

"That's good, dear." Sidney looked over at Morgan, but Morgan avoided eye contact. She spoke to her anyway. "I sure hope you kids aren't talking about ghosts and gravestones. My Lord, Ethan needs his rest now."

Morgan began to raise her head begrudgingly.

Suddenly the rustle of a distinct commotion filled the hospital corridor, narrated by the pleading voice of a female nurse, a voice that grew nearer with every second.

"Sir, you have to be on the visitor list. Sir!"

The door was thrust open and Captain Shelby cruised in.

"Sir! I can't allow you to—"

"It's all right," I said, my voice slightly unsure but loud enough. "He's a friend of mine."

The nurse, standing behind the old man in the doorway, looked at me with a confused expression. "But—"

"He's okay. I'll vouch for him," I said, managing an authoritative tone now.

The nurse looked directly at the old man and he winked at her. She left briskly, shaking her head decidedly. Morgan had gone off to the window, a subdued look of horror flashing in her eyes. Sidney sat down very slowly on the visitors' chair to the right of my bed.

"So, me Son, yer getting' on okay. That's good to see, good to see."

"Yes."

"And me duckies, how are ye gettin' on today?" Captain Shelby's petrifying gaze shifted between Morgan and Sidney. He chuckled cavernously. "Why ye both look so pale—as if ye saw a ghost!"

It began thundering outside, almost giving an echo to the old man's piratical voice. The wind picked up more and the beach pines took to a coarse whispering now, which could have been Morgan by the window muttering loudly.

The old fisherman kept looking at Sidney and Morgan. They avoided his oceanic eyes. His expression became studious now, as if he were assessing pieces of wood for their seaworthiness against the pending storm. He did not wait for any response.

"The sky be right crooked. Looks like a storm be comin', eh?" he gurgled, laughing to himself.

"Yes," I said.

Sidney and Morgan were looking at each other pleadingly now. The smell of the ocean, radically pungent, permeated the room, as if the old man's lungs were perfume spray bottles salvaged from the bottom of the sea.

"What did I tell ye, me Son, about leavin' some things alone?"

His scraggly voice was becoming raised now and I began to feel uncomfortable.

"I don't think this is a good time to talk to him about this," Sidney said loudly, but in a shrill, quivering voice.

The old man gave her a look. She covered her mouth with her right hand and sat back down again. Morgan looked as though she were trying to pass herself by sheer will through the little hospital window. A rather strong, inappropriate urge to laugh surged through my body, but I somehow managed to stow it away.

"I was doing it for you," I got out.

"All yer bringin' me is trouble, me Son. Trouble's what comes when things better left alone are bothered." The old man's eyes were becoming tempestuous, the surfaces of planet-oceans yielding to mighty descending winds.

"I'm sorry. I meant no harm."

"What did ye see down there?" His voice and the thunder seemed to speak in unison. It was a mischievous thunder, and somehow, deep in my soul, I knew that the gravestones would never be visible again.

Rain began to scathe the hospital window. Morgan looked astonished.

"I don't know. I may have been hallucinating."

"What did ye see, Boy?" His voice was still rising, leading the thunder now, a sea captain taking his ship to war and bringing the storm into battle with him.

"Well, don't hold me to it, but—"

"Tell me, Boy!"

"He doesn't have to tell you anything!" Sidney screamed out, almost crying. She looked at me heatedly, shaking her head. "Nurse!" she yelled. "Nurse, this man is upsetting my grandson!"

Sidney began pressing the nurse call button incessantly.

"It's okay, Sidney. I'm all right," I said firmly yet tenderly. "Captain," I began, looking directly into his eyes, "I—"

Morgan screamed at the top of her lungs. Captain Shelby looked at her with a face of utter bafflement. Sidney had taken to a sort of dry sobbing now.

"I think yer all crazy, if you ask me!" the old man snarled. "Right contrary!"

"You're Nereus!" Morgan shrieked. "You're Nereus, the old man of the sea!"

Just then the doctor and the nurse came in. Captain Shelby turned, his face becoming flushed, like coral red rays of a sunset tickling a rippled, rusty sea.

"What is all the commotion here?" the doctor demanded.

"It's him!" Sidney shouted, pointing unabashedly at the old man, as if she were a broad-daylight witness to a recent mugging at a police station lineup. "That man is upsetting the patient!"

Just then Captain Shelby gave me a look that I will never forget. It was a perfect symphony of forlornness, indignation, and childlike betrayal. His expression seemed to sum up all the historical anguish and longing of Pelican Bay.

A tear found my eye.

"Is this true, Ethan? Is this man upsetting you?" the doctor asked, looking at me, then at the old man, then back at me again.

"No."

Both Sidney and Morgan gave me bulging looks. The doctor was bewildered. The nurse stood in the doorway, captivated, blank-faced.

"I must ask who you are," the doctor said officiously to the old man. "There are hospital rules to be followed, and if—"

"Go on boy! *Rules*, eh? Ha! Ye know nothin' bout rules! 'Twas not yer *rules* that mended this young scopie here. He be wastin' his time here with yer fancy white coats and these crazy duckies." The old fisherman cast a formidable eye at Sidney and Morgan and they both covered their faces. "Ye fools know nothin' of the sea. But she knows about ye."

More thunder now, Poseidon driving a lightning bolt down and splitting the heavens. There was flashing outside akin to night and day seeming unable to make up their minds.

"I don't know who you are," the doctor continued, "but you're disturbing the peace and—"

The old man turned abruptly and walked out with unsettling speed. Everyone watched the captain's feet, which seemed to barely move.

He stopped in the doorway. All eyes were on him. Time felt frozen.

"The sea will take revenge on ye for the trouble ye caused! She'll have no mercy!"

The old man left.

Seconds later there was a loud banging noise outside and the room went dark, save for the dismal flickering light of the storm creeping in through the hospital window like a fog of terror.

CHAPTER TWENTY-ONE

When you live on the bay, a storm can feel like a hurricane, especially a vengeful one perhaps summoned by a god of the sea himself.

The storm came on so suddenly that the townsfolk had a tremendously difficult time putting up their storm shutters. Courageous men and women weathered the fierce winds in their attempts to protect their cottages. In some cases the shutters flew away, like giant wooden butterflies returning to a black sky of doom. And for these poor souls severe damage was inevitable. Broken glass, like the shattered dreams of all those who longed to but never left Pelican Bay, would litter their living rooms.

As soon as I put up our storm shutters, with a neighbor's son's help, he and I rushed over to Morgan's cottage to see if she and her dad needed assistance, our young bodies arguing their cases against a baying, brutal wind that almost lifted us off of our feet.

I glanced toward the docks on my way and the old man's boat was gone. This was no surprise. He would go to the Secret Spot to survive the storm in the cove, or for all I knew, perhaps he simply disappeared, watching Pelican Bay from some ghostly realm as it suffered for its intrusive curiosity.

Morgan's dad had managed to secure his shutters with the help of a neighbor, and seeing this, my neighbor's son's worried gaze turned back toward home. "Be safe," he yelled against the ferocious wind. "You better get that little librarian inside. She's going to fly away!"

I laughed, but he could no longer hear me.

Morgan was on her knees. She was soaked to the bone, trying to move some heavy rocks onto a large piece of canvas that she was using to protect her beach roses. Her dad was yelling something from the front door, almost being crushed by it in the face of a mighty gust of ocean airstream.

"Morgan," I yelled. "What on earth are you doing?"

She turned to look at me quickly, going right back to futilely pushing the rocks. She was absolutely beautiful. Her ash-blonde hair was everywhere, wet and wild, her eyes almost a navy blue in the dark daylight of the vicious storm. She could have been a regal captain's daughter at sea, battling Cape Horn out on deck against her father's wishes.

I knew that her beach roses would be gone with the storm, but that she would not leave them unprotected, so I helped her secure the last rock and then pushed her inside. Gratitude illuminated her father's face. I yelled goodbye, the word instantly swept away like a whispered noble idea, and rushed back home.

The voice of the winds was epic during that storm. It moaned and howled, whipping through the cottages, as if the avenging spirits of the now-to-be-forever-sunken cemetery.

The sea surged savagely. Maybe Captain Shelby was right after all. She would punish us for disturbing that which was better left alone. And in that moment my most recent dream of the old man, holding me in his arms, peering out to sea, suddenly began to make more sense. He was not just trying to save me from a diving accident, but me and my town from the sea, the Hand of God, a hand far greater than even his.

How I wish now that I had never made that final dive before the sea cemetery had vanished for good. How I wish that I had not pillaged the secrets of a sacred old king.

I had been through hurricanes and tropical depressions before. When you are huddled up under a stairwell, the sound of the wind can be frightening, like passing trains coming too close and rubbing against the sides of your house.

The wind had a mournful sound, too. It carried the cry of centuries of Native Americans, The Trail of Tears such a painful memory that its furious melancholy leapt into the sky and wailed its low siren song across time, across the sacred land, all the way to Pelican Bay, South Carolina. It carried the anguish of the first settlers battling for survival against famine and disease, and the rueful howl of the last Vikings fleeing the pugnacious Skraelings, the natives of Aux Meadows, Newfoundland.

Sidney and I were in a little room under the stairwell. The room was built for just such occasions.

"Sure sounds like a hurricane, doesn't it?" I said.

"I think so, dear. I really do."

"At least a tropical depression."

"But the newscast said it's only a storm."

"Well, it's not like we have our own news channel in Pelican Bay. Gull Bay might be experiencing something totally different. Honestly, Sidney, it sounds like we're going to lose the town."

"Don't say that, dear."

"Sorry, but what if the old man's right? What if the sea's going to claim us, like it did my mom and dad?"

"Now you just stop that talk, dear. I'm afraid I'm to blame for a lot of it. I should've never told you those stories about Captain Shelby."

"That's okay. You can't be worse than Morgan!"

We both laughed heartily. The wind outside laughed its profound, whirling laugh.

"You know, Sidney, it's that wind that creeps me out the most."

"I know. How are Morgan and her dad holding up?"

"They'll be fine. Morgan was out there trying to cover up her beach rose garden. I had to drag her inside."

"That little fool! But you do love her, don't you, dear?"

I was silent. The wind seemed to moan my answer for me.

"So what did you actually see down there, Ethan?"

"Do we have to talk about it?"

"No, but I'd really like to know. I'm really worried about you."

Some moments passed of just the wind hollering outside.

"His gravestone's down there, Sidney—in that undersea cemetery."

"Come on, really?"

"I saw it with my own eyes."

"Ethan, you do have quite an imagination. And you were mostly breathing your own carbon dioxide, dear."

"Well, I guess it doesn't matter now. This storm will be the last of it, I think."

"How do you know that?"

"There were a few storms in a row that had easterly winds, but it was blind luck. The past few storms have been westerly storms. Most storms that hit Pelican Bay, the big ones, like the Great Hurricane, are westerly storms."

"Where did you learn all that?"

"Captain Shelby."

"Ethan, if you saw anything down there, it's just an ancient grandfather of his, dear—a very, very, ancient grandfather."

"But with the exact same name?"

"It's very possible. What's his first name?"

"Nereus."

"Hmm."

"'The old man of the sea.'"

"I know, dear. I've always been interested in Greek mythology. Nereus is also the god one prayed to for a bountiful harvest of fish."

"It's just all so weird. I really wanted to leave it all to rest, you know? I figured I'd find nothing and we could just conclude that he has no records, no marked grave. And then I saw his gravestone. At least I think I did. I don't know. He was so angry today, Sidney, as if he *already knew* what I'd found."

"I highly doubt that, dear."

"No, you could see it in his eyes. I feel like I've betrayed him in some way."

"I know that he was really upsetting you. And Morgan, acting just like a child! Now at least I understand why she yelled out, 'Nereus.' I wasn't sure what she was saying at first. What a kook!"

"Don't say that, Sidney."

"Why not? She doesn't love you. You said it yourself. Honestly, I wish you'd move to Gull Bay and settle down with a nice girl, one who could love you back. It would do you a lot of good to get out of this crazy little town."

"I love Pelican Bay. And I love you."

"That's sweet, dear. But that's your problem—you *love* too much. Your father was the same way. At least your mother loved him back. You deserve that much, Ethan."

"I guess you're right."

"You should just say it. Say it and be done with it. At least then you could move on with your life."

"What should I say?"

"You know what, dear. Don't be coy. It doesn't suit you."

"I've tried. She always seems to be able to stop me somehow."

"I just wonder."

"What?"

"Well, if she doesn't love you, why is it so hard for her to hear you say it?"

There was a sudden, odd silence outside. The eye of the storm.

"Sidney, tell me about my grandfather—how he died."

She would not look at me for a good while. Finally, a tear started its way down her right cheek. It was in moments like these that I knew that my love for my grandmother was greater than any storm, any ocean.

"I'm sorry, Sidney. I didn't mean to—"

"No, it's okay," she said softly, wiping away the fallen tear, and then another, with her care-wrinkled finger. "You deserve to know."

A looming rumble on the sea could be heard. The eye would pass quickly.

"The Great Hurricane," she began, "was far louder and scarier than any storm you've ever heard or felt before, including this one."

My eyes expanded like a child's. Sidney went on.

"The winds did more than howl, like now. They screamed like a banshee with the voice of a thousand wailing women. I can remember having to hold my hands over my ears. A few times I screamed, even cried. Yes, the winds made quite a fuss."

"Geez."

"I remember when the hurricane first started. Things just blew away. All the lighter things were just blown out to sea. Anything that wasn't nailed down, including smaller people, and children."

The tears were streaming more readily now down Sidney's fragile, drawn face.

"We didn't have all the fancy storm tracking that Gull Bay and Lighthouse Point have now. We had no warning at all."

"No, I guess you didn't."

"Those that could find adequate shelter did so. But there was so little time. So little time."

Sidney was trembling. I put my arm around her. "You don't have to go on if—"

"It's okay, dear," Sidney said, her voice gently quaking. She held her head up straight and looked right at me, gathering herself. "Your grandfather loved the beach so much, just like you. When he was a kid, sometimes it was just impossible to pull him away from it, and his mother would have to leave him there until he couldn't see to play anymore."

Sidney sort of laughed.

"I used to love to build sand castles when I was a kid."

"Yes, dear, now you know why." Sidney sniffled a bit. "Anyway, the morning of the Great Hurricane, your grandfather was on the beach, as usual. I was making bologna sandwiches for lunch to take out there to him, when the skies suddenly grew so dark and the winds whipped up into a frenzy. It was terrifying."

"I can only imagine."

"Yes, those horrible winds came up so suddenly, dear, and all those in town who survived the storm say the sea rose ten feet in a matter of minutes."

As if telling the story now along with my grandmother, the winds outside began to howl again.

"I was very scared, so I sent his brother out for him—and—neither of them ever came back. They just—blew away." Sidney lightly wept.

The storm was back in full force, its second half winds deeply whining outside like a mountain-sized child abandoned out on the lonely sea. And the mighty thundering returned, almost the roars of surfacing lions amplified by God.

"What happened to Captain Shelby?"

"No one knows, dear. Some said his boat was carried away and he died. That's what I thought. But then I saw him a few weeks later, that rackety boat of his in the same old spot."

"I think I know where he went, where he is right now."

"Where, dear?"

"At his secret fishing spot, which seems to make its own weather."

We were both silent for a moment or so, the storm outside still whirling and hollering like an out-of-tune blues band playing on a beach pier only feet away.

"What about the rest of our town?" I said. "What happened to them?"

"We lost more than half of them, dear. Most of their bodies were never found. They turned up on the sand miles down the beach after the hurricane, some with their heads buried in the dunes, some still hanging onto things, their fingers still clutched so tightly, their knuckles as white as ghosts. Oh, Ethan! It was so awful!"

"I'm sure it was."

"The only buildings that God spared were the old courthouse and the church. I lost a lot of my friends, except those who were able to get inside the Pelican Bay Church. Minister Billingsley was quite the hero, that dear, dear man. He almost flew away himself trying to get some of his congregation inside. Eventually the winds became just too strong. He did save a lot of townspeople though, except the one that mattered the most to him. Honestly, I don't know he kept his faith after that."

"He lost his wife in the Great Hurricane?"

"Yes, dear. He doesn't like to talk about it at all. I asked him about it once and he said that God was delivering a blessing that he could not understand at the time."

"He never married again?"

"No, dear."

"He's always wanted to marry you, I think."

Sidney looked at me oddly. "I think he believes God called him to marry the church after that."

"Oh."

We were silent again as the winds spoke for us.

"How did you survive?" I asked.

It took Sidney a while, and then she said, "I don't know, dear. I really don't know. I've prayed over it many times. Many times. I believe in my heart that God spared me to raise you." Sidney was crying more fully again.

"I love you so much," I said against the winds still baying recalcitrantly outside.

"I know," Sidney said, managing to gather herself again. "It's a miracle Ethan—that I'm here. They found me in that old bathtub I still have." Sidney surrendered a half-giggle, half-cry. Then we both started laughing gently. It felt good. We really needed it.

"What about your parents and my grandfather's parents?"

And as soon as the question left my lips, I wanted with every breath that I possessed to retrieve it. Our laughing came to a halt, along with the rumbaing moan of the winds, finally.

Sidney kept herself, or perhaps her tears had run out right along with the vanishing raindrops.

"Your dear-departed grandfather's parents were among the first to fly away out to sea. God saw fit to spare them early. My mother was found miles up the coast with an old King James Bible clutched in her hands so fiercely that they had to bury her with it. God rest her beautiful soul. Oh dear, dear. Ethan, do you know she knew every verse of the Bible by heart?"

"Wow."

"I've always believed that my manners of faith and strength came directly from that dear woman. She was soft as moss but her constitution was as set as an oak. An English Oak of the Sherwood Forest. Beautiful but mighty. The stories she told my brother and me when we were kids about the hard times of our early township, the awful diseases that plagued them constantly and the Native Americans that would snatch people at night and just take them away, never to return or to be seen again. Oh, my dear Ethan, I could have written novels."

"What about your father?"

"I never knew him. He was a great fisherman who died at sea very young, dear. Very young."

CHAPTER TWENTY-TWO

Pelican Bay survived the storm. The sea did not claim anyone, only corners of roofs, windows, tree branches that downed power lines during their paranormal flights, Morgan's beach roses, and the sunken cemetery.

I ventured out toward town the next morning, to Morgan's house. It was Friday, but all the businesses were closed in order to recover from the storm. It would be a few days before power would be fully restored.

Captain Shelby's boat was not in its usual resting place, moored at the old docks. I wondered if he had vanished for good, or if he was still at the Secret Spot, waiting there for unfathomable reasons.

Storm debris littered the streets of Pelican Bay. Most of the power lines, which had not been updated since they were first installed so many decades ago, drooped lugubriously or were snapped and lay like dark, undernourished sea serpents swimming through puddles that reflected the morning sun like miniature black oceans. Pieces of wood and steel were strewn about the town as well, the storm having tasted these bites of Pelican Bay, not found them to its fancy, and spit them back out again.

Morgan and her dad were outside when I came upon their cottage. Her dad walked about their lawn, looking up and down, raising and lowering his arms, as if cursing the sea gods for their ill deeds.

"Why hello there, Ethan. As you can see, things are quite a mess," he said.

"Yes, sir. I'm sorry to see that."

Morgan was sitting on the front steps looking despondently at her beach rose garden, which was now a small lot of hapless dirt in front of their cottage, a keepsake left by the storm to remind us of the bleakness of its soul.

"Did you lose some of your roof, sir?" I asked.

He looked up and around, raising his arms again. He seemed to be murmuring something distasteful under his breath and he did not answer me right away.

"I think so, Ethan. It's a nasty business, a nasty business indeed."

"Didn't you have gutters before?"

Charles looked at me with a burning face.

"Yes, Ethan. I just installed new gutters early this summer, if you must know."

"Sorry to hear that, sir."

"The insurance company still owes me for a previous claim. I suppose they think that us small-bay townspeople won't go to Gull Bay to collect. Well, they'll have a word from me, Ethan. Oh, they'll have a word from me!"

"Is there anything I can do to help, sir?"

"I don't think so, Ethan."

"Sir?"

Charles said nothing, just kept staring up at his roof.

"Do you know anything about Captain Shelby?" I asked.

Morgan had walked around the house now and was standing right next to us. She half-smiled at me. Her unattended hair was hurriedly pulled back, which always elongated her neck and exaggerated her shoulders.

"I'm sorry, Ethan, who now?" Charles asked.

"Captain Shelby."

A vague panic seized Morgan's expression.

"You mean that old fisherman?"

"Yes, sir."

"Why are you asking about him?"

"Well, you see, uh—"

Morgan's eyes were huge and ignited now. Obviously she had said nothing to her dad about all our recent investigating. Charles was looking directly at me, his doctor eyes narrowed in an unsettling beam of skepticism.

"I treated him once."

"I'm sorry, sir?"

"He came in—let's see—it was 1953, I think. Yes, that's right. It was the spring of 1953."

"May I—"

"He had a big hook right through his hand. The biggest hook I've ever seen. I honestly can't think of what you would fish for with a hook like that."

"Well, it's probably a—"

"And the hook was old and rusted. Old and rusted indeed."

"Do you remember anything strange about him, sir?"

Charles looked at me so oddly in that moment, his face fixed almost with the look of a mad scientist.

"Well, there was no blood, that I can remember. Not impossible, mind you, but uncommon. Quite uncommon, indeed."

"Anything else?"

"Hmm, well, that was a long time ago, Ethan—a long time ago."

"I understand if—"

"Wait. Yes, I remember now."

"What?" Morgan asked.

"After I removed the hook, he would not accept a tetanus shot."

"That is strange, sir."

"Yes, indeed. We have no charts on him, either."

"Weird, sir."

"And not long after the incident the file my nurse opened for him mysteriously disappeared."

"Hmm. What else do—?"

"He refused any anesthetic, too. And he never made an ounce of noise when I pulled the hook out."

"Have you ever seen him since?"

"No, not that I recall, Ethan."

We all became silent, staring at the storm debris scattered all about. I imagined terrified-white knuckles and clasped fingers grasping their last grasps upon them and I cringed inside.

"Sure felt like at least a tropical storm, didn't it?" Morgan finally said.

"Yes," I said. "I was telling Sidney just the same thing."

"How is Sidney?" Charles asked. "Does she need anything? Anything at all?"

"She's fine, sir. Thank you for asking. Sir?"

"Yes, Ethan."

"How old do you think Captain Shelby is?"

Morgan looked at me with closed, curled lips and intense eyes.

"Why all these questions suddenly about that old fisherman?"

"Well, I—"

"Too hard to tell, Ethan. Too hard to tell. He's old all right. He appeared to be quite old when he came to my office back then. But don't go believing all those tall tales around Pelican Bay. We all die, Ethan. Now, I'll grant you that even modern science still fails to understand the full effects of the sea, especially on a man who's spent his whole life on and in the ocean, but he'll die soon, I suspect. In fact, I'd be surprised if this last storm hasn't sunk that decrepit boat of his and drowned him along with it."

An obviously sad expression captured my face. Morgan noticed. I was staring out to sea now, over toward the old docks.

Suddenly, a limousine pulled up in the driveway. The worst aftermath of any storm had just befallen my heart, worse than the property damage or the old man's missing boat or even the lost undersea cemetery.

Henry had come to Pelican Bay.

Charles's face lit up immediately. I wanted to puke.

"Why I think it's Henry, Morgan. Henry's come to visit!" her dad almost shouted.

Morgan's face became utterly blank.

The limousine was black and as long as Henry's reach all the way from New York to Morgan's timorous heart.

The driver parked and walked around to the rear passenger door, opening it quite cordially. Out sprang a dashing, dark-haired, dark-eyed, fastidious young man of medium height in his late twenties, dressed in a navy blue three-piece pin-striped suit.

Charles practically ran his way. Morgan stayed where she was, but she would not look at me.

"Henry!" Charles yelled.

"Well hello there, Charles! How's the old Pelican Bay doctor doing these days?" Henry asked, with a robust, haughty cheerfulness.

They both walked up to join us on the storm debris-riddled front lawn.

Suddenly, my heart felt as though it were among that storm debris.

"Hello, Morgan!" Henry said. Morgan just stared at her feet. She was wearing faded white beach sandals. "I was so worried about you. The news reports said that this area bore the greatest brunt of the storm, almost hurricane-force winds."

I hated how articulate and well-educated Henry was. I knew that these qualities were like tractor beams on a librarian. I cringed almost outwardly this time.

"Well, you certainly didn't have to worry on my account. I've been through worse storms," Morgan said perfunctorily, now looking toward Henry, but not at him. Her usual shyness seemed amplified.

"But you haven't answered my letters. I thought that something might have transpired that—"

"Again, there's really no need to make any fuss. I'm okay." Morgan was blushing now.

My innards felt like they were cooking.

"So how are you, Ethan? Still grinding away for the old Gull Bay Post?"

"I guess you could say that. Have you perfected the artificial heart yet?"

Henry looked at me strangely.

"Well, why don't you come in?" Charles offered.

"Don't mind if I do, Old Doctor!" Henry said, his teeth grinning whiter than the sand just beyond the flattened wild grass and slain beach roses.

Oh, brother.

"Sure beats staring at the wreckage out here!" Charles gassed.

They laughed together.

"Yes, I see my hometown is in shreds. Poor old dear," Henry said.

We all sat in the living room, except for Morgan, who chose to stand, despite Henry's many verbal and non-verbal attempts to get her to sit next to him on the couch. I grinned silently to myself.

The windows were all open and the fresh, hopeful morning breeze felt good. Morgan went to the kitchen to make some lemonade.

"So how long will you stay, Henry?" Charles asked.

"Just a few days. I have a big surgery that I have to fly back for. Can't trust the residents on this one, Old Doctor. You understand, of course."

"Oh, yes, yes. Of course."

And I would be lying here if I claimed that a morning tidal wave of jealousy was not rising in my blood. I hated Henry. Growing up, Henry took advantage of being five years older than me and Morgan, and teased and picked on me relentlessly. He was always too big back then for me to do anything about it, and he knew it. He outran me, out swam me, outsmarted me in school, etc, etc. It was back then that my natural animosity toward him took root, like a recalcitrant, blooming weed all alone in a field of sun-loved, wind-swept Kentucky Blue. When he came back home from college to visit, before heading off to medical school, my detestation reached its zenith.

Morgan had just become a senior in high school and Henry began to really take notice of her. When Morgan cared to look up from her books, all the high school boys noticed her, too. She had the best bosom the likes of which Pelican Bay had never known. But, like me, Henry liked Morgan for her intellect as well. For every ounce of bosom, came twice that in mental prowess. So Henry started courting Morgan mercilessly, asking her out on holiday visits, writing her poetry (which I caught a glimpse of once, and, thank God, he was a medical genius, but *no* poet, his prose laughable), ceaseless, voluminous letters, and phone messages left with Charles, too numerous to count.

It was all perfectly nauseating.

"So how is your surgical practice coming along?" Charles asked.

"Thanks for asking. Quite well, quite well! I've already performed my fair share of heart transplants, and now I'm conducting some unique research that will hopefully shorten surgery time, reduce the size of thoracic incisions, and significantly reduce heart transplant rejection in surgical recipients."

"Yes, yes, I heard that you just published a new article. I've wanted to read it."

I think I'm going to need a throw up bucket, please.

"Well, it took me longer than expected. I have a few new surgical residents that are keeping me on my toes."

Charles and Henry both laughed ostentatiously together. It was as if I did not exist.

Morgan came back with the lemonade and served it, staring at the glasses of lemonade and not at Henry or me.

"Great job on the lemonade, Morgan," her dad said enthusiastically. He seemed to have lost all the irritation that he had had a short while ago while talking to me on his front lawn.

Perhaps it was more my company than the wind-stolen gutters.

"Yes, Morgan, it really hits the spot," Henry added.

"Thanks," Morgan said, staring at the pitcher of lemonade on the table. She was standing, arms folded now, behind Charles's recliner chair in front of the fireplace.

Henry gave me an unmistakably competitive glance, which quickened my pulse a bit. We could have been two long-distance swimmers preparing to race each other across the Atlantic.

"Has anyone come from Gull Bay to help out?" Henry asked.

"Not yet," I butted in, piercing Henry with defiant eyes. He looked away over toward Morgan, who was still staring at the pitcher of lemonade, as if keeping it cold with her detached stare.

"I'm sure they'll be along," Charles said. "Gull Bay usually sends a deputy, at least, to investigate everything here. Will you be staying with us, Henry? I'll have it no other way!"

Henry was practically staring a hole through Morgan now. She obstinately refused to look at him. I wanted to laugh out loud, and I almost did, becoming nearly flushed in my face.

"Well, I—" Henry hesitated perfunctorily and platitudinously.

"I insist! It's done then!"

Morgan finally looked at me, though briefly. There was a flash of concern in her eyes, a small birth of rare empathy, and I relished it. However, as I sat there, the reality that Henry would be spending a night in Morgan's house suddenly washed over me like the inescapablility of a car wreck. My blood seemed to slow down. My face became the color of an early tomato and I began to fidget furiously, conspicuously. Morgan noticed immediately. Were we in another era, I would have challenged Henry immediately to a duel, right on Pelican Bay Beach, the loser's blood staining the dunes forever. I looked at him fiercely. He must have known.

"Well," I said, a bit too loudly, standing up suddenly, my voice imperceptibly quivering. "I'm going to go take a look at the rest of the town now. Morgan, would you like to come along? We could check and see if there's any damage to the library while Charles and Henry get caught up."

"Okay," Morgan said quietly, beginning to slowly walk my way.

Henry stood up phlegmatically, shock stiffening his aura, rapidly turning to a childlike disappointment.

Brilliant.
I have won.
At least for now.

CHAPTER TWENTY-THREE

Excitement did my walking for me.

Morgan and I had left her house, already on Pelican Bay Street, heading for the library. She did not look at me, but seemed to walk more closely next to me than usual. I prayed a little prayer with every step that we took that this was not purely wishful thinking on my part.

The main street was just as cluttered with storm debris as the other smaller streets, the storm having showed no bias toward one side of the town over another, just as it had never showed any prejudice against plaguing and slashing Pelican Bay at her whimsy. I had to move some tree branches out of the way a few times so that Morgan and I could pass. She stood quietly, smiling meekly at me as I moved them. I adored the task consummately. I could have been gently taking her hand aside to lavish it with a forbidden kiss. Her hair was still in a ponytail and her beautifully plain eyes were magnified behind her glasses like teal scientific discoveries.

"I know what you want to ask and I hope you won't say it," she said.
"What? About Henry?"
"Yes."
"You know, Morgan, I'm tired of asking the same question over and over again. I don't think you've ever given me a straight answer, anyway."

Morgan looked at me sullenly. We were already nearing the library.
"I have. You just refuse to believe me."
"If you've given me a straight answer, why does he act that way?"

"He just doesn't get it. He won't take a hint. That's not my fault."

"You could try a little harder to get the message across."

Morgan's face became slightly flushed.

"I don't see how it's your concern, anyway. After all, he and I are only friends, just like us."

A sharp arrow to my heart. Quick. The damage caused before I could even feel the entry.

Morgan stopped on the corner right before the library, surveying the building and roof for obvious storm damage. There was none. She turned back toward me, arms folded, staring at the ground now. Her cheeks were reddened and her eyes sported incipient defiance.

"No, you and Henry are not *just like us*. We spend much more time together, in case you haven't noticed. We're closer friends, aren't we? Plus, he has a big ego, but not when it comes to you."

"What's that supposed to mean?"

"Well, you have to admit, he's not very subtle. It's as if he's the Titanic and you're the iceberg."

"That's not funny at all, Ethan."

"I think a part of you likes the attention."

"That's mean."

"Isn't it true?"

Morgan's face took to a light crimson now, her lips curling the way that they always did when she was mad. Her eyes looked beady behind her skinny little librarian glasses. Beady and nearly diabolical.

"I refuse to discuss this any further."

We crossed the street and Morgan unlocked the thick oak library door, which was laden with seawater at least a half-inch through on the front, perhaps a barometer for the level of damage absorbed by our minute beach town.

It was dark and dank and musty inside. As soon as the door closed, I grabbed Morgan by her shoulders, pulled her toward me, and kissed her. Her lips remained hard, still curled. She was furious. I kept my lips on hers. They felt so good, even uncooperative. She did not try to pull away from me though, and after a few seconds, ever so gradually, like the mouth of a new leather baseball glove surrendering to the love of the game, her lips softened and began to give way. The kiss must have lasted for ten seconds or so before she broke loose.

"What are you doing? What's wrong with you?"

I kissed her again and she let me again. This time the kiss lasted for almost half a minute.

"Ethan, please!"

"I love you."

"No! I'm not listening to this! Stop it!"

"I love you, Morgan." I said it louder this time. "I'm so tired of all this nonsense. We spend almost all of our time together. If we're just friends, why is it so hard for you to hear me say those words? Why did you come with me just now and not stay there with Henry? Why did you let me kiss you?"

Morgan said nothing.

I could barely see her in the dim light, splashes of late morning entering from the few windows in the library. The rising sun could have been applauding my previous fit of stoic romanticism. My librarian just stared at me through her glasses, open-faced. Somehow I felt that I could have kissed her again, even more deeply, and that she would have let me.

"Do you smell that, Ethan? Oh my God! What is that?"

"I'm not sure."

Morgan found a flashlight behind the checkout counter. We walked toward the unique scent, which grew more and more pungent with every step that we took. The flashlight beamed in front of us, illuminating objects in the old library, as if we were scuba divers exploring the large quarters of an erudite captain's sunken ship.

We had approached the back of the library now, which was filled with row after row of dense mahogany shelves that appeared as old as time. We turned right, continuing to follow the odd scent.

"Ethan—it smells like—it can't be."

"The sea?"

"Yes! It's so strong. You don't think—?"

We both looked at each other, our faces tensing, our eyes growing.

"No, Morgan. Don't start all that. He's gone. His boat's not even at the docks. I think you just have a leak in the roof, that's all."

"But it smells just like we're swimming out in the bay."

"Don't start your ghost stories all over again. I think you've gone too far already. I still can't believe you yelled out *Nereus* at the hospital."

"But don't you smell it? That's so weird."

Morgan walked to the last row of the bookshelves, with exaggerated slowness, as though she expected to find Nereus there. Her little feet seemed to step rather forlornly, and her body was stiff and awkward with fright. Finally, she stopped and peered to her left.

"Ethan! Come here!"

I ran up to find Morgan pointing dramatically with her finger toward the ground at the back of the book aisle. The greenish, dingy carpet was inundated with at least an inch of what smelled like seawater.

"He was here!"

"Morgan, please," I said, dipping my finger in the puddle and tasting it. "I'm sure the storm gusts must have blown this ocean water onto the roof and it came down through a leak. This place is so old."

I took the flashlight from Morgan and shone it up at the ceiling directly over the puddle, but there was no damage or any sign of a leak.

"I told you!" Morgan yelled.

"I'm sure there's a perfectly good explanation. Isn't that what you would say? Perhaps the seawater has come in from somewhere else."

I pointed the flashlight on the rest of the ceiling over the bookshelves, but nothing.

"Maybe it came in from outside somehow," I suggested.

"I'm telling you, Ethan, he was here. Maybe he was seeking shelter from the storm."

I laughed. "If he's really Nereus, why would he need shelter from a storm?"

Morgan was silent.

"Besides," I continued, "his boat's been gone since yesterday. I'm going to go outside and look around. I bet there's a leak outside along the base of the wall somewhere."

"I'm coming with you!"

Down Pelican Bay Street you could see a few townspeople picking up debris and checking their properties. The awning of Pelican Bay Bank had completely blown away, only scrawny, protruding vestiges remained, crooked survivors of the storm yearning to regale Pelican Bay with their bleak tales. The Pelican Bay Post Office flag, as well as its pole, had gone for a swim in the Atlantic. Almost all of the town windows, denuded of their screens, were frantic with holes from crashing objects, lending the town a post-apocalyptic air.

Morgan and I carefully examined the base of the wall outside of the library near where the sea puddle was on the inside.

"See, Ethan? No leak."

"There has to be some explanation. Look, Morgan, even if Captain Shelby was in the library, what would he want there?"

"Me," Morgan said solemnly, her face turning over to resignation.

"What?"

"He knows that I know who he is."

CHAPTER TWENTY-FOUR

Morgan and her dad asked me to stay for lunch, but I refused, telling them that I needed to help Sidney out at home. Charles insisted that I ask Sidney if he could do anything for her at all.

Charles had a colossal crush on Sidney. How could he not? But there were several reasons why she was never too interested. For one, Charles was still grieving over his departed wife, and Sidney knew this. Secondly, I am not sure that Sidney liked Charles, not wholeheartedly. Part of this may have owed to Sidney knowing, deep down, that Charles did not approve of me for Morgan.

On the way back home, I passed by the docks, and as they sneaked up into view, my heart shuddered and shivered.

But the old man's boat was not there.

It's completely ridiculous. Even if he's who Morgan thinks he is, which is crazy, he wouldn't harm anyone. I just know he wouldn't harm anyone.

Sidney was trying to heat up an old furnace that had not been used in years. She had opened up all the windows in the house, and the late summer ocean breeze, placid, cool air conditioning offered with the hint of fall in Pelican Bay, the closest thing that our town knew to hope that day, pleasantly invaded our cottage.

"Sure is difficult without power, eh?"

"Yes," Sidney said, half-smiling, "and I'm willing to bet the Gull Bay deputy hasn't shown up, either."

"I didn't see anyone, and I just came from Pelican Bay Street."

"How are the Olinsworths getting along?"

"Henry's visiting."

"What? What's *he* doing here?"

"My sentiments exactly," I jabbed. "He says he's worried about Pelican Bay. But we both know why he's here."

"Ethan, dear, is that a hint of jealousy I hear in your voice?"

I said nothing, walking over to the window and peering out at the bay. I watched the few boats jostling about, loosely moored, vague in the distance, as if seen through the eyes of a landscape painter.

"There's nothing you can do about it, dear. It's up to her."

"She's so unresolved, so ambiguous about everything. A typical librarian. She drives me crazy sometimes."

Sidney was quiet for a moment. She turned her head halfway, endearment discreetly coloring her cheeks.

"Why doesn't she just tell him plainly and finally that she doesn't love him?" I went on, my frustration now blazing like the sun well past the noon point in the sky.

"It may not matter, dear. For some, rejection is like fuel to the flames."

"He's so damned obnoxious. And they're putting him up for the night."

Sidney looked at me fully this time. Her eyes revealed concern orbited by tender wrinkles.

"Did you tell her, Ethan?"

"Yes."

"What did she say?"

"Nothing. I told you. I tried to get her to confront it, but then there was a distraction. There's always a distraction."

"What distraction?"

"There's some seawater damage in the back of the library. Morgan thinks the old man was in there. My God, she's almost certifiable now. The weird thing though is I couldn't find a sign of a leak anywhere, inside or outside."

Sidney's eyes swelled.

"Also," I continued, "there's a sort of putrid sea smell in there. Morgan thinks Captain Shelby's after her because she can identify him now."

"Identify him? That's silly! What do you mean, *identify* him?"

"As Nereus."

"I'm afraid I'm partly responsible for all this nonsense. Oh, dear. Oh dear, dear!"

"Stop it, Sidney. It's not your fault."

"I'm the one that put those old stories in your head."

"It's not you. Really. Morgan found this old journal and she's done a lot of research. I must admit," I said, kind of chuckling, "her argument's pretty convincing. She even found the name Laura Hodges on this old passenger manifest."

"What, dear?" Sidney's eyes changed suddenly.

"Yeah, maybe one of our old relatives came over from England to Newfoundland back then. It could be just a coincidence, too. A common name. I must admit though, after that dream I had with Captain Shelby showing me the gravestone, Morgan's discovery kind of creeped me out a bit."

"Oh, dear. The two of you together. A kooky librarian and a writer," Sidney murmured oddly, going over to the furnace again, her body moving lethargically, one of her careworn hands held to her chin.

The day seemed to be moving quickly. We drank tea in the afternoon light, which departed quickly, maybe creeped out, too.

I did not say much. All that kept running through my mind was Henry at Morgan's house. My heart felt as though it were missing a beat here and there. Images of him fawning over her incessantly, trying to get her alone, even sneaking into her bed when the black Pelican Bay night, the shadow of our past engaged in its nocturnal hunt, fell upon us.

I could not take it anymore.

"Where are you going, dear? It's getting late."

"I just need to get out for a while."

"I was going to make dinner," Sidney said, worry weighing down her voice like ancient iron.

"There's just something I have to do. I won't be long."

"Ethan, don't do it. It's out of your control. Don't do something you'll regret!"

"You worry too much. I'll be all right."

Sidney rose slowly, disquiet now permeating her entire body and shooting out of her sagacious eyes, as if an invisible firework infused in her by circumstance.

I left abruptly, the ocean breeze stealing its way inside like a strange visitor as I opened the front door, perhaps waiting for permission to keep Sidney company, who now slid her chair closer to the furnace, feeling the stranger's nipping breath.

Of course, I took the long route to Morgan's house, the path that took me by the docks.

The wild grass was flattened everywhere, even uprooted in some spots, and the beach roses, the few that subsisted in small ditches, robbed of their radiant petals by the recent storm winds like freshly-groomed fine poodle heads, lay lugubrious in the dune sand.

The docks suddenly came into view beyond the dunes.

The old man's boat was back.

I froze, ducking down behind a nearby dune whose skin shimmered in the late afternoon sun. The creaking of his boat's ancient wood could be heard onward up the coast, it seemed, as if whispering to the great fishermen of Newfoundland.

I peered around the dune. I could barely see him, moving busily about the main deck of his boat, like a ragged pirate coming to life in a painting of a distant ship in a frowning harbor.

And then I heard something, something now ever fixed upon my memory. The light, happy wind carried a song across the dunes.

At first I could not believe it. I thought that it existed only in my childhood memory.

> *Laura lie, Laura lie, in the sea barley,*
> *in the sea barley.*
> *Hold me close, hold me close, in the*
> *sea barley, in the sea barley.*
> *Love me thorns, and this wild rose be*
> *yers—in the sea barley, in the sea*
> *barley.*

The melody seemed to dive into my bones, rearranging their marrow, composing me anew with its notes. Its beauty was deeply haunting. I found it incomprehensible that the old man could sing such a melody. His voice was so much less hoarse when he sang, as if Apollo himself temporarily lent him his Olympian vocal chords, allowing him to convey stunning tunes across the ocean wind for countless miles.

And it was then that the idea occurred to me, a sinister one, one that shall always remind me that behind the most beautiful things often lurk the most baneful.

I ripped myself away from the old man's poignant, ceaseless song, and headed straight for Morgan's cottage.

I arrived quickly and knocked on the door. After a moment, Charles answered, which was infinitely upsetting.

"Is everything all right, Ethan?"

"Yes, sir. There's something I wanted to talk to Henry about, something I forgot to ask him before."

"Oh, I see," Charles said, studying my posture. "Well, they've gone for a walk on the beach."

I must have looked quite stunned.

"Are you sure you're all right, Ethan?"

"Uh, yeah, yeah. No big deal. I'll just come back later."

"I'd ask you to wait inside, but—"

"No, no. That's all right. I have a lot to do, anyway."

I walked ploddingly back toward the dunes. I could not believe that Morgan had gone for a walk with Henry. On the beach, of all places. My blood might have been boiling.

I reached the beach and stopped about thirty feet from the shore, looking almost frantically in both directions. I spotted two figures a few hundred yards or so to the north. Thank God, they were walking separately from one another.

I hurried to catch up with them, somehow at once knowing what I was going to say and not knowing.

My heart still felt as though it were skipping beats, and it was clear to me now that I could no longer be just friends with Morgan.

They had stopped now and were both looking out to sea. As I caught up with them, Henry looked to his left and spotted me first. His face fell, and he became bent on trying to hide this fact. Morgan had not seen me yet. They appeared to be engaged in intense conversation, and this further hastened my steps.

"Why Ethan, good fellow, we were just talking about you."

"Shut up, you feigning, self-righteous son of a bitch!"

"Ethan, what on earth is wrong with you?" Morgan shouted, her face tightened by incredulity.

"Don't you think I know what you're doing out here?"

"Walking," Henry said condescendingly. "We're walking."

"That's right, Ethan, we're just walking," Morgan said, in a tone that I immediately did not care for.

"Has he kissed you, too?"

Henry instantly shot Morgan a vulnerable, clamant look.

Morgan just stared at the sand, wanting to disappear under it.

"Morgan, what's he talking about?" Henry asked.

Morgan said nothing.

"So what of it?" he said pedantically. "I'm sure she resisted you, anyway. She says you're just friends, after all."

"Is that what you said, Morgan? That we're 'just friends?' Is that what you told him? Did you tell him we kissed? Did you tell him for how long?" I asked loudly, nearly bullishly.

Henry was now looking indignantly at Morgan, and although her eyes still did not leave the sand, her reddened face looked as if it were pouting. She much resembled a hurt little girl whose sand castle had just been kicked over.

"You are probably lying. You writers are all the same—a hopeless lot." Henry chuckled pretentiously. "Besides, she's with me now, and we're spending the night together."

"What do you mean you're *spending the night together*?"

"You know precisely what I mean, Ethan. I'm staying with her, and I have her father's blessing."

"Morgan," I shouted, "are you going to let this go on?"

Morgan finally looked up at me.

"I don't love you, Ethan. I've told you that."

"That's a lie! You're just scared, and Henry and your dad are putting pressure on you."

"I'm not putting any pressure on you, am I?" Henry asked Morgan. "If you love him, go with him now."

Morgan did not move.

"See?" Henry said.

"That doesn't prove anything, you shithead!"

"Oh, that's just so original. So predictable. Ha!" Henry spouted with cheerful condescension.

"You don't think she loves you, do you, you moron? The only reason she's standing there is because her father's been pushing you on her since birth!"

"How brilliant!" Henry tossed out. "So am I to understand that Morgan's just *in peer pressure* with me?"

"She's not in love with you! Tell him, Morgan."

"You're both acting like ridiculous school children, and you've utterly ruined my walk."

"No," Henry said. "Ethan's going home. This is *our* walk."

"That's ridiculous, you bastard! You don't own Morgan. And you don't own the beach."

"And I suppose you do? Oh, let me guess, you're going to buy the beach for Morgan on your freelance writing salary?"

This hurt a bit. I have to admit.

A long, awkward silence.

"Why don't we let Morgan decide. After all, even your fancy heart surgeon's salary can't buy her free will."

This silenced Henry.

Morgan looked at both of us, and then out to sea again. Her silence was absolutely excruciating.

"My free will has decided," Morgan said, almost too quietly to hear.

Henry and I locked eyes. We could have heated each other's innards.

"I'm going home," she said.

Morgan left both Henry and me on the shore, tongue-tied, our faces both smoldering like the afternoon sun.

I watched her walk away and it felt like my heart had been sliced in two and glued to the bottom of each of her worn white beach sandals. And it was in those moments that I loved her the most—in those moments that I had to have her no matter what the cost.

I finally turned back to Henry, who had taken to covering his face with his hands now, squeezing it tightly with his fingers.

A few good moments passed, and the sun, as if out of

embarrassment, seemed to hurry for China.

"I suppose you want to fight me for her now. Is that right, Ethan?"

"She doesn't love you. She just doesn't know how to tell you."

"And you're the town shrink now, I suppose?"

Another moment passed. I thought that Henry might walk away.

"I think we're a bit old for fighting, don't you?" I asked. "And I doubt you have the balls for it, anyway. You seem to forget we're not kids anymore. I outweigh you now—in many ways."

Henry looked away, an indescribable expression conquering his face.

"Besides," I said, "I have a better idea."

"Oh, I'm all ears," Henry let out with consummate sardonicism.

"Captain Shelby's back now. I just saw his boat."

"That crazy old geezer? What does he have to do with this?"

"Just listen. Morgan thinks he's something he's not."

"What are you ranting on about?"

"You heard me. She hasn't mentioned it?"

"No. She hasn't mentioned it."

"I want you to go talk to him."

"The old man?"

"Yes, you dim-witted piece of shit."

"Is that language really necessary?"

"What, are you going to go and cry to Charles now? Boo, hoo, hoo." Henry huffed.

"I want you to go talk to him," I continued, "and find out how old he is. If you can do this, find out his real age, I won't stand in the way anymore. Morgan's yours."

"That's perfectly preposterous. And why should I believe you?"

"I swear on my parent's gravestones, over there in the Pelican Bay Church Cemetery."

"Why is this so important? I don't get it. What's your angle here?"

"It's for Morgan. She thinks he wants to kill her because she can identify him."

"What?"

"It's a long story. She thinks he's dangerous because of all our town rumors and this creative research she's done. Anyway, she'll believe you if you find out, because you're not close to the old man like I am. She'd never believe me, even if I did find out his age. This is about Morgan, not us. She may be in danger. I don't think the old man's who she believes him to be, but what if he is? We shouldn't take any chances. You finding out his real age and then telling Morgan will put an end to all of it."

Henry appeared to be ruminating soberly. The sun was just starting to dip into the sea for her evening bath. Morgan had vanished from view, had a long time ago, like a young female pelican trotting off into infinity.

"Okay," Henry said carefully. "I'll do it."

"You know what?"

"What?" Henry asked, almost softly.

"I still think you're a perfect bastard."

Later that night, with the help of a flashlight, hopelessly feeble against the merciless darkness of Pelican Bay, Henry found his way out to the docks.

Soon, he saw a lantern, almost as if suspended, tangoing on an invisible string with the night, in the dark distance.

He started walking down the dock that leashed *The Grate Hurican*.

Henry shone the flashlight in the direction of the old man's boat making dull, fake moonlight beams that could have been augmentations of his counterfeit courage.

Before long, a short figure, haloed by the black fringe of abysmal night, approached him rather quickly. It seemed to fly at him.

Henry stopped, squinting his eyes, trying to focus on the form. As it moved toward him, it personified the boundless history of the sea. It might have been a large barnacle dressed in ancient fishermen's clothes. Henry quickly realized that it was Captain Shelby.

"Hello?" he said tentatively.

The old man suddenly came within a few inches of him.

Henry winced at the insulting stink of sea before him, as if the ocean were cloaking him with itself. He instantly jerked back and his expensive New York City shoes gave way on the slick dock, the few bright stars now above the bay winking at him as he fell backward, his noble head hitting a pylon that felt like steel. The blackness of the night seemed to seize his thoughts, and he slid gently into the bay to dream with the pelicans.

CHAPTER TWENTY-FIVE

Early the next morning, there was a loud knock on our cottage door that woke Sidney and me out of a sound sleep. I peered sleepily through the peep hole and saw Charles standing there, fidgeting with his whole body. Morgan was right behind him, her eyes two slits ablaze with scientific scowl.

Standing stoically to Charles's right was Sheriff Mortimers from Gull Bay, a short, beefy fellow with eyes too small for his face and a head too small for his body. He looked much like a fat pelican without its long beak.

I opened the door slowly, avoiding Charles and Morgan's looks.

"Good morning. What's going on?" I said.

"We may have a missing person. May we come in?" Sheriff Mortimers asked.

Morgan's eyes became more open and candescent as she passed, suddenly assuming a certain defiance.

All the windows were still open from yesterday in the fashion of resilient hope. Sidney started some coffee, which was percolating now. It sounded like shallow bait fish being swallowed by bigger fish below the sea.

We all sat in the living room.

"What's this all about?" Sidney asked in a waking voice.

"I'm afraid that we have a real emergency, Mrs. Hodges," the sheriff said, strapping on an official tone.

"Please, call me Sidney."

"Okay, Sidney." The sheriff's beady eyes darted between Morgan and me. Charles had not taken his eyes off of me since he had entered. "It appears Henry Langstone may have gone missing."

"Oh my," escaped gently from Sidney, eyes gigantic, en route to the kitchen now to retrieve the coffee. Morgan got up to help her.

Weighty silence. I wanted to extract Charles's eyes from their sockets.

"Have you called the limo driver yet?" I asked.

"Yes, son. We checked with him first thing this morning, and he says he hasn't heard anything."

Sidney and Morgan came back, ears perked high like finely-bred lap dogs. They served the coffee around. "No thanks," I said, though I needed it.

"Well," I said, swallowing my nerves and praying that I had succeeded, "he could have called another driver, or a cab, maybe."

Sheriff Mortimers's eyes became almost too small to see anymore. "Why would he want to go back so suddenly, son? Did something happen that I should be aware of?"

I was wringing my hands now. The sheriff's eyes seemed not to have any eye lashes, never blinking.

"Well, we had a fight over Morgan on the beach. More of a tiff, really. Nothing serious at all."

Both the sheriff and Charles's eyes broadened now, became colossal, as if in tacit full-orchestra together.

"Is this true, Morgan?" Charles asked.

"Yes." You could barely hear her.

"Were blows exchanged?"

"No, no, of course not," I said to the sheriff, but looking heatedly into Charles's eyes. "We just exchanged a few angry words, that's all. Just jealous, competitive guy stuff, nothing more."

"And these words, you say they were about Morgan?" Sheriff Mortimers asked.

"Yes. He thinks she loves him. It's a real joke."

"Is that right, Morgan?" The sheriff looked at her. She appeared incapable of raising her head. "Morgan?"

"They were both acting like buffoons," she said, staring with quiet boldness now at the sheriff. "I left them both standing there on the beach. That was the last time I saw Henry or Ethan yesterday."

"Are you in a relationship with either of them, Morgan?" the sheriff asked.

A long bit of some of the most excruciating silence of my existence. You could almost hear the sun climb, coloring Morgan's face. She looked away and shook her head. My soul twisted into the shape of a pretzel.

"I see, I see," Sheriff Mortimers said, sipping his coffee and nodding his head stiffly, appearing to be coldly unaffected by the matter, like a veteran pelican ostracizing the stubborn tide. "Did Henry say anything to you about leaving, Ethan?"

"No, but I called him some nasty things. I suppose he could've left out of anger."

"Seems unlikely he would leave without telling anyone, don't you agree?" the sheriff asked. Charles nodded his head vehemently, annoyingly, like a Chihuahua toy with a newly installed battery.

"Do you mind if we search the house, Sidney?"

Her face cascaded. "Well, I don't see why not. Oh dear, dear." Her wrinkles looked as if they became suddenly blatant in the growing morning light. I kept trying to make eye contact with Morgan, but to no avail.

"Thank you," the sheriff said, eyeing me suspiciously. He rose lethargically and sauntered pokily off to investigate the rest of the cottage, his radio and gun chafing at his side as he walked, now deafening in the utter silence of an early coastal morning turned sullen, all of our eyes on the ground, searching it, making the vanilla Berber carpet filthy with worry.

He came back quickly.

"I want to thank everyone for their cooperation. I'm sorry to have disturbed you, Sidney. Deputy Dansby is searching the Pelican Bay area now. We may have to file an official missing person's report. You'll let me know immediately if any information turns up?"

"Of course, Sheriff, of course," Sidney said. "Oh dear, dear. Oh my, my," she added, slowly shaking her head.

Morgan and her dad followed the sheriff out. She never looked at me. Not once. Charles grimaced at me on the way to the door, raising my body temperature a degree or two with his bellicose eyes. I looked down and away, closing the door just a little harder than I needed to.

And I let myself hate Morgan.

Just for a second.

CHAPTER TWENTY-SIX

They found Henry's body early the next morning, abrading the shore incessantly, as if the sand were a washboard and the sea the arms of a stout woman of early Newfoundland. His body was bloated, twisted, undigested and spit back up by the sea. Deputy Dansby had found him and had summoned Charles posthaste to examine the body, to detect his broken skull.

Charles grabbed his old black medicine bag, forbade Morgan to come, ordered her to stay at home, but she flapped along behind anyway, barely clad against a late summer morn whispering heavily of early fall. She screamed at the macabre sight, and the shrill sound was carried by the wind like the cry of a bullied gull.

I found Morgan crying, her head almost buried in the sand, shuddering. I ran to her and held her and she let me. I let go of her when Charles started our way with stentorian steps from the shore.

The deputy bagged the corpse to protect it from the gluttonous Pelican Bay shore birds.

I glanced to my right and the old man's figure almost grew out of the docks like an ancient pylon. He was watching, always watching, a chubby silhouette fluttering against the orange peel-colored, elephantine rising sun.

"I've had enough of this," I said, storming off toward the docks.

"Ethan! What are you doing?!"

"Let him go," her father said corrosively, now upon her like a rogue shadow.

But she rose anyway, stanching her tears, and ran after me.

"Ethan! Don't! Please!"

I stopped.

"This can't go on any longer! Let me go!"

"Ethan, please!"

"What do you want? You don't give a shit about me, or anyone."

"That's not true," Morgan said, sniffling. I could not believe that she was actually crying. "I have trouble showing my feelings sometimes, you know that. And now, with Henry dead, I—"

Morgan began weeping and fell against me. I held her for a long time, feeling her body heat, wind-emancipated strands of her hair sweeping my forehead. I was a support beam holding the beating flesh of an erudite mermaid.

"I can't believe he's dead!" she cried.

"I think I know who killed him," I said gravely, quietly, pushing her gently away.

"What?"

"The old man."

We sat down on the sand. Captain Shelby stood in the same spot, as motionless as the morning horizon just beyond him, surveying us. I could feel his stare. My blood ran cold.

"What are you not telling me, Ethan?" Morgan was gathering herself now. I had never seen her eyes so pure, so vulnerable, so demolished, and so inexplicably lovely.

"I sent Henry out there the night before last, to the old man's boat."

"What?" Her eyes flew at me, teal-clothed ghosts of Pelican Bay.

"I just wanted to scare him, that's all. I never thought that any of this would happen."

"Ethan, what did you do? Tell me everything." Her tears had almost vanished now. She was launching into 'full librarian research mode' again.

"Nothing, really. I told him to go out there and find out his age."

"Do you know what you've done? You sent him to his death."

"That's ridiculous! It had to be an accident, Morgan. It had to be."

"You wanted him dead. Admit it. You didn't have the courage to do it yourself, so you sicced Captain Shelby on him like a vicious old sea hound."

"That's not true, Morgan. How could you say that?"

I looked at Morgan lingeringly. She was silent for a moment.

"That's him standing out there, isn't it?" she asked.

"Yes."

"My God, he's so creepy. He isn't human, Ethan."

"Morgan, please, not now. I'm so tired of all this. I'm going to go set the record straight. I'll bet you anything that Henry slipped out there and hit his head, just like that little kid in 1931. Those docks are so old and slimy, and if you don't have the right shoes—"

"The old man murdered Henry!"

"Shhhh! Stop that, Morgan. You're being impossible."

"It's true! And you sent him out there!"

A siren screamed in the distance like a kamikaze flock of gulls. Just then, Charles finally came up behind us, a paternal awakening amid his daughter's shouts now obliterating all the previous respect that he may have had toward our privacy.

Captain Shelby still did not move, as if a statue of Nereus erected at an ancient Aegean port.

"Morgan, you come with me now," Charles said firmly.

"You better go," I said.

She looked at me with unprecedented solemnity, her eyes glistening in the now fully awake sun, little glossy pale blue mirrors of the sea. "Don't do it, Ethan. Don't go out there," she said, her dad pulling her away.

"Don't go where? What are you talking about?" her dad asked.

Morgan did not answer him.

I started toward the docks, turning my head to my right just in time to see Henry's pitiable corpse, a long black bag stuffed with death being loaded into the back of a Gull Bay Hospital ambulance.

The wind suddenly picked up, the salty breath of Nereus, warning me to stay away.

But nothing would keep me away.

Not now.

He did not move until I was already on the dock. He could have been in some sort of shutdown mode, a regenerative hibernation perhaps. When his head turned toward me, my insides tumbled like the now swelling surf. His face looked younger somehow, as if a figurehead dressing a frigate's bow having weathered the blow of the last storm's wind, shedding its old skin like some serpent of the deep. But his eyes never changed, haloes of wrinkles of untold years, reptilian lids, and lurking inside, emeralds, brooding mood gems of the deep.

"Who they be baggin', Boy? Anyone ye know?" The old man laughed. The sound of a hundred creaking galleons.

"Who is it, Captain? Can you tell me?"

The old man's eyes ran off to the sea, the way that they always did.

"I'm serious," I said. "If you know, I want you to tell me."

"Ye better stow it, Boy. Ye got yerself right crooked." He laughed again.

"This isn't funny. Someone's dead."

"Look at yer nerves. Ye better take a rúm." I remained standing, arms folded, my eyes on fire. "Suspect 'tis the same boy who came up here night before last, sniffin' round these docks like an old hundr after scraps. He looked to be the young friend of that town doctor. Right hard to tell in the dark."

"Cut it out. You know who he is."

"Mind yer crookedness, Boy. I said he looked to be the young friend of that town doctor."

"What happened? Tell me!"

The old man's eyes grew enormous and tight. "Me told ye to mind yer crookedness, Boy. There's naught so vile as a fickle tongue."

I could not look at the old man, and boiled the sea with my eyes instead. The sky was darkening.

"'Tis the same thing happened to that young boy in thirty-one. These docks ain't been sanded or washed long as I can remember, see? Don't know what keeps 'em together. Maybe the sea." He chuckled resonantly, and then became possessed by a faraway look suddenly. "He was snoopin'. God knows it makes me right crooked when they snoop. Guess I startled him. He jumped back and slipped. Hit his head, methinks. Dark. Ye know how dark it gets. Fished round for him, but the sea was contrary that night. She was contrary with a vengeance."

"Did you kill him?"

"No, you did."

"What?"

"Ye got what ye were after, eh? Don't let yer nerves be crooked now. Go after her, I say!" A gurgling laugh escaped him again, the sea in the old man's veins bubbling and hiccupping.

"I don't know what you're talking about. You're insane."

The thunder suddenly erupted, as if coming to claim me. He closed one eye and his mouth twisted. Lightning struck a hundred feet out on the sea. Rain drops hurled at me. I cringed.

"Yer testin' me patience, Boy! Been good to ye cause I love ye like me own son, but yer testin' me, Boy! Yer testin' me!"

"How old are you?"

The bay was moving like a panoramic movie of a tango with the Devil. The rain was slanted and furious. The sky rumbled like a ubiquitous Harley Davidson.

"How old are you?" I repeated forcefully.

The boats slammed against the docks, rotten apples in a shoved barrel. In the distance, faint, failing, a female shrieked out my name.

"Go claim that ducky! She be yers now!"

"How old are you, damn it?"

"Ethan! Ethan!" The shrill, rogue, forlorn voice kept creeping over the wind.

"I'm not leaving until you tell me!"

"I'll tell ye me secret," he growled in sing-song with the ominously roaring thunder, "but get on the go to shelter. I can't stop the storm. Thee brought it, Boy! Thee brought it!"

"Ethan!"

"No! Tell me now!"

An arm, that stench of sea laminating its sleeve, reached out and grabbed me. I blinked a few times, the sea lashing my body, stinging my eyes. We seemed to fly. I closed my eyes and time abandoned me like a sinking parent.

When I opened my eyes again, the scent of dank, rotting wood inebriated me, and an old sea merchant's knick-knacks assaulted my consciousness. A paternal face, now so young in the fading light, looked over me. I lay on bundles of fetid, moth-eaten sea coats and sloppily-woven blankets, a bagged old net piece for a pillow. I was in Captain Shelby's main cabin. It looked like a dwarf's room, but I did not feel crowded. The old man was tending to something, humming that old ditty.

Laura lie, Laura lie, in the sea barley, in the sea barley—

"What's that song, Captain Shelby? It's so beautiful." I felt delirious, my speech slightly slurred.

"A ducky me knew. A lost love. A beauty. She wanted the sheltered bay of a family, but I was after the sea—always been after the sea. Not a day passes without regret, like an empty net. Had me not been bout me fishin', might've saved her."

Laura lie, Laura lie—

The old man turned toward me, and I thought that he might be crying in the feeble light. The boat rocked back and forth, as if wanting to put me to sleep along with the Captain's seductive, beautiful crooning.

Suddenly he stopped singing.

"Let me tell ye, me Son, I don't know me age. Can't remember," he groaned and croaked in the wet darkness. "But even though a man forgets how old he be, his age does not forget he."

"Are you Nereus?"

"Yes."

I think that we were making eye contact now. I felt it more than anything else, a gentle but implacable gravity.

"No, I mean, are you the god, Nereus, *the old man of the sea*?"

The old man chuckled. It sounded like an empty barrel of rum being rolled.

"Go on boy! That librarian's put a draumr in yer head! Ha! What if me was? God only knows! I love ye, me Son. Won't ever let nothin' happen to ye. Here, drink this."

I do not know what he gave me to drink, but it was warm and thick and tasted like a million heavens. And I fell into the deepest, most peaceful sleep of my memory.

CHAPTER TWENTY-SEVEN

I woke up to the smell of pork belly bacon and farm eggs, rich and flavorful, our modern preoccupation with saturated fat and cholesterol tossed aside like fish too small to sell, or a shore man's fear of the Grand Banks in the fall. The old man served them with thick, stale bread suffocated by creamy butter, and a porridge of goat's milk and oats, exhaling a dense fog of honey. A breakfast fit for the first fishermen of Newfoundland. My stomach screamed and my nostrils flared, as though breathing their very first breaths.

I rubbed my eyes and turned my head, warmed by a beam of morning sun that sang its way in, swam through the musical paper of a bright blue sky, illuminating the once dark cabin, making its square body electric with hope. The storm was gone, the main cabin door propped open like a sea hag's hair cast back over her shoulder. The melody of *Laura Lie* sank down, baptizing my consciousness. I smiled.

"If yer goin' to go get yer librarian, yer goin' to need a fisherman's breakfast, I say."

"I've already told you, she's not my girlfriend. She doesn't love me. I don't think she loves any man."

"Captain Shelby's never wrong. She be yers now, me Son, yers for the takin'. One who sees a friend roasted on a pit tells all she knows."

"She thinks you killed Henry."

Silence.

The Captain's boat rocked gently now. He shook his head over and over again.

"I told ye what happened. Don't make me crooked again, me Son. Not so early, on such a nice day. Might go fishin'."

"There's trouble in town. They're going to be coming to question you. It's inevitable."

"There he goes, with his big words. Eh boy, sure they be comin'. Good reason to be fishin', I say."

"You're going to have to face them eventually."

"Don't be tellin' me me business, Boy. Finish yer breakfast why don't ye."

And I did. And I never ate another breakfast like it again.

So real.

So primordial.

The walk back to town seemed interminable. The path through the sand and the sea barley was somehow lengthened by my colossal thoughts, and hid intermittent buds of new beach roses, stoic secrets from the storm, and wild grass-bearded dunes that made even my young knees rasp like the captain's boat out on the sea.

The sheriff's police car was waiting in the driveway of our cottage.

No surprise.

I entered hurriedly. All their eyes swelled and rolled in silent upheaval, game fish eyeing their fishermen before gallant final dives. Sidney and Charles sat across from each other, the former looking more pallid and threadbare than ever. The sheriff was pacing the carpet thin. Morgan was not there.

I took a deep breath.

"Ethan! Where have you been? We've been worried sick!" Sidney blurted out.

"I—well—"

"Yes, you've worried everyone sick, young man. Very inconsiderate. You better have a perfectly good explanation," Charles said.

"Really, I—"

"I have some questions for you, son," the sheriff let out officiously.

If someone would just let me talk.

Suddenly Morgan walked in behind me. "Ethan!" She sounded like she had just seen the ghost of a recently departed loved one. She flew past me and turned to face me, pale-faced and tight-lipped.

I was silent and swept the floor with my eyes. I went and sat down next to Sidney, who caringly rubbed my right shoulder, eyes down, too. Morgan went and sat next to her father.

"Everyone calm down, please. I spent the night with Captain Shelby."

"I knew it!" Morgan said breathily through her teeth.

"I have some questions for him, too," the sheriff said with the same officiousness.

"How could you?" Morgan shrieked.

I looked at her nearly wildly.

"Morgan, let Ethan talk," Charles said emotionlessly.

"Ethan, you need to tell us what you know," Sheriff Mortimers said.

"There's not a lot to tell," I said, looking at Morgan, who held her pastel face in her hands now. "I went out there to get some things straight, that's all. I think everyone needs to take a dose of reality here."

"What do you mean, son?" the sheriff asked.

"He's just a harmless old man, nothing else. He stays out there on his boat because people start snooping and suddenly havoc breaks lose, like the way all of you have been acting." I kept my eyes on Morgan.

"Go on," Sheriff Mortimers said.

"I asked him about Henry. He barely knows who he is."

"What did he say? What did he say?" Charles said abruptly. I looked at him impatiently.

"He said he saw someone who looked like Henry slip on the docks. He tried to fish him out, but he said the current was too strong, and it was too dark."

"Right," Morgan let out oddly, a whispery voice, as if from the sunken cemetery.

"We're going to have to question him, too," the sheriff said again, nodding a bit too firmly, eyes locked with Charles's eyes.

Charles nodded back readily.

"Good luck. He said he's going fishing."

Everyone looked at me, except for Sidney. Morgan looked vaguely frantic, the distance of a storm whipped into a watery face.

I glanced at the kitchen table and a small stack of leftover pancakes, forlorn, petrifying, syrup glued about their hips, glared back at me. A few abandoned sausages were stuck like ugly canoes in a shallow, frozen pond of accumulated regret, the white plate grinning ironically beneath them.

"This is ridiculous." Charles stood up bitterly, like a shiny swordfish's snout poking out of the Atlantic. "I demand further evidence."

Sheriff Mortimers looked downright tired, beaten sand on the beaten coast of Pelican Bay.

Sidney's gentle eyes expanded.

I thought that Morgan might blurt out something, but she stayed silent. She had fallen to staring at the decaying pancakes too, yet looking through them, beyond them, a 100-yard stare. I fancied in that moment that I was the object of her thoughts.

"Do you know when Captain Shelby will be returning from his

fishing trip?" Sheriff Mortimers said, jarring everyone, as if we were all in a dream and his abruptness, like a cane from the classic American stage comedy, yanked us out of our slumber.

"No," I said, almost too quickly.

"Look, son, if you're protecting him, it could be construed as obstructing justice."

I looked at the sheriff, shock dressing my face hazily. "What? I told you, he's innocent. There's nothing for me to protect. Why would Captain Shelby want to kill anyone?"

"There is the incident of 1931," Charles said.

"There's no proof of that," Sidney said. I smiled at her and she smiled back with her eyes.

"What about this incident?" the sheriff asked with a right-raised eyebrow. I hid my face in my hands.

"They say that he killed a young boy," Charles went on. "What happened is quite similar to the strange circumstances surrounding Henry's recent death. They say the boy saw the old man rushing at him down the dock and slipped in fright, hitting his head and falling into the bay."

"And he tried to save him, too! Can he help it if Pelican Bay's so dark at night and always has vicious currents?" I interjected, drawing suspicious stares from everyone except Sidney. I was intentionally avoiding Morgan's lashing gaze.

"Have you been out there?" I continued, practically barking. "Those docks haven't been cleaned or sanded in more years than anyone knows. What do you expect? I'm not even sure how I walk out there. And that's during the day! Why don't *you* try walking out there in the dark?"

Sheriff Mortimers eyed me analytically. Charles lent his default stare of acrid disapprobation. "So you don't know when he'll be back, or you don't want to tell me?" the sheriff asked indefatigably.

"I told you I don't know! If you don't believe me, why don't you arrest me?"

"Son, there's no need to become upset, I just—"

"No!" I shouted. "I'm tired of all this nonsense, everyone making up stories and bullying the poor old man! All he wants is to be left alone. Why can't everyone just leave him alone?"

I stormed out.

After a moment, Sidney gave Morgan a woman's look.

Finally, Morgan followed me outside.

"Ethan, that wasn't wise."

"Why not? You think the old man's a murderer! And that he and I are in cahoots!"

"Ethan, calm down."

"You know it's true!"

Morgan was silent, avoiding my stare, as usual.

"Well, if he's innocent, why doesn't he just appear and clear himself? Why's he out fishing?"

"Because he has nothing to prove or clear. Don't you get it Morgan? You just loved Henry and now you want justice."

"That's not true," Morgan said faintly.

"Prove it."

"Don't be ridiculous."

"Say it!" I yelled.

"Say what?"

"You know what!"

"No."

"Say it!"

"Please stop it, Ethan."

"Not until you say it!"

Morgan began to cry quietly.

"I don't love him."

"Don't love who?"

"Henry."

"And? Who do you love?"

"I love you, Ethan."

"What? I can't hear you!"

"I love you!"

Morgan collapsed into my arms. She raised her chin slowly. Our eyes locked like two lovers gazing at each other across oceans of time. I cupped her surrendered face with my trembling hands and began the fateful kiss, shallow at first, then deepening, our breath quickening, our hearts the raging hearts of gulls climbing up to the heavens.

In my memory that kiss lasted forever, the greatest of my life. Marshes, fetid, dark, clogged rivers separating us from the dunes, witnessed for God, and the salt blown in from the sea seasoned our lips.

And my soul.

My soul finally finding some rest.

CHAPTER TWENTY-EIGHT

I thought that I would have dreamed of Morgan that night, the way we had kissed, our hearts two shimmering schooners set adrift by the winds of fortune, rubbing bows, contemplating a grander ocean ahead, one so great that we might sink with each other and explore the depths of our souls, never reaching the bottom of our desire for one another.

No. I did not have a dream like that.

I know that Morgan did not either. If she dreamed of me at all, it would have been general flashes of me, pages in a glossy new book fluttering before her eyes like a penny arcade movie. She might have read another chapter in my novel, held the book to her bosom, closed her eyes, and found another dream within a dream.

Instead, I dreamed of the old fisherman. No surprise. I had come to accept now that dreams could be a channel somehow between the old man's maritime soul and mine, a way that he talked to me about things that he knew might be too much for me to handle in real life.

In the dream I was adrift in the rocky channel leading to the Secret Spot, adrift in a boat with no stern or bow, no sides, no keel—an invisible boat. I felt myself beginning to be tossed about, my skiff's bottom scrape and scuff, for I was too close to the snarling, fanged shore. I could feel the pointy rocks like blunt daggers of destiny, hooded departed souls of Pelican Bay waiting to recruit me into their woeful kingdom. I felt that two of the taller rocks, much less jagged, standing beside each other, might have been the cherished departed souls of my parents trying to guide and protect me. I sensed great love but no hope, for just as the sea was too crooked for them, it would be too crooked for me.

Soon I felt myself hurling toward the sharp mouth of the shoreline, riding on the tops of the waves. I closed my eyes within the dream and prepared to be chewed by the sea's teeth, sucked into her throat by the furling black tongue of her mighty undertow, and then digested in her green belly for all time, joining all those great Atlantic fisherman lost at sea.

I heard a great iron clunky sound in the front of me, the jaws of the rocky shore, my shuddering heart told me. I closed my eyes, wanting to sleep within sleep, flinching from head to toe. But I felt no penetrating fangs about my flesh as I thought I would.

When I opened my eyes there was a barnacle-ridden anchor clasping my inner-bow and pulling me ahead toward the Secret Spot, away from the carnivorous shoreline. I could see the back of the old man's boat, could see him standing at the stern of his deck and waving to me. He was smiling and looked to be in his thirties, the word, *Captain* magically visible now on the front of his hat above his head, dark hair falling out all around like trickling black ivy.

I smiled back.

The next thing that I knew I was standing on the captain's main deck and his beautiful, bronzed face, a bright blue-eyed Cary Grant of the sea, smiled gigantically at me. We were already entering the Secret Spot and when I looked back behind us my skiff was now visible, a lonely, wooden child skipping to her death. She broke up quickly upon the rocks, as if she were made of toothpicks. Acid ran up my throat.

"Captain, it is you, right?"

"Ha, ha! Eh boy, 'tis me. Who'd ye think I be?"

"You, you—look so young."

"Ha! Yes boy. But ye should look at yerself."

The captain moved in a flash to the side of his boat. I followed and soon we were both peering at the skin of the abysmal sea that filled the Secret Spot. The sea was silver-black now, darker on this side of the spot, so calm, and I could see the two of us staring back. A young man and a child.

I jumped backward.

"Go on boy! Since when have ye been scared of yer own reflection, me Son?"

"I don't understand."

"Understand what?"

"That's not me."

"Eh. 'Tis thee. Why ye be crooked, me Son? Yer handsome. Just like me, I say!"

"No, I—"

"Take a rúm why don't ye."

I sat down on top of a storage bin. I felt as dizzy as the clouds moving quickly by above. We were approaching Fisherman's Island now, so dense with foliage that it looked as if the Garden of Eden had floated out to sea eons ago, furiously growing trees to atone for Adam and Eve's sins.

The fisherman anchored his boat just off shore, removed his captain's hat and old T-shirt, rolled up his bait-stained, billowy pants, and dove playfully into the ocean off of his bow. He stood there with navy blue sea swallowing him up to his waist, smiling at me with navy blue eyes, eyes the darkest I had ever seen on him, in perfect harmony with the sea about him. His long black hair shimmered in lose curls about his head and face, his beard already coming in like a shadow of his hair under the sun. He was well-built and his swarthy, muscular shoulders and pectorals chuckled beneath glimmering chest hair that resembled a thousand wet sleeping flies. Were I a painter, I would have been known immortally for capturing, in that moment, *Man and the Sea*.

"Well what are ye waitin' for, me Son? Get on the go! I got somethin' else I want to show ye!" the captain yelled from the sea, turning and wading to shore now.

I removed my shirt, and, as I threw it to the side on top of the captain's boat deck, I looked down and saw a child's legs. And when I jumped into the ocean, I felt a child's excitement, and took the spastic arm strokes of a little boy eager to get to shore.

The sand on the shore leading into the green froth of beach pines and mangroves was the same color as the puffy clouds moving at full sail above. The sky was the busiest of my memory, awake or asleep, the sky of a famous oil painting.

As I looked ahead of me, the amalgamation of untamed green composing the bulk of Fisherman's Island seemed as impenetrable as the wrath of the sea.

"Ha! There ye be!" the old man said as my miniature legs enthusiastically caught up with him at the onslaught of crowded beach pine.

"Hi, Captain." And now for the first time I really heard my little voice in the dream. "Do you mean to go in there?"

"Eh boy. Thee need not be afraid. I cleared me a way some time ago for thee and yer mudder, me Laura."

"You did?"

"Eh."

"What for?"

"Ha! Always a book a questions!"

"Is what you want to show me at the center of the island?"

"That's me smart scopie!"

We came around to a small clearing that heralded a shadowed path toward the island's center, bridged every ten feet or so by fallen trees, rungs on a collapsed ladder to heaven perhaps.

Every time we approached a storm-blown log, the captain would lift me up over it into the air saying, "*Melrakki!*" I would laugh and he would laugh even louder. Each time I felt like a child being thrown into bed at night by a parent who was an ex-pirate. He told me later that *melrakki* was the Old Norse word for "white fox." The captain's eyes had deepened to an indigo blue now in the canopied dark of the old path.

"When did you clear this out, Captain?"

"Too long ago fer me to remember, me Son."

"It must have been a lot of work."

"Guess I carry the strength of the sea here in me arms. Here we go again me Boy. *Melrakki!*"

Suddenly, we entered a large clearing that could have been the nucleus of Fisherman's Island. The sky seemed to assault our senses with its blue light and ubiquitous clouds. I felt dizzy again.

"We made it, me Son. How ye gettin' on?"

"I'm okay. A little dizzy."

"Must be all that jumpin'."

We walked a few more feet and just ahead I could make out a very crude cabin made of beach-pine logs and calcified mud. As we came closer, I could see that the roof was an astonishing amalgamation of materials, odd flats of metal, wood, and so forth, fastened through unknown years by marsh grass. I felt that I saw all the races of humanity in it, good and evil, the battle of man versus nature, wars between settlers and Native Americans, and most notably and sadly, the countless years of the captain's trials on the sea and on the land. That roof made me want to weep and I had to look away, my eyes settling finally on the front door, which was made of tightly set tree branches fastened with more marsh grass.

"I can't believe you made that," I said.

"She's weathered more storms than I can count, but she's held true. The storms always be less contrary near Fisherman's Island. Only God knows why."

"Is what you want to show me inside?"

"Eh. Once we're inside the time'll be gettin' on bout right."

"I'm scared."

"Go on boy! Have I ever harmed ye?"

"No."

"Don't ye trust me?"

"Yes."

"Well, I need to show ye this. 'Tis important, I say."

"Okay."

Captain Shelby opened the thatch door that was cleverly hinged using carved and hollowed pieces of pine wood and secured with rope from his fishing boat. There were no windows and it was quite dark.

As I followed him inside, I was absolutely terrified.

The captain lit a lantern.

"Take a rúm," he said, pointing vaguely at a few chairs and a small table all made out of beach pine and marsh grass. I was afraid that the chairs would not hold, but they were so solid. I felt the same way about them that I did about Captain Shelby's archaic fishing boat. Miracles of manufacturing. I let my eyes wander about the room and noticed a few cots and a few other tables also made out of the same island materials.

"How did you learn how to weave marsh grass like this?"

"Me Laura. Yer mudder."

"But that would make me your son."

"Eh."

"But my name's Ethan, remember? Ethan. My mother died at sea. You told me that when I was just a kid. Don't you remember?"

"Eh boy. But that be yer children's children and so on. So many years be gone I can't count them to save me life."

"I'm Ethan. Don't you know me, sir?"

"Ethan. 'Tis a good name. A good name to have. Thee be talkin' bout things that aren't yet, me Son. Ye got me as rimmed as a tangled net, I say."

"Sorry sir, but I—"

"*Sir*? Go on boy with all this *sir* stuff!"

"I didn't mean—"

"Ethan lives in a another time, another town. He be a good scopie but tries to think too much. It's bad to be ashamed fer somethin' well done. That boy be a smart and great young scopie but needs to tell himself every now and then, I say."

"But Captain, I am Ethan. I think you're just—"

"Just what? Ye think I don't know who I be talkin' to? Did ye not see yerself Boy? Oh me nerves!"

"I'm sorry, Captain."

"Why can't ye call me dad or old man? Yer some crooked, I say."

"Sorry, but something just doesn't seem right at all." My little voice and the conversation with the captain were starting to disturb me profoundly, and I should have known right then that I was dreaming. But oh how we hang on to dreams even when we are gifted the largest of clues.

"Ye want to know about Ethan's parents? How they died? Is that it?"

"Yes, Captain, uh, I mean *Dad*."

And the fisherman's eyes became as light as the Caribbean Sea, and his smile was vast. He came over and sat next to me and all my fear vanished suddenly.

"Let me see, let me see. Well, 'twas a crooked day right sure. A crooked day. They had no business on a skiff if ye ask me. But them duckies can talk a lad into most anything, and me guess Ethan's mudder was after somethin' in Lighthouse Point. A woman's life is spent on a spinning wheel and inconsistency dwells in her breast."

The fisherman stopped for a moment and stared at the dancing flame in the lantern. He looked as though he might cry, but then went on.

"Things often take a bad turn in this here bay, ye knows yerself. I was tossin' me net just past the channel in me Secret Spot when them fiskr got right scared and started divin' deep. I knew a swell was brewin'. Ye knows yerself the sea can get crooked for no reason and come after ye. 'Tis the silent sea that can drown a man, and Ethan's father was not mindin' her vengeance that day. The sea reached out with her crooked handleggr and yanked their skiff into the mouth of that wicked channel. I scooped me net and got on the go, headin' right for 'em. I heard his mudder cry out on the wind. 'Twas a shriek that right pretty ducky let out."

The captain's eyes turned to almost a midnight blue now. The lantern began to sputter. His face began to appear lightly wrinkled in the tangoing light. My flesh crawled and ripped.

"But when the rocks are after ye," he went on, "there be nothin' anyone can do, not even Captain Shelby. I reached 'em right quick, but all me saw was a skiff like yers looked today on them rocks. No bodies to be found. 'Twas their time ye know. 'Twas their time and that's that."

We were silent for a good while, both of us almost hypnotized by the lantern flame, which looked as though it might go out. I remember the threat of darkness and of the unknown, sitting inside that strange cabin in the middle of Fisherman's Island, bringing me great terror. I wish that I had awoken. But, as the captain would say, "'Twas not me time."

"Dad, I thought you wanted to show me something in here." I could not believe that I had said it. Especially with those very words. Suddenly I realized that I was dreaming.

"Look at yer nerves, me Son. Just look at 'em."

I had lost my power of speech now.

"Don't ye know I'd never harm ye? Why ye looks like yer tryin' to wake from a nightmare. Is that how it be? 'Tis a nightmare to be here with me? Answer me, Boy!"

The captain's face suddenly began to change, his eyes so dark blue as to be almost black. A smell of rotting sea had filled the room, the same scent that Morgan and I had encountered recently in the library.

I immediately looked away and began shuddering.

"Mind yer nerves, Boy! 'Tis me, 'tis only me! Turn and look at me. Look at me!"

I could not move my head.

"Look at me! 'Tis what ye needed to see. Don't be afraid. 'Tis me."

The captain reached out and turned my head toward him.

And I woke up.

Thank God.

I woke up.

CHAPTER TWENTY-NINE

It no longer mattered to me whether or not the old man was a ghost, a god, or just a fisherman of unknown years enigmatically bonded with the sea. I loved him as the greatest, most unique grandfather of all time. But the question that rocked our tiny town now, even more than the Great Hurricane, was if Captain Shelby was a murderer. And the uncompromising flow of Pelican Bay, vicious in its smallness, would be bent on finding an answer.

The Gull Bay Coast Guard cutter scoured Pelican Bay and all its tiny surrounding bays for days, its engine struggling against the obstinate ocean current, resounding among the sand dunes, the roar of a small storm hushed to a moan.

But they would not find him. The old man was adrift at the Secret Spot, a place no normal boat had ever gone.

But this did not keep them from trying.

I was worried that the Gull Bay Police might harm Captain Shelby, but even more worried that they might harm themselves trying to capture him. I kept waiting for Sheriff Mortimers to bring the Coast Guard cutter into Pelican Bay for coffee and other supplies so that I could warn them, but they just seemed to stay out there in the bay forever. I kept thinking about the strange dream that I had had the night before, and soon decided to take matters into my own hands.

"Ethan, I made breakfast. Where are you going, dear?"

"Sidney, please don't ask me that. You're not going to like the answer."

"Oh, Ethan! Oh, dear!"

"See. I told you."

"You can't save him, Ethan. He has to save himself now."

"I know that, Sidney. But I could at least warn him, and Sheriff Mortimers, too."

"Ethan, dear, I don't think you need to warn that old man about anything." There was a forebodingness in Sidney's voice that made me uneasy. "And Sheriff Mortimers doesn't need any help. He's a professional and knows what he's doing out there."

"When it comes to Captain Shelby, there are no professionals."

I chuckled somewhat bizarrely, and hearing myself, became even more uneasy. Sidney regarded me oddly.

"I don't want you going out there Ethan. I forbid it!"

Sidney and I locked eyes together. My eyes felt like black clouds infringing upon her pale blue skies of spring. She looked as though she was going to cry, so I came over to the breakfast table and sat down.

"Sidney, I'm a grown man now. I know what I'm doing. Besides, I'm the only one who knows my way around those rocks, and the only one who knows where the old man is."

"Oh dear, dear. It's times like these that I wish your father or grandfather were alive," Sidney said softly, given over to a light weeping now.

"I know Sidney. I know. I'm sorry this is so hard on you. But something has to be done before more lives are lost. There are already three deaths linked to the old man, even more if you include all these damned rumors. I don't think he wants anyone dead, but we don't understand his ways at all, and—"

"Oh, my dear Ethan," Sidney said, trying to swab her tears with a tea napkin and to collect herself. "This may sound like an awfully peculiar time to say it, but I'm proud of you, dear. I'm proud of the man that you've turned into. I wish your father could be here to see this."

"Thanks, Sidney. That means a lot. I just wish I had started putting this all together sooner, before Henry had to die."

"That wasn't your fault."

"Well, I feel partly to blame."

Sidney suddenly stopped crying and looked at me, ample-eyed. "What are you saying?" she asked.

"I sent Henry out there."

"I'm sure it was just a prank, Ethan. A dare."

"You know what Captain Shelby said?"

"What, dear?"

"He said that I killed Henry."

"That's ridiculous."

"No, think about it, Sidney. I knew there was a risk but I sent him out there anyway. Maybe a part of me wanted Henry dead."

"Ethan! You stop that kind of thinking right now! I won't listen to it. You're a good boy, dear. Henry chose to go. You didn't drag him out there."

"What about Pete?"

"That was an accident. The way Pelican Bay's shores have been acting lately, washing up things and then burying them weeks later, tidal quick sand does not surprise me at all."

"It's still pretty rare Sidney. I looked it up. What if Captain Shelby thought he was protecting me somehow?"

"Ethan, dear, do you honestly think he caused the quick sand?"

"I don't know. There's just a lot we don't understand about the old man, that's all. With everything that's happened, all Morgan's research, and—"

"Oh dear, dear. This has all gone so far!"

"I've been thinking a lot about this, Sidney. You know, I've been having a lot of dreams about Captain Shelby. I believe that he and I are tied together somehow. What if Laura Hodges is—"

"Ethan please! I won't listen to this!"

"Anyway, I think the old man knew I wanted Henry dead, and he may have thought Pete was hurting me somehow. What if in his own strange way, out of love, he was really trying to protect me?"

"That is very strange, dear. Very strange."

"Sidney, I don't want to make the same mistake again I made with Henry. I want to do something, anything I can, to stop anyone else from dying. Sometimes a man has to do what a man has to do."

"I don't want to lose you, dear. You're all I have left."

"If I don't try to do something, Sidney, I won't be a man worth having around."

I stood up. Sidney began crying again.

"I guess I can't stop you, dear. You are a man, after all."

CHAPTER THIRTY

"Do you see that old fishing boat in the distance?" Sheriff Mortimers asked.

"Are you sure that's a boat?" the Coast Guard captain replied.

"Okay, look now."

"It's so hard to tell," the captain said, his eyes straining through the binoculars. What he saw seemed to come and go, as if a toy boat pulled under the waves and released again by some mammoth child bathing in the Atlantic. "Hard to make out. I suppose it could be a boat."

"Head that way," the sheriff demanded.

"I don't think so. See those rocks ahead? Suicide to go there."

"It's an order!"

"You can't order the Coast Guard."

"Pelican Bay and all her surrounding bays fall under the jurisdiction of Gull Bay. I have authority over all crimes that happen here. That old man's being investigated under suspicion of murder. I order you to go!"

The captain hesitated, then proceeded slowly.

The sheriff glowered.

Soon an ancient-looking fishing boat could be seen dipping just beyond the treacherous waterway, like a small ghost ship unable to make up its mind as to whether or not to materialize. It could have been a mirage at sea. Their skin crawled.

"I have to stop here. There's no passage now," the Coast Guard captain explained.

He stopped the boat. The sheriff's whole body frowned.

"How do you think he got over there?"

The captain shook his head sluggishly, his eyes loitering upon the jagged rocks.

"I order you to go through!" the sheriff shouted. "Look, you've got to. This crazy old coot has killed several people already that we know of."

Cumbersome silence.

"Better put a life vest on," the captain finally surrendered.

After a few hundred feet more, the old man's fishing boat was clearly visible. It looked deserted, not even the usual fishing poles out that always looked like the drawn legs of a faded grasshopper in the sun. The age of the old man's fishing boat, that day, seemed as indeterminate as his age, the boat perhaps robbed from some remote past by the brawny hands of time and flicked upon the mercurial waves. And a fog seemed to curl about it, like a vaporous hairdo. The boat seemed so still in the water, yet no visible anchor was cast.

"Are you sure that's his boat?" the captain asked. "It looks deserted."

"Watch out! Turn!"

And how the old man's boat was before them in that instant is still debated to this day. The young Coast Guard captain, who lived to tell the tale, says that the jagged rocks, whose distance was hard to judge, made Captain Shelby's boat appear farther away than it actually was.

And how a rotten fishing boat could crush the bow of a sturdy Coast Guard cutter is also much debated. The captain still speculates that it was all about angle of approach.

But there they were, the two of them flailing about in the murky, irascible sea near the rugged rocks of the pass. The young captain, watching the old man's boat gurgle and cough into a blur in the distance, managed to grab hold of a piece of debris from his sinking ship, madly kicking his legs to stay clear of the rocks.

The sheriff had been thrown by a crashing wave galloping for the toothed shore, the incisor of the first rock, a solitary protruding sea fang, ripping his innards to shreds. He was not capable of being saved, though the brave captain swam for him in his red life vest like a well-trained Christmas seal. Sheriff Mortimers sank pitiably and painted the bottom of the sea in blots of crimson, like a mortally-wounded sting ray.

The young captain remained marooned on the serrated coastline for many hours until he spotted a skiff heading his way, fighting the strong current of the channel, a skiff with a young man and woman inside. He waved both his hands frantically at the skiff and yelled, "Hello there! Mayday! Mayday!"

"Ethan, look! There's a man there on the shore. See? On that rock."

"Oh my God, Morgan, you're right. Ahoy there!" I yelled. "Ahoy there!"

I veered the skiff as close to the jagged shoreline as I could.

"Ethan, be careful!"

"Don't worry, I know this channel really well. I would never let anything happen to you. I still can't believe you talked me into taking you with me. Your father's going to kill me."

"The safest place for me right now is with you," Morgan said in her loud-soft voice, not even looking at me. But I could feel her sentiment and it surged through my body like the primordial smell of salt from the Secret Spot sailing down through the channel on the wind. "Don't you worry about my father. He never liked you anyway."

"Ha. You sure know how to make a guy feel—"

"Ethan, you're passing him!"

"Okay, calm down. I'll circle around again. The current's starting to get pretty rough. Hang on!"

I passed with the skiff again, this time dropping a small anchor just off the pointy channel shoreline near the stranded Coast Guard captain. His round, noble face appeared haggard with trauma.

"Hello there," I yelled through cupped hands. "What happened?"

"My name's Captain Shaw of the Gull Bay Coast Guard. I'm shipwrecked," he shouted back, also through cupped hands.

"Ethan, ask about Sheriff Mortimers," Morgan said, tapping my shoulder.

"Was the sheriff with you?"

"Yes."

"Where is he?"

"He's dead. My cutter's at the bottom of the channel. We took on lethal hull damage from a collision with that old man's fishing boat."

Morgan and I looked at each other with immense eyes.

"I'm really sorry," I hollered.

Captain Shaw looked down at the rocks. "I tried to warn him," he yelled. "Poor fool."

"Listen, I can't get any closer in this skiff. Can you swim to us?"

"Uh, I think so!"

"Be careful!"

Morgan threw out a rope with an old life preserver on it. Captain Shaw dipped into the sea and was jostled about immediately by the quickly growing current. It was frightening how deep the channel was so near the treacherous rocks. The captain was treading water right away. His eyes were calm but held fretfulness in their irises like bottomless pits of doom. He made me think of a horse being harnessed to safety through a raging river.

He grabbed onto the life preserver and we pulled him to the skiff. We helped him climb in and he sat in the middle of the boat, dripping, exhausted, and said nothing at all at first. Then, finally, as I was pulling up the small anchor that I brought, anticipating just such an occasion, he said, "Where were you headed in this awful channel? Are you kids crazy? Sure am glad you came along, though!" His eyes were much easier now, and I noticed that they were a beautiful shade of blue, a shade that seemed to belong more to a Boston lobsterman than a mid-Atlantic Coast Guard captain.

"I'm a friend of Captain Shelby's. I was hoping I might be able to straighten all this out before there are any other accidental deaths. Maybe I'm too late," I said, eyeing the center of the channel for signs of the sunken Coast Guard cutter or poor Sheriff Mortimers. There was nothing, nothing except the swirling, ravenous cross currents. The sea was swelling now, the current stronger, and our little skiff struggled and jostled about, its strap-on engine dipping in and out of the sea making the sound of a terrible fight constantly taken under the ocean.

"A *friend*, eh?" The young captain looked at Morgan but she did not hold his gaze. Instead her eyes appeared to be glued to the Secret Spot just ahead beyond the pernicious pass, now with a strange fog about it. The old fisherman's boat was not to be seen at all. "If you're really a friend, you'll find him and convince him to turn himself in. He's in a lot of trouble from what I've heard."

"What kind of trouble?" I asked innocently. The captain looked at me suspiciously.

"Well, for starters, he's been charged with the murder of Henry Langstone."

Morgan suddenly turned her gaze on the captain, her eyes betraying a certain pity and concealed despondence.

"Henry Langstone?" I asked. "They don't have enough evidence!" I caught myself. Morgan lightly scowled at me.

"Sheriff Mortimers didn't seem to think so," the captain said, "but I guess he won't be around to arrest him." An overt grief seized Captain Shaw's wrinkleless face, drooping his wonderful blue eyes. "As soon as I get back I'm going to see that the old man's charged with the murder of Sheriff Mortimers."

Captain Shaw's blue eyes began to lose their beauty now as we neared the long-surviving docks of Pelican Bay.

"But I don't understand," I said. "I thought the boat collision was an accident?"

"An accident?" The young captain laughed. It seemed that it would have been a good, healthy laugh were it not riddled with the agony of recent tragedy. "If it was an accident, where's Captain Shelby's boat? Where's his wreckage?"

"You don't think his boat sank, too?"

"No, no. I would've seen that," the captain retorted confidently. And

I believed him. There was no lying in those magnificent ugly blue eyes.

"I just don't get it. It doesn't make any sense. I've known Captain Shelby since I was just a little boy. Been fishing with him dozens of times. He's not a murderer."

"How do you know?"

"I just know. Look, you have to believe me. He's been on the sea longer than anyone, and we shouldn't try to force our limited understanding on him. It had to be an accident of some kind. His boat's made out of the same materials the Vikings used eons ago. It's strong as hell! Believe me."

"The Vikings? What the hell are you talking about? What is your name?"

"Ethan. That's my girlfriend, Morgan."

"Hi," Morgan said dimly, barely turning and regarding Captain Shaw.

"No, I want your last names."

"We have nothing to hide," Morgan said, her voice surprisingly thickening suddenly, taking me and the young captain aback. "I'm Morgan Olinsworth and he's Ethan Hodges. Why don't you go look it up. We're both long-term residents of Pelican Bay," she finished with a haughty tone.

"I don't think you realize how serious this is. That old man's killing people out here and needs to be brought to justice."

"Isn't your dad a cousin of Sheriff Mortimers?" Morgan asked.

"Uh, yes, but that has nothing to do with—"

"That's what I thought."

Captain Shaw looked irritably at Morgan. I didn't like it at all. Fortunately we were already at the docks and the captain stood up to help secure the bow line. After he climbed out of the boat, he said, "You both know I'm going to have to report all this to the Gull Bay Police."

"Of course," Morgan said with gorgeous sardonicism, peering up and managing to stare right through the hideous-eyed young man. "You go right ahead and do that."

And in that very moment I actually treasured how Morgan had the rare ability to look at one without even looking at one, to give one an acute existential crisis right there on the spot.

"If I were a police officer, I'd arrest you right now. You guys are confused and you're going to get yourselves killed, if you ask me."

"Well, it's a good thing we didn't ask you," I said.

Morgan snickered.

"Okay, funny man," the captain said, beginning to turn down the dock. "I'll be laughing when I see your corpses at the Gull Bay Coroner's Department."

Morgan and I both just sat in the skiff and watched Captain Shaw walk carefully away down the slimy dock to Pelican Bay.

"You're welcome!" I yelled out.

Morgan laughed out loud. I pulled her toward me and she hugged me, giggling, our bodies convulsing together, as if her giggles were little battery cables. I went to kiss her, and she let me.

And it was wonderful.

But we were both worried, down deep.

Confused.

Terrified.

We were so young.

And Captain Shelby was so incomprehensible.

But that did not stop me from loving him.

CHAPTER THIRTY-ONE

"Ethan, you know the shit's going to really hit the fan now."
I looked at Morgan, shocked.
"What?"
"Captain Shaw's going to go back to Gull Bay and tell all. It's going to be a zoo around here."
"Oh. I know. Do you still think Captain Shelby killed Henry?"
Morgan was silent for a moment, looking out to sea. She looked adorable and radiant sitting in the bow of the skiff. She had on her galoshes and full raingear, winter in Pelican Bay imminent. Her ash-blonde hair was pulled back and hidden in her rain hood like a coiled secret. She wore no makeup but had been sleeping as restlessly as me as of late, and a sloppy glance her way perceived too much dark eyeliner. Her eyes, an upper atmosphere blue that day with those dark circles underneath, lent her the appearance of a sexy sea Goth. She bit her lip like a frazzled child. She would make me wait for an answer.
She finally made full eye contact with me and I marveled at how I would always become a puddle every time she did that.
"No."
"That's what I thought. What about Sheriff Mortimers?"
"Maybe the Coast Guard cutter sinking was an accident, but the collision wasn't."
"What do you mean?"
"What if Captain Shelby was protecting his territory, warding them off, and things went wrong?"

"Maybe. I don't think he meant to kill them. We don't understand his ways, and I really wish we'd just left him alone the way he's wanted from the beginning."

"Too late now."

"Really."

"What are we going to do, Ethan? I'm getting cold."

"You know what I have to do. And I have to do it before the lynch mob comes."

"Have to do what?" Morgan asked with a feigned innocence and shallowness, which she failed miserably at. I giggled to myself, secretly thanking God for her razor smarts and vast depth.

"Nice try. You're not coming with me this time. High tide's coming in, and you know what high tide's like around here. I have to go back through that nasty channel to you-know-where."

"Don't try to play John Wayne with me. I'll do what I please, and I still think the safest place is with you."

"You still actually think he'd hurt you? But I thought you believed he wasn't a murderer anymore?"

"Maybe not a murderer, but *amorally territorial*."

"What on earth are you talking about, Morgan?"

"Anthropomorphism."

"God I wish I had a quarter!"

We both laughed. It felt really good.

"Whatever that old man is, our morality doesn't apply to him."

I shivered. And I was not even cold.

"Geez, Morgan. But wouldn't even territoriality be anthropomorphic?"

"Quite clever, Ethan, but remember that I'm only referring to a possible trend in his behavior, nothing more. Look at all the accidental deaths. All of them have occurred when people were invading his space, his secrets, and so forth."

"You know, I can't believe I'm saying it, but that really makes sense."

"And protecting his identity follows the same pattern."

"You still think he wants to kill you because you know who he is."

Morgan looked very serious in the early afternoon light. And her serious face was one of her most lovable expressions to me. To this day I cannot explain why, other than to say that I never really believed that Morgan loved me, and so I cherished serious moments with her, as few and fleeting as they were. I also cherished flashes of intimacy, even if they were accidental. When you love someone who may never be able to fully reciprocate, you learn to aggrandize the most feeble moments.

"Well," I said, "we're running out of daylight."

"Yeah."

"Listen, I'm not going to lie. It may get rougher out there. See those clouds coming in?" I pointed to a minatory patch of sky, like a thousand black gulls in a flock of doom. "I know the channel well, but it's going to get dangerous. We could be at great risk."

Morgan was silent for a moment. "I'm already at great risk," she said.

"Eeeeethaaaan! Eeeeethaaaan!"

"Oh my God. It's Sidney," I said. "Do you think she sees the skiff?"

"Lord I hope not."

"Eeeeethaaaan!"

"How can you stand that?"

"Morrrrrgaaaan! Morrrrrgaaaan!"

"Perfect," Morgan huffed. "My dad's teamed up with Sidney. Shit."

I looked at Morgan, astonished again.

The stretched, mournful sounds of our names sailed toward us over the dunes like Gloucester wives lullabying overdue fisherman on the Grand Banks.

"What's with all the cuss words, Morgan? That's not like you at all."

"Hee, hee. So, let me guess, we're going to the Secret Spot, right?"

"That's my librarian. Always getting right to the point. Yes. And maybe Fisherman's Island, too. We have to make sure Captain Shelby really knows what he's dealing with here."

"*Fisherman's Island?*"

"I'll explain later. Unfasten that bow line Miss Olinsworth."

Morgan smiled a pernicious smile. I'm not sure I ever felt more bonded to her again than in the chilly, gurgling throat of that surreal afternoon, a fine Pelican Bay day, as Morgan would have said, "going to the shitter."

We made our way back out to the mouth of the channel under a quickly blackening sky, our skiff now tossed about on the growing waves like a boat in an angry sea battle simulation.

Morgan's eyes, constantly on me, were filled with fear and wonder and a sort of jaded innocence as she clung to the bow, her rain hood tightened about her pastel face. All I could see were those eyes. Everything in the world to me in those dangerous moments. I felt like I was invading a part of her that had never been invaded before, our scenario somehow the key that unlocked the fortress to her quivering soul.

"Hang on. We're about halfway there," I yelled. The sky yelled back, making the pitiable intermittent roar of our engine, drowning and then saving itself, over and over again, an infant compared to the paternal roar of the caving black sky. "Once we make it to the Secret Spot and head toward Fisherman's Island, the weather will ease off us a bit."

"I hope," Morgan said with her lips instead of with any sound I could detect over the chorus of natural enemies all around us. I felt that I could have communicated telepathically, with her and the doomsday sky and the flailing sea.

And that is when the worst thing that could have happened, happened.

Our little motor failed.

"Oh my God, Ethan! What's wrong?"

"It's not fuel. I checked that before we left. The motor's got to be flooded with seawater."

"Shit."

"Shit."

Our skiff began riding the scoffing waves immediately toward the salivating, snarling rocks. Morgan covered her face with her hands and screamed. I screamed down deep in my soul, felt myself saying goodbye. But I found the wherewithal to whisper perhaps a ridiculous final prayer.

Captain, if you can hear me, if you're who I really think you are, please save us. You're all we have left. Please. Hear me now. Hear me greatest grandfather of the sea. Greatest grandfather of my life.

I looked out toward the Secret Spot as we neared the grim reaper rocks, looked out like an outlaw with a rope about his neck sweeping the horizon for his cowboy gang.

But there was no boat. Nothing. No ancient, dark knight of the sea.

Morgan and I said goodbye to each other in the beginning with our eyes, as the first rock pierced our fragile hull, and then with our bodies, as our skiff began to break in two and frantically fill with chilly dark seawater. The sky grumbled louder, as if a sadistic god laughing from its gut at a pre-written human comedy.

"I love you," I said. "Whatever happens, don't let go of me."

"Okay," Morgan said.

The sea around us reddened fiercely. "It's me," I shouted. "A rock has my right leg."

And then Morgan was lifted into the air, right out of my arms.

I thought that she was being spared the rabid fangs of the rocks, an atrocious death, and being taken early to heaven by a commiserating angel. I would have chosen that for my next prayer had I had time to think about anything at all except for Morgan's horrible expression and the nippy sea and certain death and my right leg, which ached dully, suddenly now not seeming to hurt as much as it should.

Yes, it was as if Morgan just flew away.

And then so did I, but not before I could see the rawhide face and sparkling blue eyes and the thick arms of the ocean's greatest

grandfather.
　Oh, Captain.
　You did come after all.

CHAPTER THIRTY-TWO

"Don't move, me Son. 'Tis dangerous, I say. Ye should be after takin' a rúm fer a right while."

"He's right, Ethan," Morgan said. "You're going to need a lot of stitches."

"*Stiches* ye say, me ducky?"

Morgan looked at the old man with both deep fear and a child's wonder, perhaps an anthropologist regarding a great Viking who had traversed back through time. She was sitting on the edge of the little stinky bunk that I had lain in not along ago. I never would have foreseen this moment. Not in a million years.

"*Stiches*? Ha! Here, drink this, me Son."

"Ethan, I—" Morgan nervously started.

"It's okay, Morgan. Trust me, okay?"

"Yer girlfriend's nerves always be so crooked?"

"Yeah," I giggled, wincing a bit.

"Take a rúm, me Son. Take a rúm now. Yer feelin' pain. 'Tis good. Means yer alive."

I drank the whole cup down with the faith of a child. Morgan stared wide-eyed. It was just as viscous as the last drink the old man had given me, but sour and tangy and unpleasantly mealy. And I did not sleep this time. But I did smile. The smile of a little boy.

"Go on! Me Son's on the mend already!"

"Yes, Captain. I don't hurt at all anymore."

Morgan was astonished. "Thank you," she said demurely.

"Ha!" The captain laughed from down deep—could have been the world's soul shifting.

We all laughed together. So cathartic. Such a surreal, impossibly anticipated moment. I'll never forget it as long as I live.

"Yer all lucky I came along." The old man's voice had changed. It was ominous and pensive. "What were ye after?"

"Captain, you're in serious trouble," I said.

"He's right," Morgan said, nodding her head slowly.

The old fisherman regarded her with swirling oceanic eyes, tempestuous sea globes spun by God. She looked away immediately and cleared her throat uncomfortably.

"There always be trouble on the land, but the headless army always runs away when the goings get rough."

"Captain, they've charged you with the murder of Henry Langstone," I said.

"*Langstone*, eh? Ha! A family of cowards, I say."

"This is really serious."

"Go on boy."

"Captain, I'm not fooling around here. They could capture and hurt you. They're also going to charge you with the murder of Sheriff Mortimers." The old man's fantastic eyes augmented just a little. "And it won't be long before Pete's family gets involved. You know he's the nephew of Captain Langsley who lives in Lighthouse Point."

"*Captain* be a right generous title fer he."

"We're sure there's going to be a lynch mob," Morgan said quietly.

The old man seemed to go inside himself for a moment. His reptilian eyelids closed and his eyes busied themselves, as if he were a marine god remaking the universe into nothing but endless sea.

"Enough! Me nerves be tested with all this!" the old man bellowed coarsely. Morgan and I both shuddered. We could have just awakened a terrible mummy of the sea. "Ye both mean well, but ye have said yer fill. Me understands what be at stake more than ye know. I'm takin' ye back to where ye belong now."

"No! I want to be here with you!" I shouted like a child.

"Oh me nerves! Me nerves!" The old fisherman's boat rocked and the sky grumbled in the distance. "There be nothin' more ye can do for me now. Sidney's nerves be right contrary over thee, me Son, and Charles be callin' for thee too, me ducky."

"I know," Morgan almost whispered.

"Besides, 'tis right dangerous for ye out here. This mob ye be talkin' bout will be sharks after blood, and when sharks eat they be like pigs chompin' after this and that. They'll never find me, but hid away hardly means forgotten. I may not see ye for a good while."

The captain looked away sadly. I wanted to cry. And I did.

Morgan looked at me compassionately as the old man left the cabin. A moment or so later his one-lunger coughed and belched and his boat jerked to life. Then there was that beautiful singing descending from the bridge like a prehistoric pacifying angel.

Laura lie, Laura lie, in the sea barley, in the sea barley—

"What is that?" Morgan asked, her face pleasantly baffled. "It's so beautiful."

"That's the old man singing," I said, wiping my tears away.

"It doesn't even sound like him."

"I know."

When we came out of the jagged pass from the Secret Spot the weather had already begun to clear. Dusk was imminent and a giant moon rose over Pelican Bay, illuminating a few beaten cottages, one of them mine. I could picture Sidney sitting at our breakfast table with a cup of Earl Gray, quietly weeping.

Poor Sidney.

The old man turned off his one-lunger and came down from the bridge, anchoring out of view of Pelican Bay's docks. "Yer mob's already formin', methinks," he lightly growled, looking through a tarnished-brass telescope that could have been the property of a pirate of yore.

"Can I see?" I asked.

"Here ye go."

There was a group of people all along the docks, and official-looking boats prepping to go out, one of them a police boat. *Gull Bay Police*, I thought. There were also several men in uniforms. I could not make out any faces at all.

"How are we going to get in there without them seeing Captain Shelby's boat?" Morgan asked.

The captain looked out that way and scratched his chin. His whiskers appeared as white as his eyes blue. "He who travels widely needs his wits about him."

I laughed.

Morgan wrung her hands with worry.

The old man reached into a storage bin and pulled out an old life raft. "Get on the go, me Son. Help me blow this up. I got me old foot peddle pump round here somewhere, methinks."

"Ethan, you should be lying down resting," Morgan said.

"It doesn't hurt at all."

"Let me see it. Oh my God. That's impossible." Morgan held a hand over her mouth and I thought that she might faint right there on the spot.

The old fisherman and I chuckled and his Atlantic eyes seemed to light the deck like blue lightning bugs.

"When it be right dark, I'll leave ye near the beach to paddle safely fer shore."

"Sounds good, Captain."

"Thanks," Morgan said, sitting on a storage bin now and staring, mouth gaping, at my leg.

The old man and I looked at Morgan and we both chuckled again.

CHAPTER THIRTY-THREE

The young Coast Guard captain had regaled Deputy Dansby as well as the Gull Bay Post with his surreal tale. Soon, the official word unleashed on the bay area, like a rapidly creeping fog, was that Captain Shelby was a dangerous murderer who must be captured at all costs. And the fog metastasized like a sprawling, gray tumor into every beach cottage, every bar, and every town nook.

Within a day's time, a boat mob, now already out to sea, comprised of Deputy Dansby's police boat, a Lighthouse Point Coast Guard cutter, and almost a dozen nearby fishing boats, including Captain Langsley's, descended upon the hurly pass to the Secret Spot. They looked like a group of bull ants jostled about by a plummeting late August wind attempting to funnel into a small crack in a blue-gray wall.

Deputy Dansby was the first to arrive at the old man's boat, Captain Langsley tagging close behind. Captain Shelby's boat somehow remained remarkably still anchored near Fisherman's Island at the far side of the Secret Spot, despite a strong current.

Deputy Dansby incessantly warned the bigger boats over a crackling, trumpet-like CB radio not to come through. Too dangerous.

The sky was dark for noon.

A tempest was gathering her wits.

Deputy Dansby, much to his frightful dismay, could not anchor, in spite of the nearby shoreline, and had to moor his boat to the old man's. Captain Langsley fastened his boat to Deputy Dansby's. The boats looked like wooden Gullivers floating on their backs, arms intertwined.

"She looks deserted," Captain Langsley shouted out through cupped hands, "and unseaworthy."

"Yeah," the deputy shouted back, "hard to believe anyone could fish, let alone live, on this rotting stink of a barge."

"She don't even look safe to step on."

"You stay put and keep an eye out," the deputy called back. "Don't let those overeager townspeople rip up their boats coming through that channel. We took quite a scraping coming in as it is. Probably sustained hull damage."

"You got it."

Deputy Dansby climbed carefully over the side of the old man's pride and joy. His foot gave way on his first step onto the main deck, as if attempting to tread upon the desiccated bones of a long-abandoned house, stripped of its organs by termites centuries ago.

"Son of a bitch!" the deputy yelled, managing to stable himself. "Captain Shelby, I know you're in there. Come out now before anyone else gets hurt. We promise you a fair trial."

No answer.

"This has gone far enough. Come out with your hands up."

Still no answer.

"Deputy, maybe he ain't in there," Captain Langsley yelled. The deputy looked at him wildly.

"Now where the hell do you think he went?"

Captain Langsley looked down and back toward the boat mob through his binoculars, a brown mass bobbing at the mouth of the pass like a gang of crocodiles.

The deputy found some passable footing and trod cautiously to the main cabin. The main cabin door, the color of late fall leaves, seemed rusted shut.

"My God, this boat looks like it's been deserted for centuries. Maybe we've got the wrong one," the deputy yelled.

"Can't be, if you ask me," Captain Langsley hollered back. "That's got to be it. Seen her a few times in my day."

"I need your help here."

"I ain't stepping on there! Here, use this." Captain Langsley threw an old fishing gaff onto the main deck.

"Be careful with that! Geez! Bunch of weekend warriors!"

The deputy finally pried open the main cabin door. A life-altering stench of atrophied sea escaped, as if mythical sea bats trapped for unknown time in an old barrel. He covered his mouth. Muffled curses. The curses of a son of a son of a fisherman.

An old rag suddenly landed at the deputy's feet.

"Use that," Captain Langsley shouted. It had the breath of dead squid, which quite miraculously was French perfume next to the malodor of the old man's house.

"Thanks."

The deputy took a deep breath, covered his mouth and nose with the rag, and stuck his head inside the cabin. He removed his head within a few seconds, sucking in the rejuvenating, profoundly salty air of the Secret Spot, blood gradually returning to his face like a large child just exiting a scary ride.

"Guess he ain't there?"

Deputy Dansby looked up at Captain Langsley.

And cursed again.

"Do you think he could be on that island over there?" Captain Langsley asked.

Deputy Dansby looked over toward the island. It had a low fog surrounding it, perhaps a protective spell cast by Calypso herself. Under the gloomy sky, a swelling surf beat the shore. The land resembled the primordial lost island from the movie, *King Kong*.

"I'll tell you what's on that island right there," the deputy hollered back. "Nothing. Absolutely nothing. And after that, nothing but the Atlantic, and then Europe. Do you want to go to Europe?"

Captain Langsley regarded the deputy with the oddest expression. "You don't have to be sarcastic about it."

"What?" the deputy said, now climbing back onto his police boat and walking over near the captain.

"I said you don't have to be sarcastic about it!"

"Look, I've got bigger fish to fry. There's a lynch boat mob out there. Or hadn't you noticed?"

"That son of a bitch killed my nephew, Pete Langsley."

"That kid who died in the quick sand? How do you know it was Captain Shelby?"

"I just know. And he killed your sheriff, too. Or have you forgotten that?"

"There's a proper procedure for doing these things. You go taking the law into your own hands, like those damn weekend warriors out there ready to kill themselves and each other going through that pass, and all hell breaks loose. You hear me? All hell breaks loose! Haven't we had enough deaths and accidents already?"

"I'll tell you what, Deputy, you can stay here and do your paperwork while I go check out that island. Deal?"

"Now who's getting sarcastic?"

"This is America. That's right, America, and I'm going to check out that island and there's not a damn thing you can do about it," Captain Langsley said.

A surprising sudden rogue gust of wind ripped around Fisherman's Island and took Captain Langsley's hat right off, twirling it out to sea.

The captain watched it, amazed, and then looked blank-faced at the deputy. Black clouds had gathered all around them now and the sky flashed as though ridiculing Captain Langsley. Fierce rumblings followed that seemed to shake all three boats still moored together.

Deputy Dansby looked at the sky. "Good luck," he said.

"If you think I'm going to let some bad weather keep me from bringing that crazy old geezer to justice, you've got another thing coming!"

"You can make a citizen's arrest, but that's all. There'll be no vigilantism. This isn't the old west."

The deputy suddenly raced inside his bridge and yelled into his radio, *"You hear that? Anyone who kills Captain Shelby will have to answer to me! You stay back out of that channel, too, or so help me! We're going to do this by the book. We're here to bring this man in within the law."*

The deputy went out on deck again. "We're going to have justice, but not your kind, you crazy fool."

A lightning bolt struck frightfully out on the sea, perhaps a God-made exclamation point to the deputy's last sentence. Both men looked at it, and hearing even louder thunder now, looked bellicosely at each other.

Captain Langsley quickly undid the mooring line and went to his bridge to fire up his engine.

"I'm watching you!" the deputy yelled one last time. Before untying his mooring line to Captain Shelby's boat, the deputy took out a small notepad and made notes, looking with almost wild eyes at the stinking wreck of a fishing boat. *How on earth does he get around in that thing? Un-goddamned believable. It just flies in the face of all common sense.*

Captain Langsley had already made it to the other side of the mysterious island, the waves now lashing at his fishing boat, lightning bolts in the near distance electrocuting the sea into violent surges.

Deputy Dansby anchored just off the shore of Fisherman's Island where the wind was the least fierce. He got on his radio again.

"Attention everyone. Now hear this. This is Deputy Dansby. We have a serious weather situation here, with more severe weather coming in. From the look of the seas and the weather reports out of Gull Bay, we may have another tropical storm on our hands by this afternoon. I'm asking everyone, for your own safety, to turn back now. We'll continue our search for Captain Shelby when the weather clears. Captain Langsley, that includes you, too! Over and out."

The deputy waited a good while but Captain Langsley's fishing boat did not come out from around the other side of Fisherman's Island to head back toward the craggy pass.

And the deputy had to go after Captain Langsley.

His police boat, though new and proud and strong, was no match for the rising waves around Fisherman's Island that began to beat the shore like ferocious liquid wolves.

He turned the next corner of the island too closely and became stuck in a strange dark sand bar, his engine gurgling and screaming and kicking but propelling him nowhere, as if stuck in the Devil's Mud.

He turned off his engine and walked around the deck of his boat, being blown here and there, spat in the face by a pitiless sea. He felt the odd sensation of the boat sinking into the sand and his face went blank and white suddenly. *Tidal quick sand.* Oh he had heard of it before during his tenure on and around the sea, heard about Pete's accident, but it did not seem quite real until now.

As his splendid navy blue and white police boat began to sink lower and lower, he caught a sight about a few hundred feet away that tattooed his consciousness forever. A man, stout, appearing in his early thirties, muscular, deeply tanned, curly black hair billowing in the wind, utterly nude, stood in the sea just off the shore bathing. Though the waves sprayed him, towered him, jabbed and punched at him, he remained as still as the Rock of Gibraltar.

A numbness started on top of the deputy's head and trickled its way down, soaking him from head to toe, a giant egg filled with every question ever asked by humankind cracked over his skull.

The police boat was now taking sea.

She was gone.

Deputy Dansby grabbed the radio and changed to the channel that he and Captain Langsley had reserved just for them.

"Captain Langsley, Captain Langsley, come in Captain Langsley. Mayday, mayday. On the northeast side of the island, caught in sinking sand, taking water. Mayday, mayday."

He turned and looked again out his bridge window at the young bathing man. The man had the look of a Greek god, so magically commanding in appearance.

Soon the young bathing man turned his head and set his eyes upon the deputy. His eyes were fluorescent blue, tiny lighthouse bulbs burning wistfully against the black sky and sea. Stoically stolid amidst the crashing sea about him, he may have been a human lighthouse composed by the heavens. The deputy's innards seized, froze. He could not stop staring now, perhaps unable to wake from some life-altering dream. The young bathing man flashed his glowing teal orbs and shook his head slowly at the deputy.

Sea began to seep into the bridge, and Deputy Dansby's face must have carried the look of utter defeat of all the past sinking captains of the Atlantic. He grabbed a Gull Bay Police Sea Survival Kit and strapped it on his back. He also pocketed a flare gun and two signal flares and left the bridge of his police boat. He looked to his left for the young bathing man again, but he was gone. The deputy could not decide, which was more spine-tingling, succumbing to tidal quick sand during a raging tropical storm, or the sudden absence of the mysterious bathing man.

The deputy now stood almost up to his knees in seawater. He looked around one last time for Captain Langsley's boat.

Nothing.

The police boat took another sudden drop into the quick sand below.

As he rushed to abandon ship, he looked out to sea and saw a rogue wave approaching that was as tall as a house. There was no time to think. He turned and quickly grabbed onto the side of the boat. He felt the great wave hit his back, his fingers rip loose from the railing, and a thick, bludgeoning blow to his head. He moved quickly through the sea, sensing the undulating throat of the wave swallow and then spit him forward like a mammoth underwater dinner guest bursting into laughter.

CHAPTER THIRTY-FOUR

The dreams that the deputy had were of the gritty, limy taste of primitive sea and sand, the gin and tonic of the sea gods, and of being dragged from here to eternity through sand and mud and pine needles like the half-dead carcass of a hunted castaway.

He awoke the following dawn deeply confused about where he was. He peered around at four walls of island wood and mud, a malodor swimming up his nostrils that he dared not name, and the sound of heavy winds around and above, great pines holler-whispering frantic operas. The right side of his head ached and pounded like an overbeaten native drum.

"My police boat."

"Yer crooked skip be in the sea's bowels now." The scraggly voice seemed to emanate from nowhere and from everywhere.

"What? Who's that? Oh my God. Captain Shelby."

"'Tis me."

"You dragged me here? Why?"

"I'm not what ye think I be."

"And what's that?"

"Thee be a fair man, but don't test me."

"Lord, what's that smell?"

"Don't be after questions ye can't weather the answers to."

"Can you at least tell me where I am?"

"Thee be in the center of Fisherman's Island. Yer safe till the storm thinks I not be safe."

"What?"

Captain Shelby laughed and so did the deputy's bones. "Keep yer rúm. I made some coffee. That's what ye islanders round here be drinkin', eh?"

"That would be fine," the deputy said foggily, sitting up in his bed, a cot beautifully woven out of marsh grass and covered with half-moth-eaten charcoal-colored blankets. He eyed the old man suspiciously as he brought him coffee served in a meager cup that was made of hopelessly turned brass. He could not believe how old Captain Shelby looked.

"Thank you."

"Go on," the old man said, his eyes laughing, azure blue in the cabin, which was dimly lit by a lugubriously sputtering lantern.

Two souls riding out another storm.

Looking at the old fisherman's eyes, a terrible realization grabbed the deputy.

"What yer mind be after? Ye look as if ye seen a ghost."

"I saw something—impossible—before my boat went completely under, but—"

The old man cackled. "But what?"

"Nothing. Why are you helping me, anyway?"

"Thee be a fair man, not like them others out there who be after seein' me hanged."

"I think you misunderstand me. My obligation is to the law, to bringing you in to stand trial," the deputy said, looking at his empty gun holster and patting his empty pockets. "Besides, we don't hang people in this century."

The old man laughed again. "Yer goods be in safe keepin'. Ye can have 'em back when ye head back to where ye belong."

"And where do I belong?"

"Not here in this place. And mind yer crookedness."

Silence as the two men listened to the storm argue her case outside. The old man's magnificent eyes searched the deputy's soul like a lighthouse a worried sea. The deputy could not hold eye contact with the old man. But no one ever could. However, I would like to think that a man like Deputy Dansby held it a little longer than most.

I wrote a story for the Gull Bay Post a few years ago about a drifter who was arrested by the Gull Bay Police for forced entry and attempted rape of a young woman. The story was part of a series of articles I wrote about domestic violence. The man hung around the diner where the woman worked every day saying lewd things to her, eventually following her home one night. He asked to come in, and when she said no, he pushed his way in anyway.

Fortunately a neighbor witnessed the forced entry after hearing a scream and called the police. Deputy Dansby went out there, but the man, a smooth-talking out-of-work fisherman from Massachusetts, told the deputy that she was his girlfriend now and that "she liked it rough." He also said, "You know how woman can be." The girl did not say anything, only nodded sheepishly.

I think that most police officers would have let that one alone, but Deputy Dansby, in my interview with him, told me that he felt that something was wrong. He said that he sensed an abuse or blackmail scenario at play and apprehended the man on the spot. Once the drifter was arrested, it came up in his record that he had been charged previously with several counts of battery and the attempted rape of a Connecticut woman.

"There are several murder charges against you," the deputy finally managed. "Doubtless the boy warned you somehow."

"What?"

"I know all about it."

"Go on."

"Be careful. He could end up being charged as an accomplice."

"Mind yer tone ye silver-tongued scopie!" the old fisherman roared, standing up. His eyes began to swell and shimmer, cresting waves in an afternoon sun. The deputy was utterly silenced.

"I'm not here to harm you in any way," the deputy began again, his voice and demeanor gentler like the eye of the storm outside now.

The old fisherman said nothing.

"I'm only here to bring you back to stand trial."

"Ha! *Trial* ye say? For what? Charges that ye concocted on yer own? Besides, even if I was after *standin' trial*, as ye say, I couldn't be that long on land."

"Why not?"

"Yer a good soul, but ye haven't learned yet that questions be not the way to some things."

"Well, pretty soon it's not going to matter anyway."

"Yer cleverness will snare ye in crooked ways, son. Yer right young. Chased things like thee in me youth till me learned the ways of the land matter not before the ways of the sea."

"You speak in riddles."

The captain laughed loudly again.

"Go ahead and laugh," the deputy went on, piercing the old fisherman with eyes suddenly flashing with courageous defiance. "Once the lynch mob gets through it will all be over."

The old man stopped laughing immediately and turned his eyes on the deputy.

The deputy shrank in his cot.

"*Lynch mob* ye say?"

"Yes, waiting just outside the channel. At least a dozen boats. Once the storm clears and they come through and find your deserted boat, they'll be all over this island. I was just hoping to get you back to Gull Bay safely before those revenge-crazed nuts get a hold of you."

Silence.

"The land's notion of justice holds the worth of bait fiskr to me!" the old man finally rasped. The deputy shuddered. "Even if me sees fairness in yer warning, I don't live by yer ways."

"I was just trying to—"

"Stop yer crookedness! Ye be—"

"Captain Shelby, if you're in there, come out with your hands up. We have the place surrounded."

The deputy recognized the voice as Captain Langsley's. He and Captain Shelby locked eyes in the frail light. The old fisherman's eyes churned in great calculation.

"We're also armed," Captain Langsley yelled. "No more funny business. This all ends now."

Roaring gusts of wind suddenly began to whip up and slam like fists against the outside walls. Thunder like the sound of commercial jets crashing exploded outside.

Suddenly the room went completely black save for Captain Shelby's glowing eyes.

"I've been right fair with thee," the old man whispered in the balmy darkness, the sound of dead marsh grass chafing in protest of high tide.

"He's not going to go away," the deputy whispered back loudly. "He thinks you murdered his nephew, Pete Langsley."

The thatch door was suddenly opened. Captain Langsley stood in the doorway holding a lantern in one hand with a discoing flame inside, and a cocked revolver in the other hand. Flashes of lightning illuminated the intruder's face, lending him a gaunter, younger appearance. His grayish hair twisted in the wind like the slithering snakes of a male Medusa. "I know you're in there you crazy old fool."

A grizzly laugh emanated from the corner of the room. "Rash is he who at unknown doors relies on his good luck. Go ahead and do what yer after, but be warned of heroes who may enchant thee or turn warriors into hogs."

"Enough of your foolish gibber-gabber!" Captain Langsley shouted against the din of the conspiring winds and now pelting rain. He lifted and aimed his revolver, his legs beginning to feel like saltwater taffy before the awe of the old fisherman's eyes, his shooting arm wavering in the swooshes of wind racing around the room.

"No!" Deputy Dansby yelled, running in front of the old man and putting his palms up. "Not like this!"

But the shot had already been fired. And the old man sat down and was silent.

"That is enough!" the deputy shouted, reaching for Captain Langsley's weapon. "You've done enough!"

As Captain Langsley and Deputy Dansby struggled over the gun, Langsley's lantern crashed to the ground and old pine needles caught fire, snapping and popping like boxing ring hecklers. They petered out quickly under the yoke of descending wet wind gusts.

And then a wind with the moan of a thousand freight trains came, snapping trees across the island like King Kong wading through the wild forest to claim his wrist-tied beauty. The old man let out a wounded laugh.

"Stop it! Give me that before you hurt someone else!" the deputy cried. "I'm placing you under arrest."

"Over my dead—"

The first tree split the cabin in two, its branches knocking the fighting men to the floor, the gun sounding another bullet that was dampened immediately. The second tree sent roof and wall falling on top of them. They did not move. The winds swirled and crooned and howled above them in victory song, the thick, maniacal rain providing the ceaseless snare drum roll.

The old fisherman stood up slowly and tossed the debris of his ancient island home aside. He remained stoically stolid amidst nature's chaos, his surreal eyes surveying the damage. He opened his sea coat and betook the black hole in his midsection for a moment. He rolled his grandiose eyes. "Oh me nerves," he grunted. "Look at me spor."

He walked over to where the two men had been buried, and began lifting away debris. As soon as he lifted a piece he would simply release his fingers and his fierce brotherly wind would rip it away out to sea. He could have been an old man discarding scraps and the wind and sea hungry dogs snatching them away.

When he reached the first man, he rolled him over on his back. Captain Langsley. Underneath lay the deputy, unconscious, a bloody shotgun wound near his sternum. "Me dear God, why do the good ones be right unlucky?" he grumbled under his breath. "Must it always be so?"

Captain Langsley opened his eyes and looked at the old man, stunned, horrified. The old man quickly placed his heel on Captain Langsley's neck.

"Well, will ye be finishin' what ye were after? Or are ye too yellow-bellied now?"

Captain Langsley tried to rise up but the old man pressed harder with his heel, which made him surrender a pitiable choking sound. "The beach swallowed yer swarthy young blood after he bothered things better left alone. Seems meddlin' and dull wits run in yer line."

Captain Langsley made a final desperate reach for the fallen gun and the old fisherman pushed down with his heel one last time.

CHAPTER THIRTY-FIVE

The deputy's next conscious memory was of being held by that mystifying young man that he'd seen bathing in the ocean the day before.

Captain Shelby sat on the shore with Deputy Dansby's head in his lap, letting the waves roll over them. It was already past mid-day. The weather had begun to clear and the sun, similar to the deputy's struggling will to live, burned iridescently behind gray clouds that the lighter wind now, in cahoots with the sun, shooed away. Gulls had returned to the sky and their proud squawks filled the deputy's heart with a last mainstay of hope.

Deputy Dansby knew little of mythology but what he did know in that strange moment was that if the Greek gods were real, Captain Shelby fit his image of one. As he looked up at the face above him, trying to focus his vision, he saw eyes the color of the Aegean Sea, plentiful coiled hair as black as volcanic sand, and a face chiseled by Leonardo da Vinci himself.

"Who are you?" the deputy finally managed weakly.

"It matters not who I be, but that thee be. In me long and tired travels, good souls like thee be like black pearls." Captain Shelby was cupping the encroaching sea and pouring it over the deputy's wound.

"I think it's too late for that. It's my time."

"No one knows a man's time save for God and the sea."

"Let me die."

"Trust in the sea, son. Trust in her. She flows through all our veins."

Captain Shelby betook the deputy's round, kind face and sad, dark eyes and then looked out to sea.

"They'll be coming through the pass now and swarming this island," the deputy said, coughing up blood. "There's no time for this. Save yourself. They'll kill you."

"Me thought you were after bringin' me in to stand trial."

"I know now why you can't stand trial. And I also know you didn't mean to kill anybody."

"I can't leave thee. Ye saved me before."

"Saved you before? But Langsley still shot you." The deputy turned his head, wincing, and looked at Captain Shelby's wound that had shrunk to the size of only a quarter now.

"Richard, ye saved me in a time long before this time."

The shrill sound of the Lighthouse Point Police boat siren seemed to harmonize with some crying gulls flying near them.

Sheriff Langstone saw the two men on the shore through his binoculars and as his boat approached Fisherman's Island, he shouted into his megaphone. "Whoever you are, pull the deputy ashore and remain there. You're under investigation by the L.P.P.D. We have the island completely contained and all suspects will be apprehended."

Captain Shelby looked up and down the island's coast and he could see many boats approaching now.

"If you have a place to hide, go now! That's Henry Langstone's cousin. If he figures out who you are, he'll kill you on the spot."

The young fisherman continued scooping and pouring seawater onto the deputy's wound and began singing.

Laura lie, Laura lie, in the sea barley, in the sea barley—

The deputy suddenly felt careless and resigned and lay his head back.

Sheriff Langstone anchored his police boat and jumped into the sea, sloshing his way to shore. He was a tall and slim man in his late thirties with salt-and-pepper hair, scalpel eyes, and a pointy nose. Meticulousness and fastidiousness seemed to dominate his gate. He took out his revolver and held it in front of him with his right hand, cupping it with his left.

Other boats on either side also began to anchor.

"Stay where you are! Let him be!"

"As ye wish," the young fisherman said, laying down the deputy in the shallow sea.

"Put your hands where I can see them."

"Eh," the fisherman said, lightly chuckling.

"You think this is funny? Who are you? Tell me!"

"Captain Shelby."

"Captain Shelby? But that can't be. Are you his grandson?"

"Thee be as simple-minded as yer cousin, I see."

"What?"

"'Tis me, Captain Shelby himself."

"You son of a bitch," the sheriff said. "I ought to kill you right where you sit."

"Get on the go. If ye have the nerve."

"And I'll be a witness," the deputy yelled out, suddenly regaining some strength.

"Deputy Dansby. You've been shot."

"It's a long story. Anyway, you do this by the book or as long as I draw breath you'll never wear a badge again."

Two Coast Guard men from Lighthouse Point walked up now on the right, and two Gull Bay fisherman splashing through the breaking sea in waders approached on the left.

"Better make that five witnesses," the deputy added.

Captain Shelby grinned.

"Stand up!" the sheriff hollered. "Turn around, you murdering son of a bitch."

"Sheriff Langstone, I hate to rain on your parade," one of the fisherman said, "but that's not Captain Shelby."

"Is that Captain Shelby or not?" the sheriff blew at Deputy Dansby, who was now sitting up, color returning to his face.

The deputy looked at Captain Shelby briefly, his expression betraying nothing discernible. "No," he said.

"Then what the hell was he doing here with you?"

"Trying to save me. In fact, as far as I'm concerned, this man's a hero."

"A hero? Bullshit!" the sheriff yelled. "And I think you're full of shit, too. What, you think I'm a goddamned idiot or something? You don't think I've heard about your soft police work down there in Gull Bay? Sissy." The sheriff's deputy came slopping up from behind. "Deputy, cuff that man."

"But—sir—that's not Captain Shelby."

Both the young fisherman and the deputy laughed together.

"I don't care! He's still a suspect. And cuff Deputy Dansby, too."

"What?" Deputy Dansby yelled out. "I'll see you pay for this!"

Captain Shelby and Deputy Dansby were taken to the Lighthouse Point Police boat and thrown in the small brig beneath the bridge. The police boat immediately headed back for Lighthouse Point. The other boats stayed surrounding Fisherman's Island and continued their search for the old man.

After news of the missing Captain Langsley filtered out, other boats had come from as far south as Charleston and as far north as Rocky Island. A reward of $25,000 for any information leading to the arrest of Captain Shelby was announced by the L.P.P.D.

"You're not going to make it." Deputy Dansby said. "Look at your hands."
"The lame runs if he has to."
"You saved my life."
"Eh. And thee mine."
"I don't remember that."
"'Tis in yer soul, son. 'Tis in yer soul."
They were silent as they listened to the scraping and pounding of the channel rocks thrashing the hull of the boat.
"We need a plan. I'm not going to let you die in jail. You belong to the sea."
"Thee be a good man, but I don't see what ye can do fer me now."
"You just wait until the G.B.P.D. finds out about my arrest. I'll be out of here with the shake of a lamb's tail."
"Go on." The rapidly aging fisherman chuckled softly.

The police boat stopped just north of Pelican Bay to fuel up. Sheriff Langstone came down to the brig for a moment. He looked into the small cell. "Oh my God. It's impossible," he said.
"Ye been hypnotized by the ways of the land," the old man weakly bellowed.
"He's sick and needs medical attention," Deputy Dansby said.
"What's that horrible smell. How can you stand that?"
"The stink of a coward be worse than a thousand lepers."
The deputy laughed.
"Is it leprosy that's making him that way? Why, he's not even the same man."
"Could it be idiocy that makes thee look so crooked?"
The deputy laughed again.
"Where's Captain Langsley?"
"It will all be in my report—the report that's going to end your career."
"Ha, ha, ha. Look, Captain Langsley's son has been calling on the radio every five damn minutes."
"He's dead. He was in an old cabin at the center of that island when fallen trees from the storm collapsed it. He's blown halfway to Europe by now."
"Oh," the sheriff said, not able to take his eyes off of the old fisherman.
"Why are his eyes like that?"

"Why yer eyes be so dull and cowardly?"

"I'll be damned. That is Captain Shelby, isn't it?"

"Ha! And what if I be?"

"Sheriff, you want justice for Henry's death, right? Captain Shelby's going to die any minute here unless you get him medical attention. You hear me? He won't be able to stand trial. It's your moral and constitutional duty to get him help. He has rights!"

"I'm not listening to this!"

"Sheriff, the boat's all filled up," his deputy said, coming down and standing in front of the little cell. "Oh my God. What's that?"

"It's Captain Shelby," the sheriff said.

"It can't be!" his deputy cried.

"Look, if you don't get him to Pelican Bay Hospital, he's going to die. Is that how you want it? He needs special fluids."

"Jesus Christ," the sheriff said. "All right. Let's get him out of there. But you. You can stay."

"For what?" Deputy Dansby cried.

"For obstructing justice."

"You just wait till I get out of here!" Deputy Dansby yelled, standing up. His face was a crimson red. The old fisherman looked at him omnisciently, soothingly, and he sat back down again, huffing.

The sheriff's deputy escorted the old man out of the cell. His eyes had dimmed to a dull blue-black. His gate was sluggish and his face and skin exponentially wrinkled. His once glorious Apollo black hair was now limp and platinum white.

As the sheriff's deputy went to close the cell door, Deputy Dansby suddenly stood up again, lowered his head, and charged like a human bull. The iron-barred cell door hit the deputy in the face and knocked him backward to the floor. Sheriff Langstone drew his revolver and the deputy charged him next. Captain Shelby reached out with his leathery hand, throwing the sheriff's hand off aim. A shot fired and ricocheted like a thousand thoughts riddling a philosopher's mind. Deputy Dansby continued his charge and took the sheriff to the ground as they fought for the gun.

The sheriff's deputy stood now and drew his pistol. Before he could say a word, the old man was before him, moving without seeming to move. The deputy jumped back. The old man's eyes lit up and swirled and he whispered to him, "When the glacier sees the rising spring sun, it weeps."

The deputy suddenly dropped the gun, sank to the floor, curled up, and began to blubber uncontrollably.

"Run! I got this!" Deputy Dansby cried from the floor, still struggling with the sheriff.

The old man bent down and picked up the sheriff's deputy's pistol, looking at it. "'Tis a coward's weapon," he croaked. "'Twas made fer a coward's death."

"Get out of here!" Deputy Dansby shouted again.

Captain Shelby walked over and placed the barrel of the pistol against the sheriff's head and the struggle instantly ceased. The sheriff's deputy continued weeping vehemently.

"Do it and you'll spend the rest of your geriatric life swimming to Europe," the sheriff said.

Deputy Dansby stood up now, pointing the sheriff's gun. "I told you. I got this," he said.

"How do I thank thee for what ye done?"

"You already have. There's an old story in our family going back to our first settling days about a fisherman who saved Richard Dansby's life in an attack by Indians. I never really put it together that it was you till we were on the beach. But I think I've always known. Now go on, get out of here."

The old fisherman smiled, and like a rogue gust of wind, was gone.

CHAPTER THIRTY-SIX

After the old fisherman had disappeared, Deputy Dansby surrendered of his own free will and was arrested and charged by the L.P.P.D. for aiding and abetting a felon.

The news quickly spread about Captain Shelby's escape and the death of Captain Langsley. Although Captain Shelby was never formally charged with the murder of Captain Langsley, it was widely believed that he somehow caused his death. What followed was the most vicious manhunt in the history of the area. They left his disintegrating fishing boat where it lay, for it was too dangerous to try and tow it out, but they continued to comb the nearby bays relentlessly, even many miles of outlying Atlantic Ocean, for the old man, dead or alive.

They still found nothing.

I missed the old man. I did not blame him for the deaths of Sheriff Mortimers or Captain Langsley. Perhaps they went where they should not have gone, bringing inevitable doom upon themselves. But I blamed myself for the accidental deaths of Henry and Pete. Since their passing, a question surfaced, which may plague me for the rest of my life. If we feed people to our pet lion, is the lion guilty?

I thought a lot about something that the old man always told me, that "the summer moments always pass quickly." I also thought about all that he did to win me my librarian.

A few days after the news of Captain Shelby's capture and escape, I proposed to Morgan on the beach, at sunset, reciting a poem that I had written just for the occasion. Somehow in my heart, in my soul, I felt sure that the old man could hear my words, that he was somewhere close by listening, chuckling, his eyes glimmering blue coals, smiling the proud smile of an ancient grandfather.

Morgan, morning, tomorrow, the pinnacle of my deepest joy and sorrow. I quake under your yoke of reticence and obeisance to words, shatter into a million fragments that form stars in the teal sky of your eyes, and would plummet to lost depths without the virginal paleness of your face. Without you I am a writer without a novel. Oh Morgan, marry me and save me from being nothing.

Morgan laughed at me and did not answer for days, as if she had forgotten the question.

Friday, however, a late summer night shedding its balminess, its brown cheek slowly paling before the breath of early fall, Morgan succumbed to a long, deep kiss, followed by an incinerating moment of passion, akin to falling from a plane in a hug, and whispered yes—more spoken by the Pelican Bay wind than by her.

Morgan and I were set to be married that October.

On Monday morning, around eight a.m., she called me, hysterical.
"Ethan!"
"What, Morgan? Calm down. Take it easy."
"He's here!"
"Who?"
"Nereus."
"What do you mean? There with you?"
"That puddle of seawater is back!"
"Where are you now?"
"At home. I ran home after I smelled it. I was just opening up, and—oh, Ethan!"
"Okay, hush now. Let's not jump to conclusions. We have had some heavy rain and winds the past few days."
"I checked for leaks again. Nothing. And the puddle's even smellier this time, with little puddles all along the book aisles. Ethan, I know it's him!"
"I don't get it. He's been gone for over a week. Even though they're still patrolling up and down the coast, they're about to give up on the search and declare him lost at sea. Why would he come back now?"
"He's Nereus. The actions of the gods are transparent to mortals."
"You still think he's a god?"
"Get over here now!"
"All right, all right. Let me get dressed. Geez."
"Thanks, Ethan."

When we entered the library, it was rancid with the sea, the worst that the odor had ever been. I found no leaks, either, and I began to investigate the puddle more closely.

"Morgan, what's under here?"

"I don't know. The ground."

"Real funny. I mean, does this library have a basement or crawl space of any kind?"

"Not that I'm aware of."

"Do you have something we could use to tear this carpet up with?"

"Tear the carpet up? Ethan, I do work here you know."

"All right. Forget it. You're the one that wanted me to check it out."

"Okay, okay, wait. Let's look in the back."

We found some heavy pieces of iron shelving, their sharp ends curling out like ancient, arthritic fingers. I made a crude incision in the carpet under the sea puddle, as though gutting a giant, capsized bottom-feeding fish. My hand was half-submerged in the slimy, malodorous fluid.

"Ethan, it stinks so much more than before. Why do you think that is?"

"I don't know."

I ripped up the carpet, revealing an almost black, fungus-covered wooden floor through the putrid seawater, similar to the back of a prehistoric ocean turtle at the bottom of the sea.

"Ethan, is that a handle?"

"It can't be."

It was.

I lifted the handle and pulled on it, but it would not budge.

"We need leverage. Bring me that thicker piece of shelving over there."

"Here you go."

The trap door creaked open, the seawater flooding the space below, as if the floor of the Atlantic were taking in a deep breath.

"Oh my God, Morgan, this looks like a tunnel of some kind!"

"This is how he's been coming in. Do you think he could be down there?"

"Well, there's only one way to find out."

I began to carefully climb down the ladder that groaned like Captain Shelby's fishing boat buoying in a grumpy harbor. Morgan followed.

"Where do you think it leads?"

"Near the beach, I'm sure," Morgan said, her tone suddenly becoming calm and scientific. "I'll bet this is where pirates sneaked in booty from falsely lured ships, a not uncommon practice of those times."

"How charming."

The flashlight peeks we stole at the tunnel walls that were lined with great black oak timbers and soft rock, combined with the dank earthy smells that enveloped us, made me feel like I was making love to South Carolina by candlelight.

Crouching slightly, we followed the tunnel to its end. We had crossed under Pelican Bay Street. The scent above of sun-dried oyster shells and stinking marsh waltzed together in our nostrils.

"Where's the exit?" Morgan asked.

I shone the flashlight upward and we could see an algae-colored tunnel trap door. There was a handle on it just like the one at the other end. It reminded me of a porthole to a rotted submarine, which had sunk a century ago and somehow moved through the earth's bowels like a 64-ounce steak.

"Morgan, we have to see where this ends up."

"Across from them dunes where yer librarian screamed that day like a crooked gull."

Morgan shrieked.

The old man's voice was more of a feeble growl now, the piteous roar of a lion stung by a hunter's bullet. It came from just behind us, off to the left, down a tunnel offshoot hidden by the underground darkness, as if the place from where Pelican Bay's black nights came.

I shone the flashlight in the direction of his deeply creased face, as wrinkled as the sole of an arched foot immersed under the sea over countless tides. His Atlantic eyes, always ageless, sparkled like brilliant blue diamonds. He reeked of the same smell as the puddle in the library.

"Captain, is that you?"

"Eh boy. 'Tis me."

"You don't look so good," I said, my voice breaking. Morgan had her hands over her face, fingers splayed just enough for her pale eyes to peer through. She looked as though she were watching her first horror film. The old man looked at her and chuckled—the sound of an old truck with its starter on the brink.

"Me days are numbered, me Son, unless ye can get me back to the sea. God knows I be too weak to make it on me own now. God may see fit fer me to die right here. Me old body be right crooked. Right crooked."

I began to cry.

"I love ye, me Son, but yer weepin' can't do me no good."

I glanced at Morgan. Her hands were now at her sides, an enigmatic look running away with her face.

I tried to gather myself.

"It might be dangerous to take you out of here."

"We can take him back through the library," Morgan said. "I have some old blankets we could wrap him in."

The old man's cracked face smiled without smiling, his seafaring eyes pointed toward her.

"Be much obliged, me ducky. Much obliged."

We both helped the old man back to the library entrance of the tunnel and up the ladder. I remember holding our breath most of the time lest the old man's stench might cause us to faint.

We sat him in a chair and covered him with the old blankets. He looked like an ancient turtle that had left its shell under the sea to come visit our town. Morgan brought him a cup of water, but his leathery hand was too weak to hold it.

"Try not to talk," I said.

"Happy is he who hath in himself the wisdom to make his final peace," the old man faintly groaned.

"You can tell us later, okay?"

"The summer moments always pass quickly, me Son."

"You need your strength."

"Morgan?"

"Yes?"

"Ye keep callin' me Nereus, 'the old man of the sea.' Be a right fit title fer me. But a *god*? Would a god need help to walk?" The old fisherman sniggered faintly. "Truth be told, the sea's been me mate fer so long, I can't remember some things. Don't know me age. That day during the big storm, came through the tunnel to see thee fer research. Was never after scarin' ye."

"Please, Captain, you can tell me all this when you're strong again," Morgan offered sympathetically.

"Ethan?"

"Yes?"

"That gravestone with me name ye found under the sea."

"Uh huh."

"Made me boat look wrecked back then and hid meself away. Was after a new start. Not long after we founded Pelican Bay, they started after snoopin' me out, just like in Newfoundland."

"I knew it!" Morgan almost shouted, and then lowered her head in shame.

"Hid in me Secret Spot on Fisherman's Island. Came back after a hurricane sunk the first Pelican Bay. Course she was called Bigsley Bay back then."

"Captain, really, you can—"

"Was never after hurtin no one. Been hidin' in that secret tunnel hopin' to ride out the storm of the ways of the land. Every time someone gets near me seems a death be happenin'. But would give me life for ye, Ethan. Fer Morgan, too."

The old man suddenly stopped talking. He was so still.

"I love you, Captain," I said, in a voice haggled by a rainstorm of tears.

"I love ye too, me Son.

The next thing that we knew, the gentle fall of a miniature, tap dancing rain bathed the library floor, and all that remained of the old man was a puddle of dark seawater, the old blankets now clinging to the chair, as if in mourning.

We collected all the seawater in the library the best that we could and put it in a large urn, making a sober vow to each other to never discuss what had happened.

The next morning, just before dawn, we went out to the beach and poured the contents of the urn into the ocean, as I sang.

Laura lie, Laura lie, in the sea barley, in the sea barley.
Hold me close, hold me close, in the sea barley, in the sea barley.
Love my thorns, and this wild rose is yours—in the sea barley, in the sea barley.

Later that day, a news report was broadcast from the Gull Bay Police Department: *"The old fishing boat believed to belong to Captain Shelby is gone without a trace. The search for his body was called off yesterday and he has been declared lost at sea."*

If Captain Shelby's boat sank, then it is too deep to be retrieved, just like some mysteries are too deep to be solved. But often, in my dreams, I see the old man's boat moored to some new dock, by some new fishing town, far, far away, and I say a little prayer that the people of that town will know that some things are better left alone.

~ * ~

If you enjoyed this book, please consider writing a short review and posting it on Amazon, Goodreads and/or Barnes and Noble. Reviews are very helpful to other readers and are greatly appreciated by authors, especially me. When you post a review, drop me an email and let me know and I may feature part of it on my blog/site. Thank you. ~ Jesse

JGChristiansen@aol.com

Dear Reader,

Thank you so much for investing your time and thoughts into this novel. I hope that the old fisherman has left you with an open heart and mind regarding the possibilities of life with and around the sea. We land creatures have been here so briefly compared to her. She is the greatest novel, one that we may never finish reading.

Also, I hope that this story will always remind you that everything around us may not always be as it appears, that we should always first respect and search and seek to understand before embarking on any definite course regarding others and nature.

You may have noticed that Captain Shelby's character includes a good dose of Old Newfoundland English phrases, which were translated to some degree into modern English to enhance your reading experience. Below are a few of the original phrases and their relative meanings for my readers interested in the linguistic history of Newfoundland.

Ducky - Female friend
Eh b'y - Yes son; sometimes sarcastic
G'wan b'y - No, really?
Luh - Look
Right Crooked - Grouchy
Scopie - Nickname for a fish often found around coves
Wah - What
Yes b'y - Yes boy; can be an expression of awe or disbelief

I would love to hear from you regarding your thoughts about Captain Shelby and this novel, and invite you to drop by anytime at my Web site: www.jessegileschristiansen.com.

Until then, I will look for you in The Land Between the Lines.

Yours in literature,

Jesse Giles Christiansen.

About the Author

Jesse Giles Christiansen is an American author who writes compelling literary fiction that weaves the real with the surreal. He attended Florida State University where he began writing short stories and exposing himself to the great literary classics, his greatest influences at the time consisting of London, Hemingway, and Wilde. He received his B.A. in English literature in 1993.

He wrote his first novel, *About: Journey into the Mystic* after spending a summer in Alaska working on fishing boats. His newest novel, *Pelican Bay*, part of a series, focuses on a mysterious old fisherman and the unforgettable lessons he imparts on an eccentric, nosy, sea-battered beach town.

Web Site: www.jessegileschristiansen.com

Blog: www.jgchristiansen.wordpress.com

IMAJIN BOOKS
Quality fiction beyond your wildest dreams

For your next eBook or paperback purchase, please visit:

www.imajinbooks.com

www.twitter.com/imajinbooks

www.facebook.com/imajinbooks

Made in the USA
Charleston, SC
16 December 2013